BENEATH A STAR-LIT SKY

A HOLCOMB SPRINGS SMALL TOWN ROMANTIC SUSPENSE

JL CROSSWHITE

PRAISE FOR JL CROSSWHITE

"This is a very suspenseful story and I'm looking forward to the next book in this series."—Ginny, Amazon reviewer

"I was impressed with the suspense in this book as well as the romance. Great storyline. Morality issues were great. An overall great read."—Kindle customer

"Absolutely loved it. Fast paced and kept me guessing concerning the outcome. I highly recommend it to all who like a good mystery or suspense."—Linda Reville

"Very well written, with interwoven stories and well developed characters"—Mary L. Sarrault

OTHER BOOKS BY JL CROSSWHITE

Hometown Heroes series
Promise Me, prequel novella
Protective Custody, book 1
Flash Point, book 2
Special Assignment, book 3

In the Shadow series
Off the Map, book 1
Out of Range, book 2
Over Her Head, book 3

The Route Home series, writing as Jennifer Crosswhite
Be Mine, prequel novella
Coming Home, book 1
The Road Home, book 2
Finally Home, book 3

Contemporary romance, writing as Jennifer Crosswhite
The Inn at Cherry Blossom Lane

Eat the Elephant: How to Write (and Finish!) Your Book One Bite at a Time, writing as Jen Crosswhite

Devotional, writing as Jennifer Crosswhite
Worthy to Write: Blank pages tying your stomach in knots? 30 prayers to tackle that fear!

When I consider your heavens,
the work of your fingers,
the moon and the stars,
which you have set in place,
what is mankind that you are mindful of them,
human beings that you care for them?

Psalm 8:3-4 (NIV)

PROLOGUE

Maybe it was just his conscience weighing on him, but Dalton Brandt shrugged the backpack a little higher as he hiked through the San Bernardino National Forest. Who knew a few pot plants could be so heavy? It was a cool February day, snow still on the ground in patches; drifts remained in the shadows of the trees. But he was sweating. Had anyone seen him? He'd tried to be casual as he walked away from the grow house. They had cameras everywhere. But he'd only taken a few plants. They wouldn't miss them. Their operation was enormous. What was the big deal?

Still, he couldn't wait to get far enough away and shake the feeling he was being followed. He'd parked where no one would spot his car and hiked in.

The faint sounds of a high-pitched engine reached him. He ducked off the trail and peeked back through the branches. Two guys in a Polaris side-by-side off-road vehicle. This was off-roading country, so it could be someone out for a day of four-wheeling. Though this was a pretty narrow trail, more for hiking. But they also used those all-terrain vehicles to get around the extensive grow operation.

The realization that they could be on to him twisted his gut.

The guys he stole from weren't just some low-life drug dealers. No, it was much bigger than that if the rumors were true that Beckett Lorde was involved. And given some of the phone conversations he'd overheard working at the grow house, he thought those rumors had some truth to them. If those guys on the Polaris caught him, they wouldn't play. He wouldn't be able to talk his way out of it.

His mind spun with options. There weren't many. He couldn't outrun the Polaris, but if he got off the trail and into the woods, they wouldn't be able to follow him. He turned and sprinted into the trees, dodging branches, slipping a few times on the pine needles underfoot. The ground slanted upward steeply. He cursed. If he'd been thinking, he'd have jumped off the other side of the trail, the downhill side. But that had been his problem lately. He hadn't been thinking.

Crashing brush behind him let him know the two goons were off the Polaris and hot on his trail.

He cursed again. If only he'd been in better shape. His lungs burned in the high mountain air. A thinning in the trees gave him hope that the going might get a bit easier. If he could just gain some ground on them, maybe he could find a place to hide. If the snow didn't give away his footprints.

Yes, another trail appeared running along the top of the ridge. He ignored the burning in his lungs, the sharp pain in his side, and his screaming quads. He'd be in a lot more pain if those guys got ahold of him. With a final burst, he jumped up onto the trail and sprinted down it, the going getting easier on the packed dirt. No snow either. Now for a place to hide.

A giant granite boulder poked out of the hillside just before the trail disappeared around a curve. He dove behind it just as the sounds of crashing brush and curses let him know his pursuers had gained the trail. Hopefully they'd think he'd kept on going. Maybe they'd even pick the wrong direction to chase him.

The footsteps stopped, and their voices floated to him but no clear words. His own breathing sounded loud, drowning them out. He was afraid they'd hear him if they came close. He worked on slowing his breath and listening.

The footsteps grew nearer, sounding like his pursuers were jogging down the trail toward the rock that hid him.

He tried to squeeze even tighter into the crack in the rock, hoping it wasn't home to some creature who'd resent his invasion. Though he'd take any animal over these guys right now.

The footsteps ran past and then got fainter as his pursuers must have gone around the corner of the trail. He had no idea how much the trail twisted and turned. He hoped it curved again to buy him time before they could look down the trail and realize he hadn't gone that way.

He jumped out from behind the rock and sprinted back the way he came. He'd take the trail as far and as fast as he could before jumping off, downhill this time, into the trees. Far enough where they wouldn't hear him crashing through the forest. Then he could figure out how to get back to his car.

Something jerked his arm. He stumbled. Had he snagged his sleeve or backpack on a tree branch? He turned his head and gazed into the grinning face of Goon Number One. He must've been waiting on the side of the trail while the other guy ran the other way. They were smarter than he gave them credit for. The guy's bulk let Dalton know he didn't have a chance to out-fight this guy. His only chance was to outrun him.

But the gun pointed at his stomach made that idea shrivel up and die. Maybe he could reason with him. He raised his hands and shrugged off the backpack. "Here. You can have them back. It's just a few plants." He lifted his hands. "Sorry. I know I shouldn't have taken them, but I didn't think anyone would miss them. You guys have so much."

Goon One gave a grin that showed a gold lower tooth. "You think we're chasing you over some weed?"

Goon Two showed up down the trail, huffing. "Should shoot him right now for making us run so much."

"Boss'll want to see him. Find out what he knows, who he's told."

"Hey, I don't know anything. I haven't said a word to anyone."

Goon One shoved him off the trail on to the downslope, back in the direction they'd come from.

Dalton scanned the area, looking for any opportunity. If he'd known it'd come to this, he never would have taken the stupid pot plants. He never should have taken the job Cory offered him. The cost was too high.

CHAPTER
ONE

Leading inexperienced people in the wilderness, even by someone with the skills Reese Vega had, was a recipe for disaster. The only person he would do this gig for was his brother. Even then, he was starting to regret it.

Reese stood to the side of the trail, the vanilla scent of ponderosa pines wafting around him, and wished he was hiking alone. The trip had originally been booked by Holcomb Springs Outfitters as a snowshoe tour, but the snow had melted to slushy piles on the trail and only remained in the shadows of the trees. Still, it was a beautiful day, if only he could enjoy it. Alone.

As the group of several girlfriends who had come up for a weekend away passed him, one of the women screamed and jumped, grabbing her friend's arm. "What was that? I heard something in the bushes. Is it a bear? Or a mountain lion?" She shot Reese a wide-eyed look.

He resisted the urge to roll his eyes. "Probably just a squirrel."

With all the noise they'd made, most wildlife was long gone. Even the chattering blue jays had left the area. The squirrel was probably hoping for a handout. Reese craved the quiet of the outdoors. It soothed him in a way nothing else could, especially after his injury. But this… this was not the kind of outdoors he liked.

But it was a peace offering for his brother who ran Holcomb Springs Outfitters. Maybe it would help mend the fences Reese's enlisting in the military had broken in his pacifist family. He could only hope. They had wanted him to be someone different than who he was. They hadn't exactly been in his corner.

He pointed for the group to continue on the trail while he remained behind to check on the stragglers. There were always stragglers. It gave him a chance to grab a minute of quiet. His headache had worsened from the chatter of the women. That and their endless flirting. He'd almost take another tour of duty compared to more tourists.

But due to his traumatic brain injury, that was no longer an option. And he'd told his brother, Raul, that he'd help run his outfitters shop until Raul got back on his feet. Literally. He'd had knee surgery and couldn't lead the hikes and camping trips. And being as the outfitter shop was the family's main source of income, Reese couldn't say no.

It was only temporary. He'd do his family duty and make an attempt to improve relations. And then he could figure out what he was going to do next. And it wouldn't be escorting tourists through the wilderness.

Reese stepped toward the guest who had fallen behind. The man wasn't wearing proper hiking boots. His tennis shoes were soaked from the slush, and he was breathing hard, his face red. Many people had no idea how the seven-thousand-foot altitude could affect them.

"Not too much farther. The lookout point is just ahead. Great view of the lake. It'll be worth it." Reese tried to infuse his voice with an enthusiasm he didn't feel but Raul would expect. Raul was so much better with people than he was.

The man glanced up, nodded, and then went back to staring at the trail. Not enjoying the beauty around him, missing the whole point of a hike in the woods.

Reese shrugged as the man plodded past him. Not his problem. He rubbed his temples, hoping to ease the pain. Reaching into his pack, he grabbed a bottle of Aleve and popped a couple into his mouth, washing them down with water from his bottle.

A yelp went up from the area of the lookout, and Reese sprinted up the trail. One of the women on the girlfriends' trip was sitting on her bottom a little way down the slope of the lookout, just before the sharp drop-off.

Her friend rushed over to him. "We were trying to take a selfie with the lake in the background. I think she stepped off, and then she just fell."

He nodded and knelt beside the woman. Another two steps, and she would have been over the drop-off. People didn't have common sense. He should have been up here to keep an eye on them. But then what about the straggler? He didn't know how Raul did it.

"Are you hurt anywhere?" He scanned the woman, looking for any obvious sign of injury.

"My ankle. I think I twisted it when I stepped back and tried to catch my balance." She glanced up at him and gave him a small smile.

He tugged her jeans up above her ankle. At least she had boots on. He palpated the area. "Does that hurt?"

She winced. "A little."

It wasn't swollen, but that could change quickly. "What's your name?"

"Andrea." She looked up at him and bit her lip.

He should have remembered. Raul would have remembered. He never did live up to his family's expectations. He reached in his pack for an Ace elastic wrap from the first aid kit. He eased off her boot, wrapped her ankle, then slipped the boot back on with the laces loosened. "That should stabilize it to get you down the hill. Do you think you can put any weight on it?"

"Maybe. If you help me."

A glance shot among her friends, smiles they didn't try to hide.

Great. Was this a set up? "Okay, everyone get your final pictures, and we'll head back." He slipped his arm under the woman's shoulders. "On three, we're going to stand together. Just put your weight on your good foot and lean on me."

Her "okay" came out breathy.

"One, two, three." He pushed to his feet and pulled the woman up with him.

She gingerly put weight on her foot then immediately retracted it. "It hurts to stand on it."

He should have her friends help her back down the trail. "Let's get one of your friends on the other side."

Another woman stepped to the side of Andrea, and between the two of them, she hobbled down the trail.

"It's a good thing we have a strong guy like you to help us out of trouble," the friend said, someone else whose name he couldn't remember.

And there it was. Raul was married, so maybe he didn't have women hitting on him all the time, but there was almost always one on every tour he'd done so far. "Best not to get into trouble in the first place."

He got them back down to the van and loaded up. "Do you want me to take you to the urgent care clinic? It's not big, but we have a doc who can check out your ankle."

Andrea shook her head. "No, it's not as sore as it was at first."

Her cheeks tinged pink, and he wondered if it hurt at all.

"Besides," she quickly added, "my friends can take me later if I need to go. I'll just put some ice on it back in our room."

They pulled into Holcomb Springs Outfitters parking lot. Raul came out in his knee brace to help the guests with their gear and thank them for coming.

Reese closed the van door as the last guest left.

Raul laid a hand on his shoulder. "You should thank the

guests and ask them to come back. Let them know we enjoy serving them."

"Even if we don't?" Reese brushed past him and carried the gear into the back of the shop. He'd have to repack the first-aid kit. "I don't lie." He opened the kit and rummaged through the supplies.

"It's not lying. It's good business."

Reese grunted. He never was going to see eye to eye with his family on things. Important things.

"How'd it go?"

"Fine." He told Raul about Andrea's injury. "I'm not convinced it wasn't an elaborate setup by her and her friends to flirt with me."

Raul grinned. "It's all part of the game. I should keep you around, put your face on the brochures and ads. It'd be good for business."

"I'm only here until you are well enough to lead the tours again."

The grin disappeared from Raul's face, and his whole body deflated as if more than his knee was injured.

Reese almost wished he could take the words back, but what was the point? Raul needed to know the score. Reese repacked the bag and made sure everything was ready to go for the next trip. Military preparedness had been ingrained in him.

Raul put his hand on the door leading from the back of the shop to the main floor. "Want to come over for dinner?"

Reese recognized the olive branch. "Tell Marissa I appreciate the offer." He knew it'd come from Raul's wife. "But I wouldn't be good company. My head's killing me. I'm going to go lie down."

Raul's brow furrowed, but they'd been down this road enough that he knew not to baby Reese. Instead, he gave a short nod. "Come on over if you change your mind."

Reese lifted his chin, hefted his backpack, and headed out to his classic 1978 red-and-white Bronco. In a few minutes, he was on the road heading toward Holcomb Lake and the garage apartment on Raul and Marissa's lake house, looking forward to staring at the water and appreciating the quiet, hoping it would calm his pounding head.

He should give Raul more credit. He was trying. But in the end, would anything change? He'd trusted his family to have his back and they'd let him down. Letting himself get too close, too trusting again, would only end in heartache.

ELLA SOMMER'S NEATLY ORDERED WORLD MEANT THAT ON Saturday nights, while Mom was bowling with her friends, Ella had dinner with Amanda. Ella liked nothing better than ending the week with a good meal shared with a good friend. She parked her Subaru in front of the restaurant in downtown Holcomb Springs. This time of year was her favorite, between holidays when it was just the locals and not full of tourists, when she knew practically everyone she saw.

By the end of February, her fifth-grade classes always got restless. Christmas break was too far in the rearview mirror and spring break was around the corner, just not close enough. Winter had kept them cooped up for too long. So dinner at Bella Sorgenti with her co-teacher and best friend, Amanda Elliot, was the break she needed. And they hadn't even had the opportunity to dish about the Spread the Love dinner dance last weekend, an event Ella had purposely chosen to serve at from the kitchen, where she heard some gossip but couldn't see who all had attended. It was long past time for a girlfriend sesh.

She climbed out and headed for the wooden sidewalk. Downtown tried to maintain a Western theme in a nod to its gold-rush roots. Watching that she didn't step in a pile of slush, she barely noticed that someone was holding the door to Bella Sorgenti for her.

"Thanks," she mumbled and then looked up. Her feet froze

in place. "Oh, hi, Lucas." She had avoided her ex-fiancé and coworker at school as much as possible since their relationship ended over Christmas break.

"Hi, Ella. How are you?" His brown eyes were warm, and for a moment, she thought he genuinely wanted to know. Maybe they'd moved from the avoidance stage to the cordial stage.

But before she could speak, she noticed a woman with him. A beautiful woman she had never seen before. Who had her hand threaded through Lucas's. So, not a cousin or visiting family member. Well, of course Lucas was dating again. Why not?

"Uh, good. Meeting, ah, someone for dinner, actually." He didn't need to know it was Amanda.

Lucas tugged the woman closer. "I'd like you to meet Sophie Graff, my fiancée."

Sophie took a half step forward. "So nice to meet you. You teach with Lucas, right?"

Ella didn't know what she was expecting, but it wasn't that. Too many competing thoughts and emotions flooded her, and it took all of her self-control to keep them from showing. At least, she hoped that's what she was doing.

She nodded, hoping she didn't look like a bobblehead doll. "Yep, I work with Lucas." But before she could politely extricate herself from this mess and get inside and drown her emotions in carbs, Sophie stuck out her left hand. Was she supposed to shake it? Did she not want to let go of Lucas's hand that much? Then the dazzling diamond caught Ella's eye. The ring.

She barely gave it a glance. "That's very lovely. Well, have a great evening. I'd best get inside." Sidling around Sophie, she let the warmth and comforting scents of Bella Sorgenti envelop her. Scanning the room, she didn't see Amanda. She stepped up to the podium. "Hi, Selena. It'll be Ms. Elliot and me tonight. She's not here yet, is she?" Ella had Selena in her classroom the first year she'd taught.

"No, but your favorite table is open. I'll bring her back when she comes."

"Thanks." Ella made a beeline for the private booth and slid inside, avoiding making eye contact with others in the restaurant. She just couldn't deal with being polite to anyone at this moment. Selena followed with a basket of warm, buttery garlic bread and a bottle of sparkling Italian mineral water. Ella took a bite of the bliss and closed her eyes.

So Lucas hadn't wasted any time moving on. Dating, she had suspected. After all, he was a catch. Thin, with a close-cropped beard, always dressed well, had a good job. But engaged? They hadn't been broken up three months yet. And Sophie clearly wasn't a local girl.

Amanda slid in the booth across from her. "Sorry I'm late."

"If you'd been here a few minutes earlier, you could have witnessed one of the more awkward moments of my life."

Amanda reached for the garlic bread. "Which was?"

Ella gave her the rundown, watching Amanda's face. "You knew, didn't you? That's why some of the conversations in the teachers' lounge stop when I come in. I thought it was just about our breakup."

Amanda shook her head. "I didn't know for sure. But I'd heard some snippets that made me wonder. I didn't think he'd be engaged though."

Miranda came over and took their orders, which were always the same. Spinach lasagna for Ella and whatever seasonal ravioli there was for Amanda. And a piece of tiramisu to split for dessert. The routine was as comforting as the food and company. And after the shock Ella had, she needed some comforting.

After Miranda left, Amanda leaned her forearms on the table. "How are you feeling?"

Ella shrugged. "Shocked mostly. Maybe numb, I don't know. I'm actually not sad. I don't want Lucas back. I wasn't even that sad when we broke up. What's wrong with me?"

"There's nothing wrong with you. Lucas is one of those guys

who looks good on paper, but there really wasn't that magical chemistry between the two of you that great couples have."

Ella waved that away. "That's only on the Hallmark channel or romance novels. Relationships need more than chemistry."

"I know, but they need chemistry too."

Amanda was an inveterate romantic, so Ella wasn't going to argue with her. Ella's nature was more practical. It was why, she supposed, they worked so well together. Their styles complemented each other. The best tactic was to change the subject.

"Any news from the Spread the Love dance since I was stuck in the kitchen the whole time?"

Amanda thought for a moment. "Wally and Stan put everyone to shame with their dancing, as usual. For a couple of old guys, they sure can move. You'd never guess, the way they plant themselves at the booth at the Jitter Bug Too or the hardware store."

"And we raised enough money to upgrade some of the equipment at the community center. Not every kid wants to play basketball after school in the winter." Since she volunteered there a lot helping with tutoring, she had a sense of what the kids wanted. "I'm hoping we can install a climbing wall."

Amanda pointed a piece of bread at her. "Maybe we could get Reese or Raul Vega to teach the kids."

Ella's lovely dinner turned to lead in her stomach. "Reese? He's back? On leave, or is he out of the military?"

"Yeah. Didn't you know? He was at the Spread the Love dinner with Raul and Marissa. I guess he's helping out while Raul's knee is healing." Amanda's gaze narrowed at her. "What's going on? You look pale. You didn't even react that strongly to Lucas."

Ella shook her head. "Oh, it's nothing. We just went to high school together, that's all, and not even that long. He was a senior when I was a freshman."

"Uh huh." Amanda's gaze didn't waver. "Spill."

Ella's face heated. Why? She'd had so little interaction with him, she had no idea why her body was betraying her. She shrugged. "I might have had a crush on him, but he was the high school bad boy. It was a long time ago. He couldn't wait to leave town. I'm surprised he's back."

That was the problem with letting someone get to know you. They knew you too well. Amanda still studied her. "Maybe he has strong family ties."

Ella shook her head. "I didn't get that impression. Raul is quite a bit older. I don't even remember his parents."

Amanda grinned. "I didn't think you knew him all that well."

"I didn't. It's a small town. Everyone knew everyone." They desperately needed to change the subject. It was suddenly way too hot in here. "Back to Spread the Love. Was Lucas there with Sophie?"

Amanda opened her mouth then closed it. "Yeah."

"I wonder if she had her bling and if everyone already knows what I didn't." Ella poured more sparkling water and sucked it down.

Amanda reached over and touched her hand.

Ella shook her head. "It's not that I'm upset that he's engaged. I don't want him back. I just don't want people pitying me and talking about me behind my back. That's all."

Amanda leaned back as Miranda set the tiramisu between them along with two coffees and to-go boxes.

Forking a bite of the chocolate, espresso, and creamy confection into her mouth, Ella moaned. "This is the cure for everything."

Amanda nodded, eyes closed with her own bite. After she had taken a sip of coffee, she said, "That still leaves your problem."

"I don't have a problem."

Amanda laughed. "I think you have two: Lucas and Reese. What is your plan? And I know you always have a plan."

"Eat a lot of this?" She wiggled her eyebrows as she scooped up more dessert. "How can anything be bad when this tastes so good." She leaned her head back against the booth. "Seriously, though, I can just avoid both of them. If I've managed to do it while working with Lucas, I can certainly avoid Reese until he leaves again. I doubt he'd even remember me." A flash of memory flicked through her brain, but she pushed it away before Amanda could discern something and grill her about it. "Speaking of plans, what are yours for spring break?"

"My parents are using a time share in Palm Springs, and they invited me down. At least it'll be warm, even if I'll be surrounded by old people."

"And college students."

Amanda conceded that. "Just nobody my age. What about you? Please tell me you are making plans beyond organizing your book collection or spices."

"Hey! An organized house runs smoothly and saves everyone time. Since Mom and I take turns cooking, it's important that we both are on the same page where everything is kept." She pointed her fork at Amanda. "You have benefited firsthand from my organization skills."

"Point taken. But it's not an acceptable activity for spring break. You need to get out of here and do something."

Ella sipped her coffee. "I know. I've been thinking about it. You know, Lucas accused me once of being incredibly predictable. That was one of the reasons for our breakup, even. Not that he's Mr. Adventure. I actually thought being predictable was an asset. But it's gotten me to thinking; what could I do that would be unpredictable, that I would enjoy?"

"What did you like to do as a kid? Did your family go anywhere special, do anything? You, your mom, and Evan," she quickly corrected. "Sorry."

She'd stumbled onto a sore spot in Ella's life. Her dad had left them when she was ten and then faded out of their lives. "We went camping a few times, usually with another family from church, and we borrowed equipment. It was fun. I remember running around, climbing on things, getting dirty, and none of it mattered." She put her coffee cup down and smiled. "It was like we were one big family. Mom's burden was lightened, and it was like Evan and I had a bunch of cousins. I haven't thought about that in a long time." She took a sip and tilted her head. "That actually kind of sounds like fun. Not the getting dirty part but being outdoors, not having a schedule. But I can't camp alone. Ooh, maybe I could go to one of those campgrounds that has trailers already set up. Some of them are retro, really cute. That could be fun."

Amanda scooped up the last of the tiramisu. "Talk to Anne. She knows everything and will have all the best info, saving you googling time."

"Good point. I'll swing by the library Monday after school. I need to meet with her anyway to set up the spring break reading program for the kids."

"Promise me something." Amanda turned to her as they left the restaurant. "Do something fun and unexpected, okay? If you don't have a solid plan, I'm dragging you to Palm Springs with me. Friends don't let friends organize their spices on spring break."

Ella laughed and gave her a hug. "I promise. I'll have fun, and it'll be unexpected."

CHAPTER
TWO

Ella walked the short distance to the library Monday after school. The air was crisp—it had snowed this morning—but the sun was out. Between the walk and the sun, her spirits lifted. She pushed open the door to the library and stepped through the anteroom with the brick floor and storage for snow boots and coats to the second set of doors to the library proper. The smell of ink, paper, and old books never failed to soothe her. It was like coming home to old friends.

She passed displays of local artists and slowed to peruse the new-releases table. Aggie Gilchrist had a new cozy mystery out, *Death Comes Calling*. Anne usually had a copy put back for her. That would be delightful tonight in front of her fireplace.

A group of kids she recognized were whispering at the tables around the corner. Several others slouched at the computer stations. She didn't immediately see Anne behind the circulation counter, but that wasn't unusual. Ella headed toward the section on California and then to the few books on camping, hiking, and traveling.

She'd pulled one off the shelf and was flipping through it when a voice startled her.

"I thought I saw you come in. I was in the back." Anne

slipped her arm around Ella's shoulders and gave a gentle squeeze. "What are you looking for? Rewriting the Gold Rush Days play?"

Ella slipped the book back on the shelf and turned. Anne wore a camel-colored wool jacket belted at the waist, mocha skinny jeans, and dark knee boots. Her shoulder-length blonde hair hung in beachy waves, a contrast to Ella's light-brown long bob. Anne's attention to style busted any librarian stereotypes.

"No, I'm looking for something to do over spring break. I was thinking camping, but not by myself. Maybe one of those places that has those cute, retro Airstreams." Her shoulders dropped. "Then again, maybe I should spend it rewriting the Gold Rush play. We'll be starting auditions and rehearsals not too long after the kids get back from spring break." It was the big, end-of-the-year production for the fifth graders, and a few would also play parts in vignettes performed during Gold Rush Days in August.

Anne nodded toward an alcove near the circulation desk where a few small tables were set up. This was the only place she allowed food and drink to be consumed in the library. "I brought in some oatmeal-chocolate-chip cookies. How about a few with some tea, and we'll figure this out."

Ella followed her. They often sat here planning a reading challenge or after school program. "Good idea. But first, we need to talk about the spring break reading plan."

Soon with a few cookies and steaming mugs of tea in front of them, they reviewed what they had planned and tweaked a few things. Even though Ella wouldn't be around to help, she was invested in the kids of this community.

Anne said, "I think the camping plan has real merit. When was the last time you got away?"

"Evan came up at Christmas, and we went skiing."

"In town. Across the lake."

Ella conceded. "True. But Lucas—" Why did she care what

Lucas thought? He was out of her life. As out of it as one could get in such a small town.

"Lucas what?" Anne's eyebrows raised.

"Did you know he was engaged? Of course you did. Everyone did but me."

Anne swirled her mug. "I don't think everyone knows. But what does he have to do with anything?"

Ella told of her encounter with him last Saturday. "He shouldn't have anything to do with it. I just keep thinking about what he said when we broke up, that I'm predictable and comfortable like an old sweatshirt. Not adventurous. And he wanted adventure."

Anne scoffed. "Lucas likes the *idea* of adventure. Not actual adventure. But that's beside the point. What do *you* want?"

Ella shrugged. "I'll admit I've been in a rut lately. I have my routine, and I like it. But..." She spun her mug. "I don't even know. It's like something's missing. Or... I think I want to challenge myself in some way, a way I don't normally. Nothing academic. And I don't want to run a marathon or anything like that. But I used to love being outdoors. I have great memories of that. And now I don't do anything unless Evan comes up or Mom wants to go on a hike."

Anne pursed her lips, gaze steady on her. "I have an idea. Better than the Airstreams, I think."

"I'm all ears."

"Holcomb Springs Outfitters runs hiking and camping trips here locally. I know they have one that covers the Holcomb Springs Trail where it branches off the Pacific Crest Trail."

Ella suppressed a sigh. So much for avoiding Reese. But if she didn't come up with a plan, Amanda was going to drag her off to Palm Springs. They'd play endless rounds of card games with her parents and eat dinner at four thirty.

Anne's gaze narrowed. "What?"

Ella went for nonchalant. "Nothing. Sounds like a good idea."

"Uh huh. You don't seem convinced."

This time Ella let out the sigh. "You knew Reese Vega is back in town, right? Helping out Raul."

Anne nodded.

"So it's likely Reese is leading the trip, not Raul."

"Why is that a problem?"

"It's not." She picked up cookie crumbs and popped them in her mouth. Only that she was hoping to avoid him until he left again.

"Didn't you both grow up here?"

"He and his parents moved up here when he started high school. Raul and his older sister, Rachel, were already out of college and on their own. Reese is three years older than me, so we only were in high school together one year."

Anne nodded, her gaze steady. When Ella didn't say anything, she said, "You'll be safe with him. You'll have a great adventure, prove Lucas wrong about you, and have a good memory of your trip. At least head over there and check it out, see what your options are."

"True." She could at least do that. Research. She was good at research. "My life is just so ordinary and...nothing special. Not that I need to be special, but I just have a very comfortable routine in a very comfortable town where I know everyone. I just want to shake things up a bit."

Anne touched her hand. "You are not ordinary. You are a key part of our community. What would we do without you?"

Ella shrugged. She didn't know what to do when people said things like that to her. She was just doing what any person would do.

As the silence stretched, Anne said, "Wait here." She grabbed up their empty mugs and plates.

A camping trip with Reese. What would that be like? There would be other people there. He might not even remember her, probably wouldn't. There was no way he could know she'd had a crush on him back when he'd been the distant, older bad boy. So different from her. Maybe that's what she had found appealing. Then again, she did have an encounter with him that made her think the bad boy image wasn't all there was to him. She shook her head. It'd been twelve years. Neither of them were the same people.

Anne returned with a small, leather-bound volume tied shut with a leather strap, a folded map, a guide book to hikes in Holcomb Springs and the San Bernardino National Forest. And the latest Aggie Gilchrist novel, *Death Comes Calling*.

"These should be just what you need. Something to read tonight." She smiled as she slid over the Gilchrist book. "A book on the area from someone who has hiked all the trails and talks extensively about them, a map so you can visualize what the guidebook is talking about, and most importantly" —she tapped the leather cover— "a journal, so you can record what God wants to show you on your trip."

Ella covered Anne's hand. "You're so thoughtful. Thank you."

"Just make sure you tell me all about it. Maybe you'll be like Clarissa Miller when she went camping and stumbled on a mystery in *The Finger of Death*."

Ella laughed. "Usually I prefer to live vicariously through books. But it might be time to change that this spring break."

Anne gave her a mock stern look. "Head straight over to the Outfitters, okay? I know you. You'll overthink it and talk yourself out of it."

Ella shook her head. "Okay, okay." But she had been toying with doing exactly that. She hugged Anne goodbye and gathered up her new treasures, then headed back to the school to pick up her Subaru Forester. The Outfitters was technically within walking distance, but the sun was slipping behind the trees, and it grew decidedly cooler.

She thought about Anne's words, contrasting them with Lucas's. What did she want? And would adventure help her find it? She didn't know, but she'd start like she did whenever she had a problem to figure out. She'd fact find.

Reese worked through the inventory at the back of the Outfitters shop, half keeping an ear open in case too many customers came in and Raul needed his help. But otherwise, Raul was much better with the customers than he was, though he'd do in a pinch.

Right now a father and son were talking to Raul about a spring break four-wheeling trip over the Gold Fever Trail, an overnight campout, and a little gold panning. The rumor was no one had found the big motherlode, and plenty still went looking for it. The kid had to be about ten, young enough to still enjoy time with his dad and old enough to be capable of doing a lot of activities.

He thought back to himself at that age. He had a few good memories, fishing with Dad and Raul. It made him feel important to be included, one of the guys. To have his dad proud of what he could do. Too bad there weren't more memories like those.

The bell above the door rang, and Reese leaned out.

The dad waved Raul off. "Go help them. Liam and I want to look at some of these trip maps."

Raul nodded. "Holler if you have questions."

A guy Reese wouldn't have pegged as the outdoor type came in with a woman, also not the outdoor type based on her spike-heeled boots. What could they want? Maybe they were in the wrong shop. He shrugged and went back to the inventory. The shop was moving into the busy season, transitioning out of winter sports into spring and summer. They could still get another snowstorm or two, so they had to keep a little of every-thing in stock.

The bell rang again, but Reese was in the middle of counting sleeping bags. Either Raul could handle it or they could wait.

"Ella, what are you doing here? Leading story time or some-thing?" Sounded like the non-outdoorsy guy.

"Ms. Sommer!" The boy's voice. "Are you going on a campout too?"

"Hey, Liam. I'm not sure. That's what I'm here to find out."

The boy told her all about the trip he and his dad were planning.

But Reese's mind spun. Ella? Sommer? Maybe there was more than one. Not that unusual of a name. Though it was a small town. He had to start over on his counting.

"That sounds exciting, Liam. You'll have fun. I can't wait to hear about it when you get back from spring break." Her voice was the same, maybe a little deeper, and it kicked him straight in the chest.

At moments he'd wondered if she still lived here, if he'd run into her. Reese tossed down the clipboard and moved out of the back room.

"You? Camping?" This from non-outdoorsy guy.

"Why not? Why are you here?" Ella's arms were crossed, and she shifted her weight, giving a small smile to the female companion.

"Sophie and I are reserving kayaks for spring break."

Reese raised his eyebrows. The lake would still be cold in two weeks. He hoped they were good enough not to tip over and get dunked.

The man shook his head. "Camping? That's not like you at all." He tugged the woman with him closer. "We like to bond over the outdoors."

Wow, this guy was a jerk. Reese had an urge to wipe the smug look off his face.

A satisfied smile crossed Ella's face. "Maybe you just don't know me that well. I'm thinking about hiking the Holcomb Springs Trail."

She was? Huh. Raul was back helping the father and son check out. Reese didn't let himself think about it; he just moved. In a few strides, he stood next to Ella and put a hand on her shoulder.

Her head jerked up, and her eyes widened.

He gave her a wink. "She'll do just fine. She's a real trooper on these hikes. I'm looking forward to her help with the other hikers actually." He squeezed her shoulder, hoping she'd get the hint. Hoping she'd remember him and not think him a creeper.

Her mouth dropped open a bit. "Uh, yeah. Sure. If that's what you need." She gave an overly bright smile, recognition in her eyes. "You know me, always happy to help."

Reese caught Raul glancing over at them and frowning. He'd probably thought Reese's TBI was making him delusional. He certainly wasn't sure what had possessed him to start this farce.

The man stared at Reese and then glanced at Ella, uncertainty crossing his features. "You never mentioned…"

Reese stuck out his hand. "Reese Vega."

The man reluctantly took it. "Lucas Slater, and my fiancée, Sophie Graff. How do you know Ella?"

Reese turned on his charming grin. But inside he was scowling. Lucas. He had a bad history with guys with that name. "Ella and I go way back, don't we?" He slid his hand further along her shoulders, feeling her stiffen under his touch. So maybe he was overplaying this. Not like he had a lot of experience.

But she smiled up at him and nodded. "We do."

Lucas seemed unconvinced. "She never mentioned you before."

Reese didn't know what to make of that, but clearly there was some history here.

Ella lifted her chin. "I didn't tell you everything. Just like you didn't tell me everything."

Raul stepped over. "Are you all set? Ready to reserve those kayaks?"

Lucas gave Reese then Ella one more look. "Sure." He and Sophie followed Raul over to the counter.

Reese took Ella's arm. "Let's go look at the map of where I'm thinking we'll go this time." His voice loud enough to carry to Lucas.

Ella gave him a look but went with him over to the huge map on the wall.

Reese pointed to something on the map and lowered his voice. "Who is that guy?"

"Ex-fiancé."

Reese's head whipped around. "Really? He doesn't seem your type."

"How would you know what my type is? I haven't seen you in what—"

"Twelve years." The words came too fast. He wished he could bite them back.

Her gaze was steady on him, with a curious lift of her eyebrows.

He shrugged. "You just didn't seem the type to let other people's opinions determine your actions."

Raul's "You're all set" carried over to them. Lucas and Sophie turned, giving them a slight wave before heading out.

Reese dropped the pretense of looking at the map. "So why are you here?"

"What I told Lucas. I want to see about an overnight hiking trip during spring break."

He raised his eyebrows but before he could say anything, Raul spoke up. "Here's our book that shows the different trips. What are you thinking?"

Ella moved over to the counter.

Reese was slow to follow. In his rush to defend her from Lucas, her words hadn't really sunk in.

"This one." Ella pointed to something in the book Reese couldn't see. Hopefully one of the day trips Raul could lead or Cory Grant, who he called in during the busy seasons.

Raul nodded. "Good choice. We've got a group of friends already signed up. You'll fit right in." He finished getting Ella signed up.

Strangely, Reese felt at a loss standing around awkwardly. He didn't want to hover over Ella's shoulder, but he didn't want to head back to the storage room either. He moved to a display and began straightening things that didn't really need straightening. Out of the corner of his eye, he could see Raul frowning at him.

"You're all set. We'll see you bright and early the morning of the hike. All the information is in this packet."

Ella thanked Raul then turned and waved at Reese. "Thanks for earlier. With Lucas."

He nodded. "See you around." He gave a half wave as she headed out the door. Once she was gone, he headed over to the counter. "Which trip did she pick?"

"The big one."

Reese didn't believe him, so he pulled the computer screen over toward him. There it was. Three days and nights on the Holcomb Springs Trail with Ella Sommer. He scrubbed a hand over his face.

Raul grinned and smacked him on the shoulder.

Yeah, he wanted to smack something, all right.

<hr>

Ella threw her tote bags on her counter and started a pot of tea before calling Amanda. "I did it."

"Did what? Wait, you made plans for spring break." The excitement in Amanda's voice contrasted with the swirls in Ella's stomach. She wished she could feel as enthused.

She explained about running into Lucas and Reese's response while she prepped her tea. Felt like a cinnamon-orange spice kinda day.

"Man, that's a lot of Lucas sightings in a short period of time. But you knew Reese was working there."

"Yes, but when I first came in, I didn't see him. I hadn't expected to see Lucas and Sophie either."

"So Reese is leading your hike, right?"

Ella moved to the whistling teapot and turned it off, filling her mug with steaming water. "I assume so. Raul didn't say, but I would think it would be hard on his knee. That's why Reese came back. Though I know there's another guy that works there part-time when they get busy, so that's a possibility too." She sipped her tea. Hot but perfect. "Regardless, there will be other people around. If Reese does lead it, it's not like we'll be alone. Raul said a group of friends had already signed up."

"Still, it was awfully nice of him to come to your rescue with Lucas. Wouldn't be the worst thing to spend time with a guy like that."

"No, it wouldn't." Ella responded automatically, not really thinking. Her mind went back to one other time when Reese had rescued her. She was sure he wouldn't remember. He was a senior; she was a mousy freshman. But his remark about her not letting other people's opinions determine her actions surprised her. "I'd better let you go. It's time to get dinner. Mom will be home soon. I'll see you tomorrow."

Amanda congratulated her again before hanging up.

While Ella pulled out her container of pre-prepped frozen stew, she couldn't help but think about Reese's words. How did he remember who she'd wanted to be at fifteen when she still hadn't figured it out yet?

She brushed them off. It was a lucky guess. Reese probably barely remembered her. Plus, he'd be leaving again, a fact she needed to keep front and center.

CHAPTER
THREE

Sheriff Shannon McIntyre threw the covers off her bed, the cold air replacing the warm and waking her fully. She wasn't sleeping. Hadn't been for the past hour. Might as well get up and get the day started. She slipped on her cold-weather running gear, pulled her hair into a ponytail, and grabbed a glass of water. While she drank it, she checked in on Zach.

Her son was in his final year of high school, and his lanky form sprawled across his bed. She resisted the urge to straighten his covers and swipe his hair from his forehead. The boy in a man's body wouldn't appreciate that. She didn't think he appreciated much that she did. She'd felt the same way at his age.

She twisted the small, gold studs at her ears. He'd bought them for her when he was ten. Her mom had helped him. He was so proud to get her a grown-up gift with his own money. Now he wanted little to do with her. She knew it was a natural part of the growing-up process but… She could see her life shortly stretching out in front of her, centered around her job. Coming home to an empty house. Maybe she should get a dog. No, her schedule wasn't reliable enough to take care of a dog.

Water gone, she loaded up with her phone, weapon, and

headlamp before slipping out the back door and reengaging the alarm.

The motion-sensor light turned on, nearly blinding her and ruining her night vision. She eased out of the driveway and onto the road, moving carefully. It was pitch black out. She usually ran early, but this was early even for her. She headed toward the park.

Her familiar rhythm kicked in, and soon she was on autopilot and able to let her mind run, something it had been wanting to do all night. Didn't seem to take much these days. Her therapist was helping her work through some of the reasons why, but running had been her go-to solution for stress. She needed to move and to be alone doing it.

When she'd called to check in last night, her sergeant, Jonas McCann, had mentioned a missing persons report that had been filed on Dalton Brandt by one of his friends. No one had heard from him in a week. He'd gone to work and hadn't come back. They knew he was planning on taking off for a few days to go skiing, but they thought he'd be home by now. He was a young man, so it was possible he'd stayed longer than he planned or even quit his job without telling anyone. It'd been known to happen. They had to chase down every possibility. Her deputies were good at doing that.

Shannon didn't like anyone getting hurt in her town. It wasn't unusual for a hiker to get lost, but this was a resident. Worse than that, he worked for Belle Lumber, the last place he was seen. And that did something with her gut. Belle Lumber was owned by Beckett Lorde. Shannon had no proof—yet—that Lorde was behind drug trafficking, particularly illegal pot growing in the national forest that surrounded Holcomb Springs. But he was careful. He didn't have anything tied back to him.

Still, her gut was telling her that Brandt being missing had something to do with Lorde and his operations. Or was it that she just wanted to think the worst of Lorde? She had to account for that possibility too.

What she needed to do was prove what Lorde was up to.

And she would. And this missing man might be the opportunity she needed to get her foot in the door at Belle Lumber. She had to play it smart. Time alone with her thoughts was what she needed. And if her thoughts were going to keep her awake, then she might as well get some exercise out of it.

She neared the town park, the one light in the parking lot glowing in the distance. But then she saw another smaller light bobbing up and down. Someone was walking around with a flashlight. Or wearing a headlamp like she was. Unless there was a soccer or baseball tournament or one of their festivals, the park was closed from dusk to dawn. Her deputies patrolled the area as part of their duties, occasionally finding some kids making out or drinking.

A few runners, like her, took advantage of its paths in the winter as a safe place to run during the short days and long nights. Safer than the narrow mountain roads. But no one should be up this early running. Well, no one but her.

And it was a runner. A man, by the build.

Curious, she picked up her pace, fully warm now. Ready to confront whoever it was and irritated that her alone time was being interrupted.

The other runner must have spotted her, because his direction changed, and he moved toward her. His pace was light and easy, not threatening. Still, she was alert. When he came within shouting distance, she called out. "Who's there?"

"It's me. Tony. That you, sheriff?"

Pastor Tony Stafford. He'd only been leading Holcomb Springs Community Church for a few months since their previous pastor had retired. They'd crossed paths a few times outside of Sunday mornings at church, but she hadn't had time yet to get to know him. Something she needed to rectify. She only knew that he had served on staff of a big church in Laguna Vista and that he was a widower and didn't have any kids. He truly seemed to care about the people in the church and the town. There was a lot they had in common, and she needed to connect with him.

But she hadn't wanted to do it this morning. So early and her plans were already shot to pieces. Not a good start to the day. She suppressed a sigh.

"Yep. What brings you out this early in the morning?"

He chuckled, pulled earbuds out, and shoved them in his pockets. He adjusted his stride to match hers. "Probably the same as you. Can't sleep?"

She laughed. Something about his manner put her at ease. A good trait in a pastor. "Got it."

"Guess we carry the weight of other people's burdens with our jobs."

She nodded. "Comes with the territory. I had planned to set up a meeting with you, maybe grab some coffee, talk about the town and how we can help each other." Not only had she seen him at church, she'd seen him at the community center playing basketball at lunch. And she might have studied him a bit longer than absolutely necessary. He was certainly easy on the eyes. Which was a weird thought to have about her pastor.

"I'd thought the same. I can't believe how busy I've been. I guess I underestimated the amount of work involved in taking over a small church." Tony kept his pace even with hers, though his stride was longer.

Shannon didn't like running with other people, but the ease with which they kept pace and conversation surprised her. And unsettled her. She was enjoying their conversation, perhaps because there was no one around to observe them. And his easy way melted holes in the public persona she was used to carrying.

A patch of slush caught her foot, and she momentarily lost her balance.

Tony's hand was quick on her arm, stabilizing her.

She froze as the heat shot through her. It was rare that a man touched her, especially one helping her. A whole flood of feelings rushed through her, faster than she could sort through them. All she could do was shove them back behind the door they'd burst through.

"You okay?" He still held her arm.

She tugged it free. "Yeah. I'm fine. Thanks." Her voice sounded strained and breathy. Hopefully, he'd blame that on the run, not her reaction to him. She took off again.

They made another lap around the park before the eastern sky began to lighten. The dark had cocooned them, hiding her reactions.

He was far too handsome to be a pastor. He was built like a football player, dark hair swept back, dark eyes that seemed to be looking at your soul. It made her uncomfortable in a way few other people did. Not in a bad, creepy way—that she could handle. More like it stirred up long-forgotten feelings. Things best left buried if she wanted to do her job properly. She couldn't afford any distractions. And Pastor Tony was definitely a distraction.

Which was why the words that came out of her mouth surprised her. "Let's get you scheduled for a ride along. It'll be a great way to get to know the town and its people."

His grin and the chocolate-brown eyes he turned on her made it seem like she'd given him a huge gift.

But what had she gotten herself into?

ELLA PUSHED THROUGH THE DOORS OF THE JITTER BUG Too early Friday morning. It was her turn to bring treats for the staff, and she never brought homemade goodies the way the other teachers did. Cassie made the best blueberry scones, so why bother?

Cassie smiled at her when she came in, smoothing down her apron, her diamond engagement ring sparkling. She and Brett had set a date for later this spring. Ella couldn't be happier for them.

As usual, Stan and Wally occupied their booth in the back. She'd never gotten here earlier than they did. Perhaps they camped out waiting for Cassie to open. She wouldn't be surprised. She waved at them and received a two-coffee-mug salute in return.

Cassie pushed two bags and a cardboard coffee urn across the counter. "Let me get you some of those specialty creamers everyone likes. Be right back." She disappeared into the back.

The bell above the door rang, and Ella turned, expecting to see another early-bird local.

Reese walked in.

Not who she was expecting. She gave him a polite smile. "Morning."

He nodded. "Hey."

"Cassie's blueberry scones are hot out of the oven. I highly recommend them."

"I've been here before."

She deflated slightly. Of course he had. He'd been back awhile, and where else would anyone go for coffee and pastries? She gave him a teensy smile as Cassie came back with another small bag.

"Need help getting all of that out to your car?" Cassie asked then shot a smile at Reese. "Morning, Reese."

"I can manage." Ella moved toward the counter and gathered the bags in her arms.

"Morning, Cassie." Reese snatched up the coffee and creamers and reached for one of her bags, but she wouldn't let go.

"I can get that." His gaze met hers.

"I can do it myself. It's fine." She didn't need any help. Even if it would take her two trips.

He tugged harder, and she relinquished the bag before it ripped.

A retort was poised on her lips, but a glance at Wally and Stan told her she and Reese had an interested audience, and whatever they did or said would be all over town before lunch. She gave Reese a tight smile and headed toward the door.

He got there first with his long legs and was holding it open for her.

She tossed Cassie a "thanks" on her way out and opened the passenger door of her Subaru, setting her bag on the seat. She reached for the bag Reese was holding, but he moved past her, crowding her space, and loaded his items into her car.

She tilted her head up to meet his gaze. "Thanks for your help."

He didn't back away but kept his gaze on her. "You need to know something before we go on the trip."

"What's that?"

"Individuals get hurt. Teams stay safe. If you have some big idea that you can hike the Holcomb Springs Trail without help, without my advice and counsel, you'd better just cancel right now."

Hot anger shot through her. No way. Reese was not going to keep her from going on this trip. "I hardly think a backpacking trip compares to a stop at the Jitter Bug Too."

His gaze narrowed. "It's about the attitude."

"Just because I don't need your help getting coffee and scones to my car—something I do all the time by myself, thank you very much—doesn't mean I won't take sound advice on a trip. Just because you know all about the wilderness doesn't mean you know everything about this town. Or me. You've been gone a long time."

Was it her imagination or had he winced? His gaze remained steady on her then he moved away. "Remember what I said." After a beat of silence he said, "If you still want to go, come by the shop next week and pick up a backpack and sleeping bag. You might need boots too." And with a lift of his chin, he disappeared back inside Jitter Bug Too.

Ella closed the passenger door and moved around to the driver's side and got in.

Where'd the nice and kind Reese go who had defended her against Lucas? Or maybe that was more about Lucas and some macho thing than about helping her. Fine. She was hoping for a cordial relationship, but he was leaving after all. So in a way, this made it easier. She didn't have to worry about getting too attached to him or rekindling that high school crush she'd had. As long as it didn't make their trip awkward.

Would it? She hated awkward. Maybe it would be best if she found something else to do. Surely she could come up with an idea that would challenge her and prove herself without involving Reese.

She started the car, backed out, and headed toward school. This was dumb. She was not going to change her plans just because Reese got prickly. Her goal in going on the Holcomb Springs Trail trip was not to spend time with him; it was to prove to herself that she could do it.

And she would.

When Reese re-entered the Jitter Bug Too, Wally and Stan were studying him, grins on their faces.

"Morning, gentlemen."

They lifted their mugs to him. The Jitter Bug Too hadn't been here when he was in high school, but he remembered Stan and Wally. They were town fixtures. He had no idea what they did all day beyond sitting here and drinking coffee and watching what everyone else was doing. That was not how he wanted to grow old.

Cassie's gaze was warm on him as he placed his order. She'd probably seen the whole thing between him and Ella play out through the front windows. Stan and Wally too. Great. Well, he already had a bad boy reputation in this town. No point in trying to fight it.

He stood to the side while she fixed his order, leaving room for the other customers to come in. His conversation with Ella bugged him. He shouldn't have been so short with her. But why wouldn't she accept his help? That made no sense and sent all sorts of warning bells off in his head. He didn't take to lone rangers; she could listen to him or stay home.

Except, he knew that wasn't Ella. If anyone was a rule follower, it was her. It just rubbed him the wrong way that she didn't want his help.

But it ended up being a good thing. It was better that she was mad at him. Ever since he'd seen her at the shop, she'd resurrected old emotions he'd long thought buried. Why he'd had to go and make up that story in front of Lucas, he still didn't know. But the warmth of her gaze and gratitude had loosed something in him. Something unwelcome and dangerous.

Keeping her at arms' length was the right idea. He was leaving eventually, and it was better this way.

Cassie pushed his order across the counter. "Good to see you again, Reese." There was something else in her gaze, but he didn't want to analyze it.

"Thanks." He grabbed his order and headed out the door, glad to see Ella's car was gone. He just needed to get to the other side of the Holcomb Springs Trail trip, and then he'd likely not see her much at all.

CHAPTER
FOUR

Tony Stafford was changing in the locker room at the community center after a good-but-intense game of pick-up basketball. He tried to get over there at lunch as much as possible to play. It was a good stress release for him. And since he'd burned enough calories, he figured he could indulge in a muffin at the Jitter Bug Too. The stroll there on the covered wooden boardwalk through the charming downtown in the cool air would be refreshing. And maybe it would help him figure out how to resolve his sermon issues. With mid-week services tonight, if he didn't get this buckled down this afternoon, he'd run out of time. The rest of this week was full of appointments and meetings.

He scoffed at himself counting calories. Never used to matter. But since he'd turned forty-five, staying fit was not as easy as it used to be. And being a pastor was a bit more sedentary than the construction work he'd done in his younger years.

A twinge pinged his heart as it always did. Those younger years had included Janelle, his wife. Her death was one more thing about God he didn't understand.

He stuffed his remaining items into his duffle bag and

pushed open the door from the locker room into the hallway. And ran smack into Sheriff McIntyre. Twice in nearly a week.

"Sorry, Sheriff. Didn't see you."

"That's all right. My fault. My mind was elsewhere." Her gaze traveled to his still-damp hair. "Play basketball at lunch?" A small grin crossed her lips.

He raised his duffle. "Astute observation."

"Since my office is just down the hall, I like to wander down there after school when I can, get to know the kids." She tilted her head. "Do you have a minute?"

For her, yes. "Sure." They headed down the hall to her office. The sheriff's department, as well as the fire department, search and rescue, town services, and the community center all shared one town hall building. He needed to work on his sermon. But since he'd arrived up here, he'd been trying to get to know all the major town players. And since last Friday when they'd run together, the sheriff had been on his mind. Maybe some time with her would be just what he needed so he could move on and work on his sermon.

They entered the sheriff's department through a staff-only door into a large room filled with cubicles. Toward the back was a glassed-in office with a desk stationed in front of it and a door that read SHERIFF SHANNON MCINTYRE.

An older woman with close-cropped gray hair sat at the desk and looked up, smiling at them.

He searched his mind for her name but couldn't come up with it in time.

"Hello, Pastor."

He spied her nameplate. Donna Littrel. "Hi, Donna. How's your week going?"

"Can't complain. Can I get either of you coffee?"

The sheriff pushed open the door to her office and turned to him. "Or water? I have bottles in here."

"Water would be great." So this could be more than a quick

conversation. Interesting. He nodded at Donna as he followed the sheriff.

She gestured to a seating area of a small couch and a few chairs in the corner of her office while she reached into a small refrigerator for two bottles of water and handed him one.

He chose a chair, and she took the couch opposite him, a touch of weariness evident in the way she lowered herself. He imagined there weren't many people she could share the burden of her work with. He'd learned she was a single mom of her eighteen-year-old son Zach and that his dad wasn't around much. That alone would be a lot to handle.

A bowl of peanut M&Ms sat on the table between them. She took a handful and set her phone next to the bowl. "Help yourself. My afternoon pick-me-up, and my only bad habit. I think." She smiled at that.

"I'm surprised it's not coffee from the Jitter Bug Too." Cassie was the sheriff's younger sister. They had different coloring. Cassie had dark, curly hair. Shannon's was blonde, pulled back into a bun at the nape of her neck, but on Sundays he'd seen it curl down around her shoulders. Perhaps they took after different parents. But their builds were similar. Tall, lithe, high cheekbones, athletic in their movements.

"I often head there when I need to get out of the office. But then she usually has something fresh out of the oven that I can't resist. And I need to resist."

He laughed. He liked her easy humor, something he wouldn't have expected.

"After our conversation last Friday, I'd planned to get something with you on the calendar, just hadn't done it yet. But when I saw you today, I thought perhaps it was a divine nudge. I try not to ignore those. So, how are you liking Holcomb Springs so far?" She twisted the cap off her water and leaned back against the couch.

"I like it a lot. Different from Laguna Vista, for sure. But it's been a good move. A lot more than I expected in some ways, with managing staff and stepping into the shoes of a beloved retired pastor. But you can't beat the location. Sure, I can't go surfing in the morning, but there's so many more outdoor activities to make up for it." Writing a sermon every week had been more challenging than what he'd expected. He'd only preached once a month in Laguna Vista as one pastor on a staff of pastors. The urge to get back to his sermon pulled at him, but he resisted it. The sheriff had started this conversation; he was going to see it through.

Her phone buzzed on the table. She glanced at it then picked it up. Something flickered across her face—annoyance?—before she tamped it down. He didn't think anyone but him would have even caught it. But he was good at reading people. He had to be.

She met his gaze with a tilt of her head. "Want to take that ride along now? We could get out of here and tour the town. I can guarantee I can show you places you haven't been." That grin again.

He smiled back. "Sounds great."

A moment later they pushed out the back door of the sheriff's department to the gated lot and climbed into her department SUV. He spotted a bag of peanut M&Ms in the console and smiled.

Soon they were tearing down back roads, dirt trails, and things that didn't even seem like they were roads, with tree branches brushing the sides of the vehicle. He'd been on ride alongs with the Laguna Vista PD, but nothing like this.

"I've definitely never been this way before. I'm not even sure where we are."

"We're not too far from Belle Lumber's land and the national forest. We have a possible missing person, Dalton Brandt, early twenties. I doubt he ever showed up at church."

Tony shook his head. "Doesn't sound familiar. I've made it a point to reach out to all the teens and young adults that are even tangentially connected to the church. I know church isn't often the cool thing to do. But I've never heard his name mentioned."

"He worked for Belle Lumber, but he'd requested some vacation time. He didn't come back when he was scheduled to. His friends reported him missing last Thursday. Which means he's been missing for close to two weeks. Maybe. Depending if he left on a trip or not. It's possible he just hasn't come back yet. But I thought we'd look around out here, see if we could spot his car while we talk."

"Multitasking. I'm familiar with it." The woods crowded into the road. The scent of pine filled the air, even in the car with the heat blasting. It was a beautiful place to work. For both of them.

"What's the adjustment been like for you? I know Pastor Johnson was beloved by all. That can't be easy."

"It's had its challenges, but overall, the people have been great and welcoming. People don't like change; I know that. So I'm trying to move slowly, take my time. Not my strong suit. But I see us having a unique opportunity. We get a lot of tourists who come up for rest, relaxation, and renewal. I'd like to add *spiritual* in front of all of those too. The only true rest and peace is found in Jesus."

"I agree. And there are definitely two camps in this town. One who welcomes the tourists because they truly are the lifeblood of our small town. And one who hates them and wishes they'd leave us alone. So you may get some pushback from folks who want the church to be just for the locals."

He nodded. "I figured. But I used to run a construction company. If I can get a bunch of stubborn guys to all work together on the same project, I think I can get church members to sing out of the same hymn book, so to speak."

She laughed. "Nice. Well, the construction experience explains a lot. But you might need a bit more finesse. I've had some experience in that area."

"I bet. That's why I'm hoping we can join forces. We're in

unique positions, having a lot of responsibility for others, having to maintain confidences. Not too many people understand."

She pulled the vehicle over on a high ridge overlooking the valley. "Let's take a look around." She climbed out and headed to the back of the SUV. He followed. She opened it up, rummaged in a compartment, and handed him a pair of binoculars, taking one herself. They walked out to the brow of the ridge, the mountainside, lake, and valley opening up before them. "This is a good spot to see most of Holcomb Springs from here. You take that side. Pan down whatever roads you can find. Anything that looks manmade, sunlight glinting off it, let me know. Though I suspect if his vehicle was left anywhere around here that it is either chopped into pieces and sold off or on its way to Mexico right now."

They were both quiet for a while, intent on their job. But it was a companionable silence, just the wind blowing through the trees.

"From here we can see just how bad that fire was that came through last August," Shannon said. "It's only by God's grace we didn't lose the whole town or more houses. And it was started by an illegal marijuana grow operation. They're dangerous to the community. So I might be a bit intense about getting them shut down." Her stomach twisted at the idea of more loss, of how close they'd really come.

"I came up after the fire, but I remember watching it on the news from down in Laguna Vista. Some members of our church were up here for the weekend, and a group of them got trapped on the lake and had to be rescued by helicopter. I was shocked at what I saw when I finally got up here. I think everything we can do to prevent it from happening again is a worthwhile effort."

"I agree. And as you can see, it's a lot of ground to cover. But speaking of Laguna Vista, how is it going with Ryan Bradley?"

Tony turned at her question. She was still scanning the area with her binoculars. "It's been interesting. When we worked together at the church in Laguna Vista, we both reported to Pastor Tom. So I don't think he's taken too well to now reporting to me. He likes to do his own thing. There's no doubt he's a gifted singer and worship leader. I think he thinks his gifts are wasted in this small town. But he's open to doing some concerts this summer to introduce tourists to the church. He acknowledges he's made some missteps and errors in judgment, but I don't think it's all really sunk in yet. There's a lot of immaturity still." He scanned his area and looked back at her. "You must deal with that with some of your younger deputies."

She laughed. "Some feel like it's punishment to work in a small town when they want to see the action of a big city. I've had a few come through here who made it clear this was not their first choice and they were moving on first chance they got. It's a challenge for sure."

Her radio crackled and she reached for it. "Cell service is unreliable up here, so we use our radios a lot. Though the mountains can get in the way of them too." She responded then listened for a moment. "Copy that. I'll head over there now."

She glanced at Tony. "Got time for one more stop? HR at Belle Lumber is expecting us, and I'm hoping to talk to Beckett Lorde while I'm there." She studied him a moment. "You're good a reading people. I could use your impression of him. Since this is a community service visit and not anything criminal, you're fine to come along if you have the time."

The sun was rushing toward the trees. He'd given up any sermon prep time to spend it with the sheriff. It had been a good trade off, but one he'd pay for later. "Sure, sheriff."

They headed back to the SUV and climbed in. After a short trip down more back trails, they turned onto a proper road and soon saw the sign for Belle Lumber. She pulled the SUV up front, and they walked up the stairs to a wide, wooden porch and a building that resembled an oversized log cabin. Inside there was a lobby area with a receptionist's desk and a hallway disappearing behind it. The sheriff announced them. "We're here to get information on Dalton Brandt. I'd like to speak to Beckett Lorde directly."

The receptionist nodded. "He's expecting you. Head down the hallway, last door on the right."

"Thank you."

Once they were in the hallway, the sheriff turned to him with raised eyebrows. "Interesting." Her voice was barely above a whisper.

The door was open, and they stepped in.

Beckett Lorde spotted them, rose from his desk, and came around. Tony had never met the man before, but he'd seen him at a few town meetings.

"Sheriff McIntyre. Good to see you as always." He shook her hand then leveled a questioning gaze at Tony.

"This is Pastor Tony Stafford." The sheriff made the introduction. "He and I are working together on a community building plan, and he's part of our search and rescue team. Considering Dalton Brandt's disappearance, I thought his presence could be helpful."

Lorde nodded and shook Tony's hand with the kind of grip men use when they're trying to prove something. Tony hid a smile. He'd been around a lot of macho men during his construction years. He could handle Lorde.

Lorde gestured to the chairs in front of his desk. "Please, have a seat. I had my secretary print out Brandt's file. I have his emergency contact information, if that would be helpful." He handed over a piece of paper to the sheriff. "He clocked in Friday right on time for his shift; clocked out at quitting time. That was the last anyone here saw of him. He'd applied for some vacation time, so no one thought of anything until he didn't show up for work for two days last week. His supervisor marked him down as no show, no call. As of Monday, he was let go. Of course, if we discover that he's been sick or injured, he's welcome to have his job back. We just have plenty of kids who stop showing up for work, so our policy is to terminate after two no shows."

The sheriff scanned the paper. "Do you have him on any security cameras? Or his car?"

Lorde smiled. "Already ahead of you." He turned a computer monitor to face them, tapped a few keys. A video window came up of a young man in a coat and backpack swiping a security card at a door and entering. "The cameras are synced to the security cards. That's him clocking into work. You can see the date and time stamp at the bottom."

It read 7:58 on Friday, February 16.

He tapped more keys and another window came up. It looked like the same young man swiping his card again and walking away. The time stamp had the same date, but the time was 15:02. Three in the afternoon. "This is him leaving. And this is his car." Another window popped up. A security camera of the employee parking lot. The same man in the coat and backpack got into a light-colored two-door car, like a Honda Civic, backed out, and drove out of sight.

Tony let the sheriff put the pieces together; he kept his eyes on Lorde, watching the man's body language. But there was nothing there but helpfulness. Maybe a little smugness and superiority.

"If you could get us a list of people he worked with, his supervisor. I'd like to talk to them, see if he mentioned any plans or going any place on his vacation. Hopefully he just decided to extend his stay and hasn't told anyone."

Lorde handed the sheriff another piece of paper. "I thought you'd probably want that information. This is everyone on his shift and anyone the supervisor thought he might know or talk to. I like giving young people a chance at a good job, but many of them are just irresponsible. In Brandt's case, I hope that's all it is."

The sheriff was silent for a moment. Lorde wore a pleasant expression and didn't seem bothered by the silence.

Finally, the sheriff rose. "Thank you for your diligence and cooperation. I or one of my deputies will be in touch if we need anything further."

Lorde rose too. "However I can be of help."

The sheriff shot a glance at Tony, and they left the office.

Once they were in the SUV and heading away, she turned to him. "What did you think?"

"He was awfully helpful. A little macho with that hand squeeze. A little smug at being able to out-maneuver your requests."

She nodded. "My thoughts too. If he gives us everything we might want, we have no excuse to come back and poke around." Her phone buzzed an alert. "Shoot. I've got to get Zach from school. Mind if we swing by there before we head back to the station?"

"Whatever you need." Zach was eighteen. He knew a lot of kids were getting their driver's licenses later these days, so perhaps Zach didn't drive himself to and from school. But surely he could get a ride? He didn't know where the sheriff lived, but she'd run to the park, which wasn't far from the high school. It was a small town, but it seemed like there would be plenty of days when the sheriff would be too busy to pick him up. It was an interesting thing to learn about her, and he wasn't sure what to make of it.

"Zach doesn't have his license yet?" he ventured.

She shook her head. "I haven't encouraged it. Hazard of the job, I know. But he doesn't really need it. Either I can give him a ride or there are plenty of people in town he's approved to ride with. I'm sure he'll end up getting it this summer because he'll need it for college. His dad has already promised him a car." She grimaced.

He supposed what she saw in her line of work made her more protective of her only child. Still, he'd seen plenty of kids rebel against overly strict parents. It was tough being a parent under the best of circumstances. Something he'd likely never experience, a thought that always put a bruised feeling in his heart.

He moved away from the painful subject. "So what makes you think Beckett Lorde isn't everything he says?" The man was likely a jerk pretending not to be, but that wasn't a criminal offense.

"I've suspected for some time that he is behind some of the drug rings in the area. His company is a good front for laundering money, having access to illegal grows. He's got the transportation. For the past two years, one of my deputies, Brett Chang, had suspected someone inside the Spread the Love event of embezzling money. Last year they were able to catch the lady who was doing it. She'd run up a large gambling debt at the casinos down the hill. But she'd done it by overbilling a paper goods supply company. That happened to be owned by an LLC that was traced back to Belle Lumber. Lorde played it like he was the victim, getting ripped off by Yvonne. But if he needed to launder some money, it would have been a good way to do it. Plus, he's lied to me in the past. I hate liars, and I'm not sure I believe they can change. I certainly can't trust one."

"I agree with you, sheriff. It's hard to trust someone who's lied to you." Tony stared out the window as the small downtown came into view. He'd enjoyed spending this afternoon with her, even if it meant he'd be up late working out the kinks in his sermon. But that wasn't the foremost problem in his mind right now.

She pulled into the high school parking lot and glanced at him. "Call me Shannon." She gave him a genuine smile. Had she enjoyed today as well?

He returned her grin. "And it's just Tony, not pastor. Kind of nice to take that hat off once in a while."

"I know what you mean."

Any further conversation was interrupted by Zach piling into the backseat. They chatted about school, but when Shannon dropped Tony off at the church and he was able to get into his office, he couldn't get his mind on his sermon. He'd enjoyed spending time with her today. And he thought the interest was mutual. It had been so long since he'd been interested in a woman. After Janelle's death, he'd figured he'd be alone the rest of his life. And he'd been okay with that.

But Shannon was different. Still, if he wanted a chance to have anything more than a collegial relationship with her, he knew he'd have to be honest with her about the one thing no one knew about. And he'd have to do it sooner rather than later. Because she hated liars. And his whole life was based on a lie.

CHAPTER
FIVE

Ella blew her hair out of her eyes as she filled the watering can in her classroom sink. The kids had dashed out of her classroom as soon as the bell had rung, searching for the freedom of spring break. She was ready too. She hoped.

She moved around the room, giving her plants a drink before the vacation. "A little something for you. And a little something for you. At least you guys are steady and reliable. A little water and sun, and you're grateful." She didn't know if it helped the plants to talk to them, but she liked it.

Amanda appeared in her doorway. "Why does the day before vacation always feel a week long?"

"I don't know, but I'm glad it's over. Hiking the Holcomb Springs Trail will seem like a piece of cake after trying to keep fifth graders engaged in their lessons today." She watered the last plant, touched its leaves, then replaced the watering can on its hook by the sink and washed her hands. Kids were such germ magnets.

Amanda glanced out the window. "Hopefully the weather will be better. This rain just turns everything slushy and muddy."

"It's supposed to be nicer. No snow or rain. Highs in the fifties. Nothing like that Palm Springs weather though." Ella walked over and nudged Amanda's shoulder. "You'd better come back with a nice tan."

Amanda nudged her back. "You'd better come back with some great stories."

"I'm planning on taking pictures. I want just enough adventure, like sore muscles from hiking and carrying a pack. Not being-chased-by-a-bear adventure." She packed up her tote bag at her desk.

"Reese will keep you safe. I have no doubt of that."

Ella stared at her. "How do you know that? You don't even know him."

"Town gossip." She crossed her arms over her chest and leaned back. "He's the new guy. Plenty of people are happy to talk about him. He had some heroics as a soldier; also had some sort of injury that caused him to leave the service. Though it doesn't seem to be slowing him down any. People in town have lots of good things to say about him, even those who remember him as a high school kid with a bad attitude."

"Huh." Ella checked her desk for anything else she might need to bring home.

"I can't believe I know more than you do about him." Amanda peered at her. "I know you. You didn't ask because you didn't want to know. Maybe you're afraid of that crush of yours fanning back to life."

Ella swung her gaze around the room, anywhere but at Amanda. "I guess I'm all packed up." She glanced out the window. "Not looking forward to going out in that. At least snow isn't as messy."

"You're avoiding the subject."

"What subject?"

"Reese."

"How did he become a subject? You know more about him

than I do. You've told me everything. He's leading the hiking trip that a lot of other people will be on. What else is there to discuss? I'll take pictures and have a good time. I promise." Ella hiked her tote over her shoulder and pulled out her keys. "Are you all packed up? I'll walk out with you."

Amanda just gave her a look. "You always do this."

"Do what?"

"You don't want to talk about your feelings."

Ella dropped her tote while she looked up at the ceiling. "What feelings?"

"Your feelings for Reese."

"Good grief, Amanda. It was twelve years ago." And she knew that because Reese had reminded her. He had mentally retrieved the number quicker than she had. A fact she had noticed but had no idea what it meant. "We were in high school. Do you still have feelings for your high school crush?"

"Considering it was Chad Michael Murray…maybe." Amanda giggled.

Ella re-shouldered her tote. "I think all of this is a misdirection. What about you? You're headed to Palm Springs to hang out with old folks on vacation. Yes, the weather will be great, but what about you? It's not like you have a robust dating life."

Amanda picked up a paper on Ella's desk. "Not easy in this small town."

"Precisely." Ella put her arm around Amanda's shoulder and guided her toward the door. "So try to break away from the parents once in a while. Go crazy and have dinner at six. Or seven even!" They both laughed as they exited Ella's classroom, and she locked the door behind them.

As they walked down the hall, they passed the trophy-and-display case. And the plaque that listed each year's graduating class valedictorian. Her name was on it. She'd attended this school. She and the school secretary were fixtures here. And she knew how often people would come and go from this place.

Teaching in a small town K through eight school wasn't too many people's idea of career advancement. But she liked the predictability of it.

Just before they left the building, Ella reached over and hugged Amanda. "Have fun, and I promise I'll share pictures and stories when I get back." She popped up her umbrella and ran for her car. Not that there would be much in the way of stories, she was sure. Definitely nothing about her feelings for Reese, which did not exist.

She slid into her Subaru, tossing her umbrella and tote on the seat next to her. Amanda was one of her dearest friends and a good teaching partner. But there was only so far she could let someone in. It was just too risky. Someday Amanda would find a man and get married, maybe move down the mountain and leave teaching or get a different job. Because everyone left eventually.

Still, the hiking trip would be good for her, stretch her comfort zone, and give her a feeling of accomplishment in a different area of life. How bad could that be?

But as she headed home—the one she'd grown up in, the one she still shared with her mom—she couldn't help but wonder if Amanda was right. Maybe there was something more out there she was missing.

When she pulled into the driveway of the house, Evan's car was there. She didn't know he was coming this weekend. Had she missed a text from him? She pulled out her phone. No text. Hmm. That wasn't like her younger brother. He usually texted before coming up. He lived down the hill—what locals called anything off the mountain—where he had a good job as a physical therapist and a girlfriend, Chelsea, who Ella adored.

She grabbed her items and bounded inside, not bothering to open the umbrella for the short jaunt up the wood stairs. She burst into the mud room, dropping her bag, umbrella, and taking off her boots, replacing them with fuzzy slippers. Voices drifted in from the kitchen.

She stepped into view. Evan and Chelsea sat around their kitchen table cradling mugs. Mom wouldn't be home from work for another hour. "Hey, guys. I didn't know you were coming up." Her mind thought through dinner plans that could be stretched for two more.

"Hey, sis." Evan stood and gave her a hug. So did Chelsea. "Sorry. I texted Mom, and she said it was fine. It was kind of last minute, and I didn't want to bother you during class."

"I'm always glad to see you. Anything in particular you have planned? How long are you staying?"

Evan's eyes darted to Chelsea and—was that a faint hue of pink creeping up his neck?—he drummed his finger on the table. "It's supposed to snow tonight and tomorrow morning. We thought we might grab some fresh powder on the slopes before the spring break rush."

Hmm. He was nervous about something. He'd tell her eventually. He always did. "Well, anything sound good for dinner? Mom and I were going to have leftovers, but I can see what we have in the freezer or make a run to the store."

"Actually, I thought we'd get a lasagna from Bella Sorgenti. I've already ordered it. Mom will pick it up on her way home."

Ella grinned. "And that's why you're my favorite brother."

He gave her a wry grin back. "I'm your only brother."

"Still applies. Let me get out of these clothes into something cozier. You guys up for a board game night?" She started for the stairs.

"Sure. But I need to tell you something." He glanced around then gestured upstairs. "It's about the furnace. Let me just show you."

She frowned. The furnace? What was he talking about?

He put his hand between her shoulder blades and guided her upstairs to her room, closing the door behind them.

She cocked her head. "This isn't about the furnace."

"No." He let out a breath, then reached into his hoodie pocket and pulled out a ring box.

Ella's jaw dropped. "Is that… an engagement ring?"

He nodded and popped it open. A beautiful diamond nestled in a band of smaller ones sat inside.

"Oh, Evan. You did good. She'll love it." Then it dawned on her. "Is that why you're here? Are you going to propose?"

He grinned. "I thought I would up on the slopes where we had our first date." He closed the box and slipped it back in his pocket. "I'm terrified I'm going to lose it."

She hugged him. "You'll do great. She'll say yes, and you'll live happily ever after."

"You and your romance books."

"Yes, but I'm also a teacher, so I have to be right. Plus, I'm your big sister. But now I want to change." She opened the door and shooed him out. "Thanks for that advice about the furnace filters. I'll make sure to get them changed." She closed the door behind him, giggling.

They chatted around the kitchen table until Mom came home bearing lasagna, garlic bread, and salad.

In between bites, Evan asked, "So what are your spring break plans, sis?"

She told him about hiking the Holcomb Springs Trail with a group. "We leave Monday. I have a pile of gear started in my room. Should be a great trip." Luckily when she'd gone by the Outfitters to pick up her backpack and sleeping bag, Raul had helped her. She hadn't seen Reese.

Mom looked at her over the rim of her glass. "Just stay with your group. I'd hate for you to go missing like that young man, Dalton Brandt. They've been talking about it at work."

"I'm the last person you have to worry about wandering off, Mom." Ella helped herself to more salad.

"I know, but I'm a mother, and it's my prerogative to worry."

"We don't even know if this guy is missing. Or if he went missing anywhere near here. There's a lot we don't know. He didn't do all the things you should, like telling people his itinerary or keeping anyone informed. There's a reason to follow best practices." Ella took a bite of her salad.

Evan laughed. "Spoken like a true teacher."

"I'm just saying, if he'd done what he was supposed to, everyone would have a better idea of where to look for him." Ella gestured with her fork. "Rules help keep you safe. I'm not going to go missing, and nothing bad is going to happen to me because I'm a rule follower." Even if it meant following Reese's directions. Amanda was right though; he'd keep her safe.

After dinner, they set up Risk in the living room in front of the roaring fireplace and played for world domination while they sipped hot chocolate. Contentment spread through Ella at having her family in one place enjoying each other's company. But melancholy tinged it as she realized this might be one of the last times they did this. Things would change. Chelsea would be part of their family. Evan would be part of Chelsea's family now.

Ella's world—which had always been centered around Mom, Evan, and her—was tilting. And nothing would ever be the same.

SHANNON CARRIED TWO PLATES TO THE LIVING ROOM AND set them on the coffee table in front of the fireplace. It was more comfortable here instead of the dining room. Zach was spending the night at Isaiah's house, celebrating the end of the school week and the beginning of spring break.

Tia was already ensconced on the couch, a cozy throw over her lap, her natural hair spread out over the back cushions. She lifted her head. "Thanks for cooking tonight. It's been a week."

Shannon sat next to her. "Just a new Instant Pot recipe I'm trying. Pork chops and mushroom sauce. My therapist says I need something in my life more than work."

Tia laughed as she picked up her fork. "You and me both. So

how was your impromptu ride along with Pastor Dreamy, I mean Tony."

Shannon nudged her. "I'm not going to even ask about how you know about that." She took a bite. The recipe was a keeper. Some days, it was the small victories.

"Answer the question." Tia talked around a bite.

"It was nice. Collegial."

Tia raised her eyebrows. "Really? How academic. So, no sparks?"

"It was work." She paused. "But he is easy on the eyes. And easy to talk to. We have a lot in common."

"Uh huh."

Shannon's cheeks warmed. Tia's needling never bothered her; they were best friends. She told her things she told no one else. Tia was the only one who knew she was seeing a therapist. So why did this subject twirl her stomach? "What?"

Tia sat up and set her plate on the coffee table. "Just that this is the first eligible guy for you to show up on this mountain in a long time. You should explore the possibilities. You're not getting any younger."

"Thanks for the reminder, Miss We're the Same Age." This conversation was going to require ice cream. Maybe brownies. Did she have the ingredients?

"You're a determined woman. You have to be to do your job and get where you've gotten. I'm just saying, put a little of that determination towards Pastor Dreamy and see what happens."

"Flirting seems ridiculous."

"I'm not talking about flirting. I'm talking about putting yourself in his same proximity. Get to know the man. Let him get to know you."

Shannon sighed. "You really think so?"

"Girl, unless you make a concentrated effort to get to know this man, you'll just drift around with everything else taking priority. Your personal life gets to be a priority, not just work."

"Like you should talk."

"I'm preaching to myself too."

Shannon got to her feet. "Want some ice cream? I think this requires ice cream." At Tia's nod, she headed into the kitchen, thinking about Tia's words. Maybe it was time for her personal life to be a priority. And if she didn't do it, Tia would never let her hear the end of it.

CHAPTER
SIX

Early Saturday morning, Reese ran away from the lake and his garage apartment and toward town, his stride comfortable and familiar. It was about three miles, easy enough. And somewhere along the way, he'd run into Pastor Tony. Though with the fog and light flurries, he wouldn't see him as quickly as usual. Saturdays had become their day to connect through running.

The Sunday Reese had come back to town, the pastor had spotted him and made a point of introducing himself after the service. Given Pastor Tony's build, he clearly worked out and soon had invited Reese to join them for basketball at lunch most days in the community center.

Reese had gone a couple of times, but he and the pastor had actually connected better over their love of running.

"Clears the fog out of the brain and helps me settle down for the day," Pastor Tony had said.

Reese couldn't agree more. He'd run a lot in the Army, but before that even, running had been his salvation. Running track in middle and high school had given him strength and purpose. He'd found something he was good at. It didn't hurt that it helped him get away from the one particular bully who had plagued him in elementary school. Reese had been a late bloomer physically, and growing up in a pacifist household—his parents were proud hippies—had only made him a bigger target for being picked on.

But his body knew how to run, and he found peace pounding the pavement.

Most Saturdays it was just him and Pastor Tony, but he'd also met a few other guys who ran, played basketball, and enjoyed the outdoors. Deputy Jonas McCann and firefighter/paramedic Marco Valdez would join them on occasion. It wasn't the same as his Ranger platoon, but it gave him a taste of the camaraderie he'd found in the service.

As he got closer to town, the fog thinned, and he spotted a figure in the distance. Tall and broad shouldered with a loping stride, it had to be Pastor Tony. Didn't look like anyone was with him today. In a way, Reese was relieved. This upcoming trip with Ella had rattled his brain a bit, and he wouldn't mind running through it with Pastor Tony. He'd become a counselor of sorts, and Reese trusted his confidence implicitly.

Reese raised a hand. "Hey, Pastor."

"Reese. Good to see you." He slapped hands with Reese before turning around and heading back the way he'd come. They typically ran to the park, took a few laps then headed back. The pastor lived just outside of town, so it wasn't as far of a run for him.

Then again, Reese didn't think Pastor Tony had the same demons chasing him that Reese had.

They made a little small talk and mostly ran in silence. Reese liked that the pastor didn't feel the need to fill the air with words.

"Got some trips planned for spring break?" Pastor Tony matched Reese's stride.

"Yeah. A three-day trip starting Monday along the Holcomb

Springs Trail. A group of friends scheduled it." He waited a beat then added, "And Ella Sommer is coming too."

"I'm still trying to connect the dots with everyone here." He paused. "She's lived here her whole life. You used to live here in high school. Did you know her from before?"

Reese nodded. Pastor Tony had an amazing memory for details. It must come in handy being a pastor. "Yeah. She was a freshman when I was a senior. But our paths didn't cross often."

"Have you seen her much since you've been back?"

"Some. She came into the shop to sign up for the trip, and I ran into her at the Jitter Bug Too."

The only sound was their feet slapping the pavement and their breath puffing as the park came into view. The fog created a private bubble around them.

Pastor Tony nodded. "It'll be good for her to get away. Maybe the two of you could reconnect." He slid a glance at Reese.

Reese shrugged. "I can't imagine she'd have any use for someone like me. We're so different."

"Not that different, really. Both of you understand family obligations. You have a strong sense of duty and responsibility. You both care about people under your charge. Apparently you both like being outdoors, since she's going on this hike."

"She's a teacher. I'm a Ranger washout. She likes books. I don't."

The pastor shook his head. "You're not a washout. You had a traumatic brain injury. And book smart isn't everything. Lots of smart people don't enjoy reading. It's not the only way to get information." A touch of vehemence had slipped into his voice.

They ran in silence another hundred yards. "I'm still having nightmares. I haven't done an overnight trip since I've been back." A few more strides then, "What if I have one on the trail? Are Raul's clients going to think he set them up with a lunatic?" And what would Ella think?

"Do you have them every night or are they triggered by something?"

"Not every night. Sometimes once a week. Sometimes not even that often. I haven't figured out what triggers them, if anything."

"Do you get them the nights after you've led a day hike?"

Reese thought for a moment. "I don't know. I'd have to think about that."

Pastor Tony shrugged. "It's possible the physical activity helps. You like being outdoors. Mostly, though, you can't live your life in fear of the what ifs." They were about halfway around the park before he spoke again. "That goes for Ella too. Just be open to the possibilities. Give her a chance. You're living a solitary life, Reese. It wouldn't hurt to let someone in."

Reese huffed a chuckle. "It might." He elbowed the pastor. "Besides, look who's talking. You could take your own advice."

Tony shrugged. "I was married before. Had a wonderful marriage to a wonderful woman."

Reese couldn't imagine what it would be like to marry the love of your life, only to have her taken from you. The pain would be unbearable. And yet, Pastor Tony was still serving God and not bitter. But he'd hinted at a long season of wrestling with God after his wife's death.

Still, it wasn't something Reese wanted to face. He'd known loss. Two of his buddies had died in the same explosion that had given him his TBI. High-school Ella had a special place in his heart, completely blown out of proportion, he was sure. But he kinda hated for that memory to come crashing down with the reality of spending time with her hiking.

"I'm sure Ella is a different person than she was in high school. I know I am."

"Probably. But change is a good thing."

A few people had trickled into the park, but they were on the far side.

"So what's eating you?" Pastor Tony asked.

Reese shrugged. "I don't know. I was kind of a jerk in high school." He let out a breath. "I had been bullied in elementary school because I was small and my parents believed words could solve any problem. By the time we moved up here when I was in high school, I was bigger, faster, and had a chip on my shoulder. I figured if I had an aggressive attitude, no one would mess with me. And no one did."

They waved to a few people as they passed the parking area. "It was a small high school, so we all knew each other, at least by name and by sight. Ella never really seemed put off by my attitude. She even went out of her way to help me with a paper one time. And I never forgot that."

"Seems someone like that would be worth getting to know again."

Reese let out a breath. The pastor was right, but he didn't like it. "I was hoping you'd have some people-management techniques. Raul's always so good with the clients. You're good with people. I was hoping there was some secret or technique you could share."

Tony laughed his big laugh that fit his frame but not his profession. "The secret is to actually care about people. You want to get along with Ella on the trip? Ask her about her life. Find out what's important to her."

Which meant letting her into his. Not on his agenda. Still, he had a feeling his agenda wasn't going to matter much. After three days on the trail, High School Ella would get blown out of the water by Current Day Ella.

He just hoped he wasn't too disappointed. High School Ella had been one of the few people who had seen through his attitude and spent time to help him. And he'd never forgotten that.

SHANNON THOUGHT SHE COULD GIVE SOME OF ZACH'S high school classmates a run for their money in the silliness department this Saturday morning. Why else would she be out here running to the park hoping to spot Tony instead of just calling him like a normal person? She could have asked him to coffee or lunch. Though it was hard to find a place in this town where they could go and not be gossiped about. And that was the last thing she wanted. She had to navigate taking Tia's advice without making a fool out of herself.

Maybe she was waffling because she wasn't sure what she wanted to ask him. No, she knew what she had to confide. She just wasn't sure she wanted to. But her therapist had encouraged her to find a few trustworthy people to lean on. That her insomnia was part of her carrying too big a load by herself.

She had Tia. But even she had encouraged her to let other people in. And after finding out that Pastor Tony suffered from insomnia, too, and seeing him at work on the Dalton Brandt case, she thought he was someone she could trust. So she figured she'd feel out that idea during a run.

This was not like her at all. She prided herself on her decisiveness and ability to make decisions. She picked up her pace and headed for the park. As the fog thinned, she spotted Tony's build and stride.

But he wasn't alone. She should have considered that possibility. There were a few guys that ran with him, her sergeant Jonas McCann was one of them. But for some reason, she'd spent all of her energy debating the wisdom of this trip. She'd never run an investigation like this. Why couldn't she manage her personal life better? Probably because she didn't really have one.

So who was with Tony? Not Jonas or Marco. She knew them well enough to recognize them even with the fog. So it was someone she didn't know well. Who could that be? Only new person in town was Reese Vega.

She'd heard about Vega's past and also that he was a decorated soldier. She had no reason to think that he was trouble now. But she should talk to him about Dalton Brandt. Vega was an outdoors person. Maybe he'd seen something. Her deputies already had talked to him and Raul, but they were sifting through leads and information that came in daily after the BOLO—be on the lookout for law enforcement agencies—and Brandt's description had gone out to the media, trying to figure out what was relevant and what wasn't. The county sheriff's department was lending their resources too.

Her gut still told her that Lorde was behind this in some way. But she had to be objective and not let her dislike of the man blind her to other options.

As the men came into view, she waved. "Mind if I join you gentlemen?" she asked as they came closer.

"Sheriff, happy to have you." Tony motioned to Reese. "You know Reese Vega?"

"We haven't officially met, but I heard you were back in town."

Reese held her gaze. "Good to meet you… officially." He smiled.

She came along side Tony and nodded for them to resume their pace. Running three across wasn't great for conversation, or even running. "How long have you been running this morning?"

"Reese has an extra three miles on me, but we've been pounding the ground for a while."

Reese pushed back his sleeve and looked at his smart watch. "And I've got another three to get back home."

"You're young." Tony patted his shoulder.

"While you're here" —Shannon leaned forward around Tony to look at Reese— "I wanted to ask you about Dalton Brandt."

Reese nodded. "Yeah, Brett came by last week and was asking if Brandt had ever booked anything with us or we had any thoughts on where a guy like him might go. Neither Raul or I had ever met the guy, but we told Brett to check with Cory Grant. He sometimes does solo trips."

Cory Grant was on their search and rescue team and also

helped out at the Outfitters during peak seasons. He was an experienced outdoorsman. Brett had talked to him too.

"If you were a young guy Brandt's age and took off somewhere, where would you go?"

"Depends on what he was into. Skiing, hiking, snowboarding, rock climbing. This time of year, the better skiing and snowboarding is in Utah. But it takes money to get there. Most guys just hang around here. There's enough decent stuff to keep busy."

That had been Shannon's thought too. The guy wasn't making a lot of money, drove an old car, and didn't have parents who funded his lifestyle. Unless he was involved in Lorde's side business, and then he could have a lot of untraceable cash. It kept coming back to Lorde. "His snowboard and ski gear were still at his apartment. So either he wasn't planning a snow trip or he hadn't collected them yet."

"Maybe he wanted to do a solo hiking trip. Some people like winter backpacking. Lots of solitude and quiet. No one on the trails. No issues with it being too hot or not having enough water."

"There wasn't any camping gear at his apartment. Which meant he either had it with him or that wasn't something he was into." Shannon liked how Reese thought.

"Did his friends have any clue? Did he say anything about where he was headed?"

Shannon shook her head. "I don't think they knew him that well. He came up to work for Belle Lumber and made some casual friends there. When he didn't show up for work, they went by his place and then reported him missing."

"Lots of possibilities then." He was quiet a moment. "Well, if he was going to go on a solo trip, the odds are he'd take either the Pacific Crest Trail where it runs near here or the Holcomb Springs Trail. Those are the two big ones. I'm heading out on Monday on the Holcomb Springs Trail with a group, so I'll keep my eyes open for anything unusual. It's a lot of territory to cover to find one person. Could have had some sort of emergency or gotten injured. No good comms up there either."

Shannon nodded. "My thoughts exactly. I'd appreciate your eyes up there. And stay safe. You know about the illegal grows near there, right?"

He nodded. "Raul has mentioned it. We'll stay to the trail and not wander off. I'll let you know if I see anything. I'd better head back. Good to meet you, Sheriff."

"You too."

Reese peeled off from them and loped off into the fog, headed toward the lake, as she and Tony turned toward another lap around the park.

"You about done too?" she asked him.

"I got a few more in me if you do." He studied her. "Seems we're establishing a pattern of running into each other every few days."

She laughed. "It is at that."

They ran a bit more with neither saying anything.

Tony broke the silence. "I'm a good listener, and I think you have something on your mind."

She nodded. But it was a few more paces before she spoke. "You know how we said we both have the welfare of so many people on our shoulders but there's no one we can talk to about it?"

He laughed. "Oh yeah."

"What do you do?"

He scrubbed a hand over his face. "Well, I have insomnia, something I think we have in common."

"Any good solutions?"

He slowed until they came to a stop. "I think we should help each other. We have a unique position in this town, both of us. Instead of these chance encounters, why don't we make it a regular thing?" His gaze held hers and something about how his voice got quiet and soft did something to her insides.

Maybe Tia had been right about her being open to possibilities. She was feeling things she'd thought long dead. But not completely dead because she found herself agreeing as they talked through the options.

Her phone buzzed. Maybe Zach was up. She pulled it out of her pocket. A text from Dan.

Sorry. Something came up and I'm not going to be able to take Zach for spring break.

Yeah, she could imagine what came up. Dan had never remarried after their divorce, preferring a series of girlfriends instead. Something Shannon hated that Zach was exposed to and could do zero about. But what she hated more was how often his dad disappointed him.

You'd better let him know.

She'd learned long ago not to be the bearer of Dan's bad news. She would be there to pick up the pieces.

"Something wrong?" Tony's voice broke into her thoughts.

She let out a sigh as she stuffed her phone back in her pocket. "Yeah. Dan—Zach's dad—was supposed to have him over spring break. Now he can't. Zach's going to be disappointed. And I don't know what he's going to do over spring break." Another problem she'd have to figure out.

"The community center has programs going on for kids whose parents work."

"I'd forgotten about that. Though Zach would consider himself too old for any of it."

"Does he play basketball?" Tony cut a glance at her.

Was he just being polite or was he helping her game plan this? "Yeah. Some. He prefers video games these days though. But anything I can do to pry him out of his room is a good thing."

"Well, a group of us play at lunch most days. He'd be welcome. I've been getting Ryan to join us, so maybe Zach could relate better to someone cooler than us." He chuckled.

"That's a good thought."

"Let me know if I can swing by and pick him up. If that'd make your life easier."

She let his words roll around her head. Make her life easier. Wow. She couldn't remember the last time anyone had offered to do that.

Tony was going to be an interesting person to get to know.

CHAPTER
SEVEN

Ella lugged her stuffed backpack out to her car. It wasn't light, and she was going to have to carry it for three days. Could she do it? This was her last chance to bail.

She closed the hatch on the back of the car and leaned against it. The day was sunny and bright, the sun warm on her skin, a contrast to the cool air. It was a perfect day for hiking in the woods. Mom had left for work after giving her a hug and saying she couldn't wait to hear about her adventures. She'd said she was even looking forward to some time alone.

Evan and Chelsea had left happily last night, Chelsea sporting her sparkling new ring. Both of them radiating joy. And both of them making her promise to tell them all about her trip as soon as she got back Wednesday night.

Ella couldn't live that down. She slid into the driver's seat and headed toward the Outfitters. It was a short trip, and she pulled into the parking lot and around to the side of the building next to a van bearing the logo of Holcomb Springs Outfitters.

The side door of the building opened, and Reese strode out, hands shoved in his front pockets.

She climbed out. "Hey, Reese."

He didn't smile as he walked toward her. "So, bad news. The group that was scheduled to go on the trip just called. They all have food poisoning. They were staying at a cabin together, and it was something they ate, maybe the potato salad or hamburgers. Anyhow, they are all too sick to go on the trip."

"Oh, that's too bad. Food poisoning is miserable." She headed to the hatch to open it, but Reese put a hand against it.

"The trip's canceled, Ella. It was their trip. You were just added on."

His words were like a punch to her gut. *Canceled* and *added on*. Yeah, that could describe her whole life. She wrapped her arms around her middle and leaned against her car, trying to absorb his words.

"But I'd planned for this. This was my whole spring break adventure."

"I'm sorry, Ella." His dark-brown eyes actually contained some regret.

What was she going to tell everyone? Her big adventure was derailed by food poisoning. Her life, as usual, controlled by someone else's choices. Anger rose, fighting with disappointment. She was sick of this. An image of Lucas's face rose in her mind of his reaction to the news. He'd be smug. Maybe he'd even think she made up the food poisoning thing to call it off. She fisted her hands. There had to be another option.

"What are you doing, then?" She met Reese's gaze.

"What do you mean?"

"I mean, you had this trip planned. What are you doing now that it's not happening?"

He shrugged. "I don't know. Hadn't thought that far. They just called. Probably help Raul around the shop. The time was already blocked off, so there's nothing scheduled for me."

"So you're just going to hang around the shop all day?"

"I guess. Why are you so interested?"

"I'm just thinking about what we could do instead." She pushed off her car and paced through the gravel. She had to come up with something to salvage this spring break. And Reese was her best shot at adventure. "I mean, we both have the time off, why can't we do something adventurous without the group?" She stopped, an idea flooding her brain that she hardly dared to voice to him. Being alone with Reese caused emotions and ideas to wash over her, forcing her to get them under control while her back was to him. Being alone with Reese was a bad idea. Wasn't it? They were so different.

But this was supposed to be about adventure, right? And he was a professional. She was only asking him to do his job. It wasn't personal. So nothing ventured, nothing gained. She turned and faced him.

"Why can't we just go on the trip together? Just the two of us."

"No." The word was out of Reese's mouth before he could even think. He did not want to be alone with Ella. He had just gotten his brain around being with her for three days with a group. Alone? No way.

Ella planted her hands on her hips. "Why not? The trip is already planned. It's just with fewer people."

Reese turned to go into the shop. "Follow me. I'll get your money refunded."

As he stepped inside, she grabbed his arm. Heat filtered through the layers of flannel and thermal shirt down to burn his skin, freezing him in place.

"Wait. I don't want my money back. I want to go on the trip. I still don't see why we can't go."

"Store policy. Raul's never on a trip alone with a woman."

"Good policy for Raul. He's married. You aren't." She paused and looked up at him. "Are you?"

He shook his head and continued into the store. Ella scrambled after him.

Raul was at the counter talking with his wife, Marissa. She also helped out during their busy times. He looked up, frowning. "Problem?"

"The group got food poisoning. The trip's off. I'm just going to refund Ella's money."

Ella leaned on the counter and spoke to Raul. "I don't want a refund. I think Reese and I should still go. You don't have a problem with that, do you, Raul?"

Raul glanced between Reese and Ella. He cleared his throat. "Reese, can I see you in the back?"

Reese shot a look at Ella and headed back with Raul out of earshot. "You don't want to go?" Raul asked.

"Do you think it's a good idea for me to be alone with a woman in the wilderness?"

"I think it warrants some caution. But I know Ella, and I know you. And you guys know each other. What's your objection to it?"

Reese ran his hand through his hair, now longer than it'd been in years, reminding him of everything he'd lost. Ella felt risky. He couldn't say that to Raul because he didn't know why. It was just his gut telling him that. And he'd learned to trust his gut.

"I don't want to disappoint a customer. Ella's a good woman. She's done a lot for this town, and never takes time for herself. I want her to have a good spring break." Raul pointed to the schedule tacked to the backroom wall. "Cory's got a day trip meeting at the trailhead. You guys could join his group for today. He's got day trips each day this week, or else I'd see about having you all join up. I'll call around and see if I can get someone else to join you for the rest of it. Have any ideas of who I can call?"

Reese thought for a moment but came up blank. He just didn't know enough people. Hadn't tried, really, since he didn't plan to stick around. Especially people willing to give up their plans last minute to spend three days in the wilderness packing their own supplies.

"No, I can't think of anyone. You know more people than I do. I'll take Ella today with Cory's group, but if I don't like how today goes, I'm bringing her back. She can do day trips with Cory's groups."

Raul studied him for a moment. "Fair enough. I'll radio you with details if I can get someone else to join you. In the meantime, I'll drop you off at the trailhead."

Reese turned to tell Ella the decision, but Raul stopped him. "Hey, just give it a chance. Ella could be a good friend to you."

Reese didn't say anything, but Raul continued. "You're bringing a weapon, right? Early spring could have mountain lions out with cubs and bears prowling around looking for food."

"I have bear spray."

Raul raised his eyebrows.

"Look." Reese lowered his voice, feeling the tension in his throat. "I don't want to take the risk. I'm still having nightmares. I can't be responsible for having access to a weapon when I wake up in a cold sweat thinking I'm back in a gun fight." His weapons were safely locked up in the storage room of Raul's garage.

Raul didn't say anything, but his expression softened.

Reese headed out front. He did owe it to Raul to give it a chance. And Ella. It wasn't her fault the group got food poisoning, and she deserved a good spring break. He thought about what Pastor Tony had said. And Ella had helped him before. Maybe he could return the favor. He came out on the main floor.

Ella greeted him with questioning eyes.

And behind her stood Lucas and his fiancée. Yeah, they were here to pick up their kayaks. He'd expected to be gone by now.

Lucas gave a smug grin. "I'm surprised you guys haven't left yet. Where's the rest of the group?" He cast a sideways glance toward Ella, one side of his mouth tipping up. He didn't believe there was a trip. Great.

Ella seemed to shrink, like she was collapsing inward.

Reese strode past Lucas and took Ella's arm. "We're meeting them up there. Ready to go?"

Her gaze shot to his, her eyes wide and hopeful. "Um, yeah. Yes, yes I am." She tilted her head slightly, clearly a little confused by the turn of the events.

"Careful with those kayaks. The water's cold, and you can get hypothermia quickly," Reese tossed over his shoulder at Lucas as he and Ella headed out the door.

"We'll be fine. You be careful yourselves. I'll be waiting to hear about your adventure, Ella."

Marissa turned to help them.

"See you at school, Lucas. Have a good time, Sophie." Ella let Reese guide her out the door to the van and lowered her voice. "Were you serious?"

"Yep. Grab your stuff." He opened the back of the van where his gear was already stowed and added the backpack she handed him. In minutes they were both in the van and Raul was driving them away. He filled her in on the plan.

She was agreeable to it, probably realizing it was the best she was going to get.

Reese was sure it was the worst decision he'd ever made.

ELLA'S HEART RATE PICKED UP AS RAUL DROVE THEM further back into the woods and turned into a dirt parking lot. A number of cars were already there, and a group of people with day packs milled around. After explaining the plan, Reese had been quiet the rest of the drive out here, and she left him to his thoughts. She wanted to do everything in her power to convince him that keeping the trip was a good idea.

They hopped out of the van and went to the back, where he

handed her her pack. She felt a little funny shrugging into and buckling up a backpack while everyone else had day packs. She and Reese had garnered some curious looks while they were getting their gear on.

Cory Grant wandered over. She knew him, of course, but not well. The sun glinted off his short, blond hair. He had the rangy build of an outdoorsman, wore the gear well, and she saw some of the female hikers checking him out. "Hey, guys. Glad you could join us. We waited for you, but we're late getting started. I'll head out if, Reese, you'll take the rear." He waved at Raul.

"Sure. We'll catch up." Reese turned and examined Ella's set up, tugging on a strap, adjusting her load. "You brought every-thing on the checklist, right?"

"I did."

He and Raul sorted through the items in the back, clearly not needing everything for just the two of them.

She held her breath, hopeful that it meant he was committed to extending this beyond a day hike.

"Don't get your hopes up." He slid her a small smile as he added some communal items and a first-aid kit to her pack. "I just want to be prepared. Doesn't mean I've decided we're staying out there."

She nodded. "Sure. I get it." She'd agree to anything he said right now.

When he was satisfied they were all set, he nodded to Raul. "If I don't hear from you before, I'll likely see you at the other end of the trail when you pick up Cory's group to shuttle them back here to their cars."

Raul nodded. "Have a good trip, Ella. Enjoy yourself. You deserve it."

His warm smile gave her all the encouragement that had flown away at Reese's words this morning.

Raul climbed in the van and pulled away, and they headed down the dirt trail. A few of Cory's hikers were visible in the distance. Reese's long legs ate up the ground, and Ella struggled to keep up, but she didn't want him to know that. Still, he must have noticed because he slowed his pace a notch.

Ella took a deep breath and enjoyed the view around her. Tall pines, firs, and incense cedars swayed in the breeze, the sound giving the illusion a rushing river was just around the bend. Snow dotted the ground in the shade, but the sun was warm on her face. She'd be shedding layers before too long.

As they approached the main hiking group, she recognized a few people, but most were tourists. Spring break was a busy time for most businesses in Holcomb Springs, so the teachers were the few people who got the time off. Most residents ended up working overtime.

They hiked up an incline that led to a lookout point.

Cory stood at the brow directing the hikers to the best view and keeping an eye on everyone. He answered a few questions then smiled when Ella neared. "Hey, Ella. Glad you joined us."

"Thanks. It's a beautiful day for a hike in the woods."

"We got lucky with the weather." He cocked his head. "I didn't expect you to be out here."

"I wanted to do something different for spring break. A little adventure to liven things up. I used to camp and hike with my family growing up, but I haven't done it in a while. Decided it was a good time to change that."

He grinned at her. "I just never pictured you as the outdoorsy type. Everyone knows how much you like books."

She was surprised he knew anything about her. Yeah, it was a small town, but she and Cory didn't cross paths much. Why would he have spent any time even thinking about what she might like to do?

A hand landed on her shoulder over her pack strap, and she turned. Reese.

"Holding up okay? Pack's not rubbing anywhere? Boots okay?" His gaze skimmed over her in an analytical way, different than Cory's more—appreciative?—gaze.

"Yeah, everything's great. No trouble at all." And even if there was, she wouldn't tell him. She didn't want to give him any reasons to back out.

"Good. You said you wanted to take pictures. There are some good spots up here." He guided her toward the top of the hill, away from the group that had gathered.

The view was amazing. The whole Holcomb Valley spread out before them, nearly bisected by the Holcomb Creek that ended in Holcomb Lake. It sparkled like a sapphire in the sun. She took a moment to simply soak it all in before retrieving her phone from a pocket on her strap.

She'd taken a few pictures when Reese's voice came from over her shoulder, closer than she'd expected. "Let me take some with you in it, so you'll have proof." He grinned.

She smiled back and handed him her phone, ignoring the sparks that came as their hands brushed. When did anybody ever truly leave high school? At what point did those memories fade? Because she hadn't reached it yet. And if she didn't get them shoved down, this could be an awkward trip. Smiling, she let him take pictures of her, more than she was comfortable with.

Finally she said, "You get in a few too. Proof I didn't do this by myself."

He studied her a moment then moved next to her and extended his arm. When they both didn't fit in the frame, his arm slid around her waist, tugging her close until their packs collided. He took a few more then handed her phone back.

She couldn't wait to see how they turned out, but Cory was calling them back to head on down the trail.

As Ella came even with him, he touched her arm. "Why don't you walk up here with me? Reese can handle the stragglers. I've got a few things to point out that I think you'll find interesting."

She glanced back at Reese. His face was unreadable. She shrugged. "Sure."

Cory and she headed out along the trail while the rest of the group followed. It was an easy pace, and Cory was a good guide. He pointed out features along the trail that highlighted this area's history of gold mining. There were still a lot of mines scattered in the area. At least once a year someone hiked off the path, fell into one, and had to be rescued. A warning that Cory gave several times.

She wouldn't be surprised if that's what had happened to Dalton Brandt. A shiver ran through her at the thought.

Cory surprised her with how much history he knew of the area. He told the story of William Holcomb and Ben Choteau coming up here in 1860 to look for gold. They shot a bear, followed the blood trail, and came across gold instead, setting off what would be a huge gold rush. Not only did it keep the more inexperienced hikers' minds off their physical discomfort, it kept them close enough to him to hear his stories. It was a good technique, and as a teacher, she admired it.

When it was time for lunch, they stopped in a meadow with a stream running through it. The water level was higher due to some runoff from the melting snow and the recent rain. Fallen logs and a few sun-warmed granite boulders made a natural picnic area, and the trickling stream was the perfect soundtrack accompanied by the rushing wind. She didn't think it was possible to be stressed in surroundings like these, and she was glad that Anne and Amanda had pushed her to do this.

Reese had staked out one of the granite boulders and had slipped off his pack. Ella joined him. He helped her with her pack and leaned it up against the rock. She instantly felt twenty pounds lighter. He opened his pack and pulled out their lunch supplies of packets of peanut butter, jelly, and pita bread, along with some dried fruit and nuts.

Ella had been warmed on the hike and contemplated taking a layer off, but as they sat eating lunch—which tasted as good as anything Bella Sorgenti served—she began to cool down. She drained the water from her bottle.

"Ready for some of the best water you've ever tasted?" Reese pulled a couple of plastic bladders connected by a tube out of his pack.

"That sounds promising." Ella followed him to the stream.

Reese dunked the upper plastic container in the stream until it was full. Then he hung it from a branch. Water trickled through the tube, which contained the filter, and down into the lower container. Once it was full, he disconnected it and filled their water bottles.

She took a sip. "Wow." It tasted clean and fresh, like the outdoors.

A few other hikers wanted their water bottles filled and remarked on how fresh the water tasted. Cory's slide glance and narrowed eyes made Ella think he wasn't thrilled with Reese's water demonstration.

Reese refilled the upper container once again. While the water was filtering, he packed up their items, even though Cory seemed in no hurry to get started again. He grabbed the water bladders. "Come on, I want to show you something. Grab your pack."

As she loaded herself with the pack again, noting that it felt twice as heavy as it had when she'd put it on this morning, she caught Cory's gaze.

He stood and came over. "We've got another fifteen minutes here before we move on."

Reese kept on checking Ella's pack. "That's fine. If we're not back by then, go on without us. We'll catch up."

Cory's hands went to his hips. "This is my hike, Reese. We don't split up."

Ella's gaze darted between the two men. "What did you have in mind, Reese?"

"There's an ephemeral waterfall up this creek. It only appears in the spring when there's been some significant snow melt. No real trail, but it's one of the prettiest things around here."

A few of the hikers had tuned into their conversation. "Ooh, that sounds great. I want to go."

"No." Cory's tone was sharp. "It's not safe. Nobody's going."

Reese patted Ella's pack. "You're good to go." He turned and headed toward the stream.

"Reese." Cory's tone had a warning note in it. What was the history with these two?

Reese didn't stop.

Ella started after him, but Cory grabbed her arm. "Don't go, Ella. It's not safe. Reese takes risks, and I don't want you put in danger."

She slipped her arm away. "It's fine. I trust Reese. He wouldn't take me any place unsafe."

Cory snorted. "Tell that to the two guys in his unit who got killed because of his risk taking."

Her stomach free fell. What was Cory talking about? For a moment, she was torn. Was Cory right?

"Ella. Coming?" Reese looked at her from by the stream. Something in his gaze—pleading?—flashed before turning hard. If she wanted to continue her adventure, she had to follow him. But what had Cory been talking about?

She turned to Cory. "I'll be fine. I trust Reese."

Did she? Or was she making a mistake? One look at Cory's face gave her his answer. But she turned and headed toward Reese, the cool air of the tree shadows goose bumping her arms.

CHAPTER
EIGHT

Tony checked his duffle bag to make sure he had everything he needed for basketball before leaving his office at the church. He and Ryan were going to pick up Zach and head to the community center. Where he expected to also run into Shannon, since her office was in the public safety wing of the same building.

He'd been enjoying getting to know her on the ride along and running with her. He liked seeing the softer side of her than she presented to the public, though she was well loved and respected in the community. They had a lot in common, and he definitely wanted to get to know her more. Up to the point where he'd have to reveal his struggle with dyslexia.

Janelle had known and helped him. He had a hard time picturing Shannon in that role, coaching him through sermons and books. And to be honest, he'd figured out a way to make it all work without help. It was the being vulnerable and admitting his weakness that he didn't want to do. Didn't want to see the disappointment, or worse, pity in her eyes.

He knew at some point, if their relationship progressed enough, that he'd have to tell her. Relationships didn't work when there were secrets and lies. And she'd made her feelings clear about liars.

But the big *if* was would their relationship progress? Until he was sure that it would, he wasn't going to risk it. He'd always believed in beginning with the end in mind, which meant he had to tread carefully. They would have to work together, no matter what, which made the entire proposition tricky. And almost made him want to forget the whole idea.

But she intrigued him in a way a woman hadn't since Janelle. Her care and concern for the community matched his own. And she was still completely feminine despite her uniform and weapon. He would continue to pray for guidance and leading, hoping his own stupidity didn't get in the way.

In the meantime, he could help her out by getting Zach to play basketball with Ryan, him, and some other guys. And get to know Zach.

Ryan leaned in through the open office doorway. "Ready to head out?"

"Yep." Tony hefted his duffle, and they headed out to his truck and made their way to the sheriff's house. He'd bet they'd have a lot more spectators to their basketball game today. Ryan's good looks were always drawing female attention. And with it being spring break, there'd be a lot more kids at the community center.

They pulled into the sheriff's driveway, and Zach hustled down the stairs. He had the same athletic build of his mom but with dark hair and eyes. Was that from his dad? But Shannon's sister, Cassie, had dark hair. He climbed in the back seat of the truck.

"Hey, Zach," Tony said as he backed out of the driveway.

"Hey, Pastor. Hi, Ryan. Thanks for coming to get me."

"Happy to help." Tony mentally shook his head at the scintillating conversation. Teenage boys were tough in that department. Luckily Ryan asked Zach about the video games he was playing, and that kept him talking until they got to the community center.

Inside, a bunch of kids were milling around on the basketball court. A few of the regular players wandered around, looking lost. It didn't seem right to kick them off, but a number of adults liked to play basketball on their lunch break. He headed into the locker room to change. When he came out, he looked to see who was in charge of the kids' programming. He spotted Anne Cartwright, the librarian, and headed in her direction.

"Hey, Anne. Do you know who's running the kids' programs today? I know a group of us are looking to play basketball, but I don't want to kick the kids off. Is there another event they could get involved in?"

Anne scanned the room. "Michelle Sanders is running it. I know she's pretty overwhelmed, which is why I came over to help. She's at the craft station."

Tony spotted her, nodded his thanks, and headed in Michelle's direction.

When she noticed him, she gave him a harried glance. "Come to make some bookmarks, Pastor?"

He smiled. "Actually, a group of us usually play basketball at lunch, but there are a lot of kids on the court. Is there something for them to do? Do you have something planned?"

"That *is* the plan. Those that have a ton of energy and don't want to do crafts or read with Miss Anne can run around the gym. We had some other activities scheduled, but the help fell through." She wiped the back of a glue-and-glitter-covered hand across her forehead. "Sorry about your basketball game. I just don't know where else to put them."

"That's okay. We'll figure something out." He turned to walk away and then stopped. He'd never been in charge of children's programming at church, but he'd bossed around contractors. How hard could a bunch of kids be? "Hey, mind if we play some games with them in the gym?"

Relief eased the tension lines in her face. "Oh, would you? That would be so helpful."

"Sure." He headed back to the gym. Now to tell the guys they were going to be playing with the kids too. He ran through some ideas. Maybe Ryan would have some suggestions.

A group of the regular players were standing around, some less than pleased at the kids' presence. Jonas and Marco had joined them. Zach sat on a bench, phone in hand.

He approached them. "Hey, I told Michelle that I'd help keep the kids busy. There's no place else for them right now. So looks like we won't have our regularly scheduled game. Anyone have any ideas of activities we can do with the kids?"

There was some muttered grumbling, but he'd learned to ignore anything that wasn't a direct comment or question.

"I have an idea," Ryan said. "We can teach them basic basketball skills—passing dribbling. We've got enough basketballs to break them into groups of four."

"Good idea." Tony scanned the gym. "Hey, I think we can make it so some of you could still play half-court, if you want to."

Jonas and Marco agreed to help with the kids. Given their jobs, they spent a lot of time making sure kids felt safe in their presence. It was one of the things Tony appreciated about Shannon's community policing style. Ryan stepped over and said something to Zach, who got to his feet and reluctantly put his phone away. The remainder of the players started their half-court game while Ryan got the kids' attention and broke them up into groups. Some of the older girls were more than happy to do whatever Ryan asked. Each man took a group and demonstrated basic basketball skills.

Tony stepped next to Zach. "You want to help me with this group? I bet they'd rather see you demonstrate it than an old man like me." He grinned.

Zach laughed and took the basketball, showing the kids how to dribble.

Tony surveyed the gym. They'd made it work, and everyone seemed reasonably happy. Occasionally one of the kids' balls would get loose, and they'd have to warn the basketball players, but no one had broken an ankle yet. It's too bad they didn't have something like a climbing wall here. It would take up less space than another sports court, and it would give the kids a way to burn off energy. He'd mention it to a few people. The community center was one of the recipients of the Spread the Love event.

Shannon entered the gym. His heart rate picked up as he waved her over. He couldn't help but be a bit proud of what he'd accomplished. Maybe he'd look a little bit like a good guy in her eyes.

"So you're adding activities director to your resume?" Her eyes sparkled and laughter laced her words.

"You know us pastors. Always wearing all the hats."

"Yeah. I saw. Sunday's service was bigger than usual. Lots of guests."

He nodded. "I'm expecting that for the next several weeks. Which is good. We've been making sure we have invitations in all the hotels, motels, and cabins that we can get them into." He studied her as her gaze landed on Zach working with the younger kids.

"You've worked a miracle prying him away from his video games and getting him to help out."

"He's a good kid." And he meant it. "He just needs some direction and structure."

Shannon winced, and he realized that his words sounded like a criticism of her. He had to salvage this. "They all do. It's the age. Grown-up bodies and not fully developed brains. Not always a great combo."

She nodded. "Oh, I know."

The conversation between them faltered even as noise and chaos surrounded them. Rarely was he at a loss for words. But now…

Anne headed in their direction. Relief. "Hey, Sheriff. Come to help out?"

"Just came to see what was going on. Looks like you all have it under control." Shannon snagged a runaway basketball and tossed it back to the freckled girl with braids.

"Well, control might be too strong of a word." Anne turned to him. "I actually came to see if you'd have a moment to read to some of the kids while I help Michelle get the lunches set out." She glanced at Shannon. "We're short staffed. A few of our volunteers couldn't make it." Back at him. "It would just be for a few minutes."

Both of the women's gazes turned to him.

His throat went dry. Was his forehead getting sweaty? The two people who would naturally expect this to be no big deal for him stared at him expectantly. There was no way to say no. And yet, how could he read to children? He'd stumble all over the words. They'd dance across the page and not stay in place. He had no time to even prepare so he could fake it.

"Uh, sure." *Lord, I need a miracle. I know it's selfish, but please don't let me embarrass myself in front of them.*

Anne smiled. "Great. I'll show you the selection of books I've picked out." She turned and headed across the gym.

Now would be a good time for Shannon to leave. He turned to her. "So I'll just bring Zach home later this afternoon, okay?"

"Stop by my office first, if you would. Depending on what's going on, I might just be able to keep him here."

"Sure." He followed Anne and settled in the plastic chair in front of a group of young grade school kids seated on the floor.

Anne pointed to a stack of chapter books next to the chair. "We've been reading through a few of these. You can pick any one of them." Then she was off.

He thumbed through the books, buying time. No picture books. These kids were too old. And he wasn't familiar with any of these stories. He glanced up.

Shannon stood in the doorway between the gym and activity room, watching.

Great.

He took a deep breath and slowly let it out, focusing on the kids in front of him. "Hey, guys. How's it going?"

He got a chorus of answers that he responded to while his mind whirled for a solution. "What's your favorite story?"

The kids shouted out answers. "Captain Underpants!" "Diary of a Wimpy Kid!" "Pete the Cat!" "Halley Harper: Science Girl Extraordinaire!" "Junie B. Jones!"

He had no idea what any of those were. But hey, he was a pastor, he could tell them a Bible story. He didn't dare look to see if Shannon was watching. Instead he began, "Once there was a boy, about the same age as most of you. But he had an important job for his family. Do any of you have jobs?"

He listened to their answers about chores around their homes. This was the ticket. Get them involved in the story by asking questions along the way. He continued telling them about David the shepherd boy. They were so enraptured that they insisted on hearing the end of the story even when Michelle called them to pick up their lunches.

By the time they'd filed off for lunch, he was as exhausted as if he'd preached three sermons. Anne waved her thanks and he wandered off. Ryan and Zach were collecting basketballs in the gym. The lunch time players had exited the court, along with Jonas and Marco. It was weirdly calm after the earlier chaos.

"You guys want to grab some lunch before heading home? I'm thinking Belleville Flats." Their famous onion rings, usually just an occasional indulgence given the amount of time he spent behind a desk these days, seemed like a necessity to recover from today.

"Sounds great." Ryan shoved the basketball cart against the wall. Zach just nodded.

"Oh, we've got to stop by your mom's office, Zach. She wanted us to check in." Tony led the way to the locker room.

Once they'd changed, they headed down the hall to the public safety department, only to be told the sheriff was out.

Tony wasn't sure whether to be relieved or disappointed. He shelved those thoughts aside and concentrated on looking forward to some onion rings and a juicy burger.

REESE IGNORED CORY'S WORDS AND MUTTERED CURSE AS he picked a path next to the stream, checking only to make sure Ella was behind him. She was. The tension eased a bit from his shoulders. He wasn't sure if she'd stay with Cory or go with him. He hadn't had a problem with Cory before now, but today something about the guy set his teeth on edge. Part of it was probably the slow pace of the hike, though Reese was used to that from the hikes he led. Whatever it was, he felt nearly driven to break away from the group and take Ella somewhere else. This waterfall was a perfect excuse.

Of course, at this time of year, there were all sorts of waterfalls in the area caused by snow melt. They weren't too far from the San Andreas fault, and there were a number of natural springs too. Probably what contributed to the area being settled long ago, considering the mountains were surrounded by desert on one side and a Mediterranean climate on the other. Water wasn't always easy to find.

Still, the farther they got from the group, the better he felt. The shade was cool, and he picked a path for them through the slushy snow piles and across the rocks, finding places for Ella to step that wouldn't be too slippery. He stopped and looked back.

She was right behind him.

"Doing okay?"

"Yeah. It's so pretty back here. I love how the water cuts through the snow. There's so much more of it than you find in the summer."

"Wait til you see what's ahead." Reese started hiking again, and soon they could hear water cascading over granite. They rounded a bend, and he stepped aside, waiting to see Ella's reaction.

She was watching her steps carefully then looked up. Her eyes widened. "Oh, wow!"

The runoff got caught in a crease in the hillside, gathering speed and water until it hit a granite outcropping and spouted out into the air, landing about ten feet below in a tree-surrounded pool that emptied into the stream they'd followed.

"I never knew this was here." Ella eased closer and took out her phone.

"Most people don't. I stumbled on it when I first got here. I chased the creek upstream to see where it started. It wasn't this big then, just a trickle, but I figured it might be pretty spectacular today."

"You were right."

Reese moved closer to the waterfall, examining it. The way the hillside cut around, there might be a way to get to the top. He tilted his head. "Follow me. I want to check this out."

She did, stepping where he stepped as they forged their own path, not something he would normally recommend, but he was curious, and they weren't on a timetable. Lately, he hadn't had any hikes just by himself where he could explore. He was always leading groups, which felt a lot more like babysitting than enjoying the wilderness.

A series of granite boulders piled up next to the waterfall. He scrambled up a few then held out his hand to pull Ella up.

She studied it a minute before taking it.

He almost regretted the offer. Her hand fit snuggly in his, almost like it belonged there. The idea terrified and comforted him at the same time. He pulled his hand back as soon as she was safe.

As they crested the last boulder, he could see his gamble had been a good one. The water created a small pool before plunging over the edge, creating the waterfall.

Ella joined him, and they leaned against the boulder, just taking it all in.

This wasn't too bad. Ella was a good sport, so far. He hadn't heard from Raul, but they weren't in an area with good comms, so he didn't expect to hear from him until they were at a better location.

He was just stubborn enough to milk this side trip so that Cory would leave without them. Probably already had. Cory had seemed too interested in Ella, though she didn't seem eager to get back to the group either.

Her face had relaxed, and she leaned against the rock, taking deep breaths and letting her gaze travel over the scenery. When was the last time she'd had an outing like this? He thought back to what Pastor Tony said about Ella. Maybe he could give her the adventure she wanted. In a way, he owed her. Even if the debt was twelve years old.

"How far back does this creek flow?"

Her words startled him. "Not sure. It disappears over that ridge. Want to check it out?"

"Sure."

They pushed off the boulders and stepped carefully along the moss-encrusted rocks and mushy ground, picking their way along the creek's edge and up the slow incline. It was a scenic trek through the woods, and they could easily retrace their steps by following the creek back down.

Reese scanned their surroundings, wanting to maintain situational awareness and not get caught off guard by anything. Which was why it was strange that it took his brain a minute to register what he was seeing. An irrigation pipe and pump coming off the water and disappearing into the woods. And a worn path into the woods.

A more thorough scan showed pieces of heavy plastic and other trash scattered about.

His heart rate ticked up. An illegal grow site wasn't far from here. Likely there were trail cams around here, and when someone checked them, they'd see Reese and Ella. The best hope was to make like they didn't see what was going on. But he wanted to record their location so he could report it to the sheriff.

"Let's head over here." He nodded to an area away from the creek and the grow.

Ella frowned. "Why? That's away from the creek. I thought we wanted to see where it went."

"Trust me. Please?"

With a slow nod, she followed him.

They side-stepped around the slope of the hill until the creek was out of view. He reached around the side of his pack for his map to ascertain where they were and where the grow operation might be.

Ella studied him. "We're not lost."

"No. But we've stumbled on something we shouldn't have."

"What do you mean?"

"Did you see that irrigation pipe running out of the stream?"

"Was that what that was? I thought it was weird that there was some sort of pump thing."

"Someone's running an illegal pot growing operation back here."

"But it's legal to grow marijuana in California. Why would someone want to grow it illegally?"

"Lots of reasons. They don't want the permits and oversight. They're expensive and take time to get approved. They want to use the natural resources up here of water and land, and they leave their trash all over the place, contaminating it. Often they're connected with drug runners and money laundering schemes. It's a health hazard, not only for what they do to the land and water, but for anyone who stumbles across it."

Her eyes widened when his meaning sunk in. "Will they know that we discovered them?"

"Possibly. They likely have trail cams up here. They wouldn't have a live feed this far out with such bad cell service. But someone probably comes by and checks them regularly. Hopefully we'll look like hikers who didn't know what we saw. I just wanted to mark the location on the map so I can tell the sheriff when we get back. Speaking of which, we need to get out of here." He folded the map up and looked around. "We can parallel the creek this way, but we should be far enough downslope they won't spot us."

Ella nodded and followed him as he started across the slope, weaving in and out of trees. His mind spun with possibilities. He was betting the trail cams weren't monitored, but he wasn't sure. If his plan to get away from Cory had put Ella in danger… He flashed back to another bad decision he'd made; one that had killed two of his friends. He couldn't let himself go there. He had to get them out of here.

He turned to make sure Ella was within arm's reach of him. She was, her gaze focused on his footprints.

The scent of something foul reached him on a gust of wind. Then it got stronger. He knew that smell. Something had died around here, probably an animal of some sort. Whatever it was, they were getting closer to it. But there was no way around it; they weren't going back the way they came, and he didn't want to deviate too far from this path and get them off course.

He spotted the jacket first. He held his hand behind him for Ella to stop.

"What's that smell?" She held her hand over her nose and mouth.

"Stay here. And look away." Reese took a few steps forward, watching where he stepped and checking the surroundings. Between the animals and being out here at least a few weeks, it would take the coroner to make a positive identification. But Reese would bet they'd just found Dalton Brandt. He pulled out his phone and snapped pictures. Then grabbed the map to estimate their location. He didn't think it was a coincidence that they'd found Brandt's body close to the grow site.

Which meant he and Ella needed to get out of here. Fast.

CHAPTER
NINE

Ella didn't want to look. She kept her gaze on the scenery all around them, anywhere but what Reese was doing. She looked back at where they'd come from. The peaceful forest now seemed foreboding and dangerous. All she wanted to do was get down and get back to the trail. Maybe she didn't have the adventurous spirit after all. Then again, most people didn't find dead bodies when they were hiking in the woods.

Unless they were Aggie Gilchrist's heroine Clarissa Miller. Ella's only experience with death was through books. Gilchrist's *Death Comes Calling* was sitting next to her bed at home. She distracted herself by thinking about what Clarissa would do in a situation like this. Probably just what Reese was doing.

She thought she saw something move on the slope above them. A flash of color. Were there other hikers…? The pieces slipped together.

"Reese." She pitched her voice low. "I think we've got company."

His head swiveled around, and he looked where she pointed. He swore. "Let's get out of here. Quietly but quickly." He shoved the map and phone in his pockets and grabbed her hand.

His strides were longer and more sure than hers. He nearly pulled her down the slope, and she scrambled to keep her feet under her.

She didn't know if they'd been spotted or not. She only saw the flash of a jacket or a hat. Her legs burned as her quads engaged to keep her upright on the slope. Reese's grip was firm on her hand, comforting in this situation that quickly felt like it was spinning out of control. She kept her gaze on Reese's pack and prayed that she wouldn't stumble and fall. For what seemed like an eternity, with her legs feeling like wooden pegs, they scrambled down the hill until she got glimpses of a trail below them. Hopefully it was the one they'd been on earlier.

But then what? Would the bad guys chase them? Was anyone else even around? Cory and his group would be long gone. Could they get to the other trailhead where Raul was to meet them? Would Reese be able to use his radio to get help? Too many questions, and she couldn't focus on any of them for fear she'd stumble and fall.

A sharp report as bark splintered off a nearby tree. Two more mini explosions happened nearby before she realized they were being shot at. Which meant they'd been spotted. Her arm and her cheek burned with what felt like fire brands.

"Get ready to jump. Land with your knees bent."

"What?" Ella couldn't understand his words until he was tugging her over the edge of the hill onto the trail below that she'd just spotted.

She hung in the air a moment longer than expected, then the ground came up with a force that jarred her jaw and made her ankles sting.

Reese jerked his head toward her. "You okay?"

"Yeah," she breathed out. And without a chance to catch her breath, he was dragging her across the trail—not the one they'd been on earlier she could now see—and across into the woods.

They dodged trees and slipped on pine duff before the ground sloped upward again.

Ella grew lightheaded. Even though she lived up here, there was less oxygen at seven thousand feet, and she didn't regularly do this much exertion. Her legs burned, her arm burned, and her face burned. If Reese wasn't dragging her, she didn't think she'd make it another step.

Finally he tugged her behind a granite outcropping. This side of the valley had some rock climbing areas. They must be near those based on the geography. She didn't care. She laid back against the rock and closed her eyes, sure her gulps of air could be heard back in town.

Reese squatted and moved in various positions. She didn't care what he was doing. She closed her eyes and concentrated on breathing.

"Ella, you're bleeding."

CORY'S ANGER SIMMERED JUST BELOW THE SURFACE. HE kept a good front up for the clients, but Reese had torqued him off. When Reese and Ella hadn't returned after a short period of time, Cory had gotten the rest of the hikers back on the trail. He knew the trip well enough to spout facts and keep it interesting, even if his mind was elsewhere.

He kept going back to Reese and Ella. He knew the waterfall Reese was talking about. And he also knew that it was near somewhere they shouldn't go. He tapped out a text message with little hope that it'd go through. But he didn't want Reese's actions to blow back on him. He needed his supply too much to risk it on a washed-up soldier trying to prove something to a woman.

They were halfway between their lunch spot and the trailhead when a series of sharp reports echoed through the valley. A chill ran through him.

"Were those gunshots?" one of the men asked.

"Someone hunting out of season?" A man next to him speculated.

Cory shrugged. "It's probably granite boulders coming loose and colliding. You'd be amazed at how much they sound like gunshots. A good reminder to keep your eyes open. You don't want to get in front of one of those coming down the hill."

But he knew they were gunshots. And he knew what they meant. *Stupid, Reese.* If he'd gotten Ella hurt… He didn't particularly care if Reese got hurt. But it would raise too many questions and create more complications. Far more than Brandt going missing did.

When they reached the trailhead, Cory was glad to see Raul already there with the van. Cory was ready for this trip to be done with. He had other things to take care of.

Raul met him outside the van as the hikers loaded up. "How was the hike? Where's Reese and Ella?"

Cory shrugged. "It was good. Reese and Ella, uh, decided to go off on their own at lunch." He smirked. "I think Reese wanted to get her alone." A little misdirection could buy some time.

Raul frowned. "Really? That wasn't his attitude this morning."

"Dunno. He just seemed real eager to get her off on her own. I tried to warn her, but she went with him anyway. He told us to go on without them."

Raul studied Cory for a moment.

Cory resisted the urge to squirm. What could Raul know? The guy wasn't even capable of leading his own hiking trips. Cory shifted his weight and grabbed the van door. "Let's get these folks back to their cars."

It was a long moment before Raul nodded and climbed in.

They backtracked to the original trailhead. It always amazed Cory how a day-long hike was such a short car ride. As soon as they pulled into the lot, Cory hopped out. "Raul, you can handle the rest of this, right? I've got somewhere I've gotta be."

"Sure. Head on out. I'll see you tomorrow." Raul lifted a hand then turned to the hikers exiting the van.

Cory hopped in his truck and gunned it, leaving a cloud of dust in his wake. Raul would say something to him about that tomorrow, he was sure. As soon as he had some bars, he pulled over and placed a call.

"Don't know if you got my text, but that's Reese Vega and Ella Sommer out there that your muscle went after. They were stupid enough to fire their guns. We could hear it miles away."

A string of swear words came back as the response. "That makes things complicated. Keep me informed."

The line went dead.

⸻

REESE PEERED THROUGH THE GAP BETWEEN TWO GRANITE boulders. Their pursuers returned back up the hill where they'd come from. He and Ella had lost them. For now. But he had no illusion they were actually safe.

He eased back from his position and shrugged off his pack before studying Ella. Her eyes were closed. Blood streaked her face and soaked her flannel shirt. He squeezed her shoulder and gently shook her. "Ella. Wake up. Are you with me?"

"Um hmm." Her head moved slightly.

"Open your eyes."

After a long second, she did. "Are we safe?"

"For now. Let me look at you. Sit up. Let's get this pack off of you." He undid the straps and worked it off her, setting it aside. Opening the top, he pulled out her packable down jacket and laid it over her. He didn't need her going into shock. Then he dug around in her pack for the first-aid kit.

He examined her arm first. The flannel was ripped as well as her SmartWool base layer, and there was a gash in her arm underneath. But it wasn't deep. "Looks like one of their bullets grazed you. Or a piece of bark or rock. We're lucky it wasn't worse." He cut her shirt and base layer away with his knife, rinsed the wound with water, and slathered on some antibiotic cream before putting on gauze and tape. "It could probably use a few stitches, but I don't think that is going to happen. It's going to be dark in an hour, so I need to find a safe place to set us up for the night."

He winked at her. "Looks like you'll get your overnight trip after all, and have a badge of honor as proof."

She smiled. "Thanks, Reese. As crazy as it sounds, I feel safe enough with you."

Her words did something deep inside, something he didn't have time to think about. He wet another piece of gauze and wiped the blood off her cheek. It was already drying. "Probably got hit by some flying bark. Not more than a scratch."

Their gaze met. Her soft brown eyes so full of trust. Had anyone ever looked at him that way? He wasn't sure he deserved it. He gathered up the gauze and shoved it in a bag before putting it in her pack.

She touched his hand. "Thank you. I mean that."

He nodded and pulled away, pulling out the map. Where could they go that was close enough to get them set up before dark and yet safe from their pursuers?

"Do you think they're still after us?"

He shook his head. "No. They won't go far from the grow they're protecting. But it's not going to be hard to figure out who we are. I'm sure they'll have our faces on their trail cams. And if they don't recognize us, it'll be easy enough to find someone who does. They don't have to get us out here. They can get to us anywhere."

Ella paled a bit. "So what do we do?"

"We'll get to them first. And by 'we' I mean the sheriff and the feds, since this is national forest land. When we get out of here, we'll give them the info we have, and they'll take it from there. If these guys are smart, they'll figure that out too, shut down their operations, and get out of town." He tapped the map. "There's a good spot not too far from here where we can set up for the night. You ready to get back on your feet?"

She nodded and sat up, shrugging into her coat, wincing a bit as her injured arm went through the sleeve. When she got to her feet, he helped her on with her pack, avoiding brushing against her injured arm.

They eased down the backside of the rocks, Reese careful to guide her. Her first steps were a little wobbly, but she found her feet soon enough. They were quiet as they made their way through the trees. The homey vanilla-butterscotch smell of the ponderosa pines was such a contrast from the danger they'd just come from.

The shadows were getting long, so they were walking in the shade for most of the time. Which made it better to keep them from being seen, if anyone was still looking for them.

They didn't talk much as they moved across the ground toward their campsite for the night. He'd picked a spot up against some granite pinnacles with enough trees to provide screening. They were able to walk side by side for most of it, allowing him to keep an eye on her. She didn't complain at all, which surprised him. Most of the trips he led had folks quick to mention what was bothering them. He didn't know how Raul was always so upbeat and kind to everyone.

Actually, Ella was a lot like that too. She'd chatted with various people on the hike today, always seeming to have something to say to everyone. And she'd gotten along well with Cory too, not something he liked thinking about. And wasn't that interesting? Why should it bother him if she wanted to talk to Cory?

Luckily they reached the site he'd picked out, and he didn't have to do any more soul searching. The area was as he'd remembered. There had been a season in his life when Raul had come back from college as often as possible to hike these mountains. A lot of times he took Reese with him. It had developed their shared love of the outdoors, bonded them through the family rupture that his enlisting in the Army had created, and gave them something to talk about during their infrequent communications during his long deployments. His brain was full of maps of this area, and he'd enjoyed getting reacquainted with those old memories.

"Home sweet home for tonight." He swung his pack off and helped Ella with hers. "Let's get the tents set up before it gets full dark. Then we'll worry about dinner."

"Sounds good." She was a little breathy, but she pitched in, getting their lightweight, one-person tents set up on fairly level ground they cleared of sticks, pinecones, and rocks. The tents were small and well hidden in among the trees.

A weird twinge shot through him at the idea of her being out of sight at night. What if she needed him? What if she started bleeding again? He shook his head. When had he become a worrywart? She'd be fine, and he'd hear her if she called out.

Of course that meant she'd likely hear him if he had a nightmare. He prayed that wouldn't happen.

He snapped on his headlamp and grabbed his phone and radio. "I'm going to climb up the ridge before it gets any darker and see if I can reach Raul. We'll eat when I get back. Eat this if you get hungry." He tossed her a bag of trail mix.

"Okay." She caught the bag and shoved it into her pocket. She had put her headlamp on and was shuttling items into her tent.

He watched her a long moment and then scrambled up the pinnacles, the granite molded into pillar-like formations, giving plenty of places to scramble to higher ground. The sun had gone behind the trees. If it were summer, the sky would stay light for a while, but this time of year it would be full dark shortly after sunset. He had to hurry. He didn't mind cooking in the dark, but he didn't want to climb back down in it.

When he'd gotten as high as he could go, he scanned the area. He didn't see any other lights or hear any sounds of engines, anything that might alert him to the men on his trail. He hoped they were smart enough to realize their gig was up and to bug out. But he wouldn't bet on it.

He tried the cell phone. No bars. He sent a text message anyway, hoping it might go with little connectivity. Then he tried the radio. No response. He likely wasn't high enough. And they were about as far from civilization as it got. Definitely not line of sight to wherever Raul was. And Raul would have his radio with him. He was good about that when either Reese or Cory were leading a trip.

Reese let out a breath. It was what he had expected. That was why they had SOPs—standard operating procedures.

He headed back down, picking his way carefully. The last thing they needed was for him to get hurt. He spotted Ella's headlamp as she sat on a downed log near their tents, snacking on the trail mix.

She looked up at his approach. "Any luck?"

"Nope. It was a long shot. Let's get dinner started." Out of his pack he pulled the bear canister, which contained all of their food and cooking items, and handed her the water bladder. He started off about one hundred feet from their tents, looking for a good place to cook as well as a convenient place to stash the bear canister.

There was a small clearing with a downed log to sit on. A small stand of sagebrush was off to the side. That would work. He squatted on the log and unpacked the canister with the camp stove, food, and cooking utensils. He pulled out a freeze-dried bag. "Mac and cheese for dinner?" He started to rip open the pack.

Her hand on his stopped him. "Is there another option?"

His headlamp caught the expression on her face, a weird mix of fear and revulsion. Who didn't like mac and cheese? "Um, sure." He rummaged through the canister and pulled out another one. "Beef stroganoff okay?"

"Yes, thanks." Relief laced her voice. "That's great. Sorry."

"Not a problem." He got the food and water into the cooking pot and stirred.

"Since you weren't able to get a hold of Raul, what happens?"

"Our standard operating procedure is that he'll pick us up at the trailhead at the far end of the lake at noon on Wednesday. We're about halfway between where we started and where we'll end up, given our little shortcut jaunt today." He tried to infuse some humor into his voice. "So the wisest thing is to keep on going. If we don't get ahold of Raul before then, we know when and where we can meet him."

The blue glow from the camp stove and their headlamps made a little pool of light enveloping just the two of them. They ate, the silence companionable. After what Ella had been through today, she wasn't complaining. Other than not wanting mac and cheese.

They cleaned up the dinner dishes and stowed everything in the bear canister before heading back to their tents. He held out his hand to her. "Give me your good arm. I don't want you to stumble in the dark."

She hesitated. "I've got my headlamp."

"Yeah, but you've had a lot going on today. No need to court trouble."

She reached out her left hand and he took it. That same feeling of connection from before came back, almost like this was something they'd done before. But they hadn't. Not really. He didn't hurry them back, on the pretense of making sure she didn't trip on anything. But really he just enjoyed feeling her hand in his, just for this moment of time he could pretend the world and its trouble didn't exist.

Back at the tent, he dropped her hand. "Normally I'd light a fire, but I don't want to attract any undue attention. I do want to look at your arm, however." He motioned to a log for her to sit on while he grabbed the first-aid kit from her pack.

She did as she was told, shucking out of her jacket, shivering when the cold air goose-bumped her bare skin where her sleeve used to be. She watched him, her headlamp adding light to the area.

The dressing was soaked with blood, but when he eased it off, the bleeding appeared to have slowed. He added more antibiotic cream, a butterfly bandage to hold the cut closed, and another layer of gauze on top to protect it. He didn't think Raul had ever had one of his clients shot at on a trip. This was an area Reese had more experience in, unfortunately.

"Just be careful using it, okay? I don't want it to rip back open."

"I'll be careful." She slipped her jacket back on, turned off her headlamp, and tipped her head up. "The stars are so bright and clear. So many more than I can usually see, even up here."

He switched off his headlamp and looked up. "Yeah, without a fire, our eyes can adjust to the dark better and see more stars. And the moon hasn't risen yet." The odd sense of contentment continued to envelop him.

He thought about Cory's comments about getting his men killed. It was exactly what he hated about small towns. Everyone knew his business, or thought they did. He didn't know what Ella knew or had heard. She deserved to hear the truth from him.

But the night was peaceful, and they were getting along. He was enjoying her company and didn't want to wreck the moment. And that story would.

Ella was exactly like what he had remembered. And also… not. She was kind and friendly. She had no problem talking to people in Cory's group on the hike. And yet she didn't demand that Reese be anything other than who he was.

"Thank you, Reese, for taking care of me today. For getting us out of that mess safely. If I had been with anyone else, it wouldn't have ended as well."

He couldn't see her expression in the dark, but her words

washed over him like a balm. "It was my fault for getting us in the mess in the first place."

"No, it's not. You wanted to show me something special. The illegal growers are at fault for everything. Including poor Dalton's death." She shuddered next to him. "If anything, it's my fault for pushing you on this trip."

"No. It's not your fault. Not at all. I was enjoying showing you that waterfall, exploring the area." He let a smile creep into his voice. "You're a better hiking companion than I expected."

She laughed, as he hoped she would. "Well, considering I can imagine what most of your hikes are like with tourists complaining about lack of cell service, blisters, and wanting selfies with bears, it's a pretty low bar."

He laughed. "Have you been on my hikes? Seriously, though, you've been great. You didn't even complain when you were shot. I've seen Rangers bellyache more about a bullet wound than you did."

"You're just trying to make me feel better. And I'll let you." She stifled a yawn. "But as beautiful as these stars are, I want to crawl in my sleeping bag and get some rest."

"Good plan." With a final look at the stars and a whispered prayer of thanks, he flipped his headlamp back on and turned toward the tents, lighting a path for her. "Don't be afraid to call out if you need anything. I'll be right next to you."

She squeezed his shoulder as she stood and flipped on her own light. "Thanks for everything."

He watched until she crawled into her tent and zipped it up. Then he switched off his light and studied the stars some more, praying for wisdom and protection. And no nightmares.

Once again, he wondered about his decision-making abilities. Should he have brought a weapon? Now that someone or some*ones* were after them, he wished he had something to defend them with. Would that choice ultimately get them killed? If he hadn't been worried about nightmares, he would have brought his gun without thinking about it. Was this TBI ever going to stop messing up his life? And those around him?

And then there was Ella. They were going to be together a lot more than he'd bargained for.

Hopefully, he could keep his heart protected.

And her alive.

CHAPTER
TEN

Light seeping through Ella's tent woke her. Her nose was cold, but the rest of her body was snug in her mummy sack. She pushed up on her elbows before registering the pain in her upper arm that told her that was a mistake. Her legs ached from all of yesterday's running up, down, and across hills. Small price to pay for their safety though. Once again, she breathed a prayer of thanks for Reese's capabilities and his ability to protect her. He knew what he was doing. She wasn't sure there was anyone else she could say that about.

She hadn't even been certain she'd be able to sleep. But something about Reese's presence—and her exhaustion—had her nodding off quickly.

Better get up and get going. The only way her muscles would loosen up was to get the blood flowing through them. The tent was barely big enough to sit up in. She pulled her hiking pants out of her sleeping bag. It was a trick she'd used as a kid when they'd gone camping. Clothes left out were cold to put on in the morning. She'd grabbed a clean shirt last night too. She only had the one underlayer, which was now missing a sleeve. Once she'd gotten dressed, with contortions that would have done a gymnast proud, she finger combed her hair. The nice thing about her straight hair was that it didn't tangle too much and had a propensity to lay flat.

Once her boots were back on, she unzipped the tent and climbed out.

Reese turned. He was sitting on the log from last night, his back to her. "Morning. How'd you sleep?"

She stretched and eased her muscles into movement. "Not too bad. I went out pretty fast. How about you?"

He stood, dropped the map he was studying on the log, and handed her a metal cup. "Coffee." Dark scruff coated his cheeks, making him look like a model for some outdoors magazine.

"Thank you." She took it and sipped. Heavenly.

"Slept fine." But his gaze darted away from her. "Let's check that wound again, then we can get breakfast going."

She sat on the log while they reprised the events from last night in caring for her arm.

"Looks good. Very little blood today." He slid her sleeve back down her arm, causing tingles to run up and down.

Being in such close proximity to him—not to mention having him rescue her—was bringing back the high school crush in full force. And yet, it was more than that. Reese was no longer a misunderstood bad boy. He was a grown man with a strong sense of duty and responsibility. There was so much more to him than she'd known twelve years ago.

He handed her a couple of ibuprofen from the first-aid kit. "To help with the headache and the soreness."

She squinted at him. "How did you know I have a headache?"

"You lost some blood yesterday and had trauma. How could you not have one?"

Perceptive. She finished her coffee, and they headed down to the cooking area. He retrieved the bear canister, and they soon had powdered scrambled eggs with flecks of bacon reconstituted into a breakfast that rivaled any she'd ever had. Probably had something to do with the exertion. "I remember how good everything tastes when you're camping. I think it goes double for backpacking."

He nodded. "I thought the effect might wear off when I lived up here all the time and was out in the woods. That maybe it was just the novelty of it. But no. It's something about the whole thing."

The companionable conversation ebbed and flowed. It was like they'd been friends forever. Maybe going through trauma together would do that. But she felt easy with him, much more so than the awkward fits and starts they'd had in their encounters before this trip. She didn't know what to make of that.

After cleaning up from breakfast, they headed back to the tents and packed up the site. Soon they were on their way.

"What's the plan for the day?" Breakfast and moving around had helped eased the soreness, but her muscles still let her know that she had put them through a lot yesterday.

"Make our way toward the rendezvous spot with Raul by tomorrow noon. There's a few higher areas I thought I'd try to make contact from. But I also want to keep us off any main trails where our 'friends' from yesterday might find us. Might make the going a bit rougher."

"Beats the alternative."

"True."

Reese picked out a path for them in and out of the trees, clearly familiar with the area and not needing a trail. It was another beautiful day, cool and sunny. And if she forgot about her sore arm and yesterday's adventures, this could be a perfect hike. And Reese? Her heart gave a little thump. This was his environment. This was where he shined. She had complete confidence that he'd get them out of this place safely.

But could she get out of here with her heart intact? He was helping Raul out until he had healed. Was he planning on staying? Everyone else in her life had left her, so why wouldn't he? *Okay, Debbie Downer.* Not everyone. Just… her dad.

She had to get out of these thoughts. "Who do you think is behind the illegal grow?"

Reese shrugged. "Could be any number of people. You know this town better than I do. Who do you think?"

"While Shannon tries to keep her cards close to her vest, I know she doesn't like Beckett Lorde of Belle Lumber. I don't know if she thinks he's behind the illegal grows—which she hates with a vengeance—or if she thinks he's just involved in shady business. At last year's Spread the Love event, Yvonne Pettis was convicted of embezzling money from the event. You know Deputy Brett Chang?"

At his nod, she continued. "Well he had suspected something wasn't on the up and up since the previous year, and he and Cassie set out to figure out what was going on. Anyhow, Yvonne skimmed the money by overbilling for supplies. But the company on the bill was a paper company that eventually linked back to a company that Lorde owned. I think Shannon suspected him of money laundering. But he's good at covering his tracks. Nothing sticks."

Reese was quiet for a few steps. "Sounds like a good suspect. And with enough funds to hire muscle and security for his grows. Makes him a more formidable opponent than some low-level fly-by-night operation." He grew quiet again.

Ella kept quiet too. She could see the wheels turning in his head, and if he was working out a plan, she wanted to give him space to do it. He was the one who would get them out of here safely. So she was going to follow him and not complain.

Besides, the view was pretty. Nature seemed soothing and protective. It was hard to believe anything bad could happen out here.

"You stopped talking."

She glanced at Reese. "What?"

"You stopped talking. Why?"

She shrugged. "You looked like you were thinking. I wanted to give you space to do that."

He held her gaze for a moment. "Huh."

"What?"

Now it was his turn to shrug. "In my experience, people who like to talk keep talking. They aren't comfortable with silence."

She laughed. "I enjoy silence. I spend a lot of time in it, usually every night with a book. Mom and I lead a pretty quiet life." She waited a beat. "What about you? What's life like with Raul and his family?"

"It's good. We haven't lived in the same house together in over twenty years. Not that we really live in the same house now since I live in the apartment above the garage. So I have my own space. But Marissa usually invites me for dinner. And I like spending time with my niece and nephew. It's different, that's for sure."

She hesitated before asking her next question. "So what are your plans for the future?"

He glanced at her then stopped and looked around. "Let's head up this way." He took off up a bit of a hill that had no trail.

She dutifully followed. Was that because he didn't want to answer her question or he had a reason for getting up here? She was partway up when he turned. "You can stay there."

He kept on going before stopping his climb at little farther up from her and looked around, studying the area for some time before heading back down.

"See anything?" she asked as he neared her.

"Nope."

Once they were back down on more or less level ground they continued in the direction they had been going. She had given up hope of ever getting an answer to her question.

"I told Raul I'd stay and help him with the shop until his knee had healed and he was able to lead hikes and overnights again. With the amount of soft tissue injury, it could be another six months. A guy from my unit who got out when I did has a shop in San Diego, kind of like Raul's. He's been wanting me to go into business with him."

Ella kept her face neutral as her heart plummeted to her stomach. She supposed a hero complex was a real thing. Even though she knew there was a good chance Reese wasn't going to stick around and she'd determined not to get attached, her heart had gone and done its own thing. Stupid heart. Why didn't it listen to her head?

This trip was turning out to be a very bad idea. Why had she thought she was any kind of adventurer? Why had she let Lucas goad her into it? Okay, it hadn't all been Lucas. She'd been restless and wanted something different. But not this kind of different.

Between getting shot and her stupid attachment to Reese, this might be the worse spring break ever. And she had at least another twenty-four hours before it was over.

Shannon took her coffee and slid into the back booth at the Jitter Bug Too. Stan and Wally had vacated the coffeeshop for their afternoon down at the hardware store, which was why she'd picked this time. She and Tony could meet during the slow period, and Cassie wouldn't say anything.

Tony entered the shop, the bell above the door jingling.

Shannon lifted a hand, and he spotted her and smiled. He stopped at the counter. "Cassie, I'll take a large coffee. And whatever you've freshly baked."

"I'll bring it over." She shot a smug look at Shannon, who pointedly ignored it. The downside of your sister knowing you well. And having strong opinions about your personal life. Now that Cassie was engaged to Brett and planning her wedding, she wanted Shannon to find happiness too. And she was all for it being with Pastor Tony.

Shannon wasn't so sure. In her experience, men didn't want a personal relationship with a woman in a position of authority. At least her ex-husband hadn't. And anyone that had been interested since then had been few and far between. Which was fine. Her job was demanding, and she needed to raise Zach and keep him safe.

Tony slid into the seat opposite her. "How's your week been?"

"Crazy. Lots of tourists doing stupid things. How's yours been? You seemed to have survived wrangling kids yesterday. And my son."

Tony's gaze flickered shut before it came back to hers. "He's no problem. He was a big help with the kids."

"How are things going with Ryan?" Shannon looked up as Cassie slid Tony's coffee mug in front of him and two plates of still-warm blueberry scones. Her sister knew her too well. She couldn't resist. She should, but she couldn't. She picked up a scone and took a bite. Warm, buttery pastry with hot, tart blueberries melted in her mouth. The perfect afternoon treat.

"He's adjusting, but it's hard for him. He's used to being in the limelight with a big audience. It's humbling for him. He's finally gotten it in his head that this isn't just a temporary assignment. He's been willing to make some long-term plans. He's even helping with the community youth outreach Friday night we're hosting so parents can drop their kids off at a safe place and have a night out. I think a few preteen girls from yesterday have developed a crush on him."

Shannon laughed. "Well, he looks like Chris Hemsworth, so no shock there."

The bell tinkled again, and Raul Vega came through the door.

Shannon caught his gaze and nodded.

Raul ordered his coffee and then approached their table. "Hey, Pastor, Sheriff. Sorry to interrupt. But I'm glad I ran into you. Something happened out on one of the trails yesterday that I think you should know about."

"Grab a chair." Shannon pointed to the next table.

Raul slid it over and took a seat. "Cory took a day trip out, and Reese and Ella went along. Reese's group had come down with food poisoning, so it was just the two of them. When I met Cory at the end of the hike, Reese and Ella weren't with him. He said they wanted to be off on their own."

Shannon raised her eyebrows. "They know each other from before, right? High school?"

"Yeah, but as far as I know, they've hardly talked since Reese has been back. He didn't want to take her on the trip once the group canceled but agreed to the day trip. I was going to try to find another group to meet up with him and Ella, so I was pretty surprised they weren't at the trailhead."

"Do you think something happened to them?" Shannon shifted into work mode, her mind sorting through the information she needed to know.

"Reese is experienced. Neither of them are the type to do anything foolish. But some of the folks from the day trip thought they'd heard gunshots. They said Cory played it off as boulders colliding, but one man said he knew what gunshots were and made a point to tell me."

Shannon was on full alert now. "Where were they? Do you have a map?"

He pulled out his phone and messed with it a bit before putting it down on the table between them, a map app open. "Best I can figure, they were somewhere around here. This is a good spot for a lunch break, and that's when Reese and Ella went off on their own to explore a waterfall."

Cassie brought him his coffee and he thanked her.

They all studied the map a minute before Raul spoke again. "It's not an easy place to get to, but it can be done with four-wheelers. I'd go check it out except that I wouldn't get too far up that hill with my bad leg. And Cory's got hikes booked every day this week."

With all the vacationers up here for spring break, Shannon didn't have any deputies to spare. And Cory was one of their search and rescue guys. Reese was capable. She shouldn't be overly concerned. Maybe he and Ella had hit it off and wanted to spend some time alone.

But after the disappearance of Dalton Brandt—and all the questions it raised—she wanted to err on the side of caution. And the gunshots were troubling.

"Reese was a Ranger. Ella has a good head on her shoulders. They had planned for a three-day trip, right?" Tony took a sip from his mug.

Raul nodded. "Yeah. They had enough supplies."

"So maybe they decided to go on the trip. When are you supposed to touch base with them?"

"Tomorrow at noon at the lakeside trailhead."

Shannon leaned back, appreciative of Tony's cool head and wisdom. "That's less than twenty four hours from now. I'll keep an ear out for any reports. But if they don't show up when they're supposed to, we'll work on assembling a search and rescue team. The gunshots are troubling, but people do hunt out of season. I'll ask forestry if they've got anyone out there or caught any poachers. It's their turf, though we do work together."

"Thanks, Sheriff." Raul slid his chair back and rose. "It's probably nothing, but I thought you should know."

"I appreciate that. Let me know if you hear anything else."

"I will." Raul shook her hand and then Tony's before leaving the coffeeshop.

Shannon sat in silence for a moment, appreciating that Tony didn't pepper her with questions. And he didn't seem bothered by her shift from personal mode to work mode. The two were so intertwined that anyone involved with her life—family, friends —had to put up with that.

She sipped her coffee before speaking. "If it wasn't so busy, I'd send a couple deputies out on four-wheelers to check it out. But that's not an option. Let me call my forestry guy and see if he knows anything." She pulled out her phone and searched for Walt Longrin's number. When he got on the line, she gave him a quick summary, focusing on the reported gunshots.

"We're at capacity too." Walt's voice came over the line. "With the opening of a few campgrounds and all the off-roaders, we have our hands full. I'll check out the reports of gunfire. Keep me posted on the missing hikers if they miss their rendezvous."

She thanked him and hung up.

Tony studied her.

"What?" She felt…uncomfortable, something that was a bit foreign to her. She wasn't used to the appreciation and admiration she saw in his eyes.

Tony shifted his gaze to his coffee before bringing it back up to her. "You're good at your job."

"Thanks."

He reached out and touched the back of her hand. "I mean it. You could let this job make you hardened and jaded, but you haven't. You still care."

Shannon didn't know what to say. Only Tia seemed to read her this well. "This is my town, my people. I care about what happens to them. They're my responsibility."

He nodded. "I know how you feel."

Yeah, he probably did. But, time to change the subject. "What concerns me most about Reese and Ella is the timing. Brandt's missing; there are reports of gunfire. Reese and Ella aren't careless. They wouldn't wander off and not let Cory know their plan to relay to Raul. It's possible it's something as simple as a sprained ankle. But a small injury can become a big deal in the back country."

She leaned forward, arms on the table. "I can't help but feel Beckett Lorde is at the root of all of this." Suspicions she would never divulge to anyone except perhaps Jonas. But Tony had been with her to visit Lorde. She leaned back. "I'm sorry. This was supposed to be our coffee time. I guess that's what happens when you have a meeting with the sheriff."

He tilted his head. "Actually, I liked watching you work. Gives me a bit of insight into your thought process. And we both know that our jobs have no real office hours. Helping Reese and Ella is something we can do together. I'll make some calls and see who might have four-wheelers and be available to do a search tomorrow afternoon if Reese and Ella don't show up. Doesn't have to be anything official."

A strange, unfamiliar lightness came over Shannon. Someone was lifting her burden, helping her with her job, taking her concerns on themselves. She wasn't sure what to make of it. It threw her off balance.

"Thanks." Her radio was turned down, but part of her was always tuned in to pick up anything that might require her attention. She listened for a moment then turned back to Tony. "I appreciate that." She gave a small laugh. "I'm not used to having help. Other than my staff."

He gave her a long look. "Get used to it."

Shannon wanted to believe that she could. But it would require taking a risk, and that didn't come easy to her. But what if there was a reward on the other side of this risk? Could it be worth it?

CHAPTER
ELEVEN

They stopped for lunch near one of the springs Reese had remembered. It was a good opportunity to refill their water bladders and to rest their legs. Ella had to be hurting, but she hadn't said a word.

"Rest for a bit. Take off your pack. I'm going to run some water through our filtration system." He shrugged off his pack and pulled out the collapsible plastic jugs connected by a filtering tube. He ran the first one into the spring. Spring water was generally safe to drink, especially in an emergency. But why take the chance? The last thing either of them needed was stomach trouble.

He'd thought a lot about her question regarding his future plans. Did she have any further interest other than making conversation? Two days ago he would have thought they were about as different as two people could be. But he'd learned a lot about her on this trip and erased many of his misconceptions.

The container filled, he hung it from a branch so gravity could pull it through the filtration system into the lower container.

He joined Ella on the log in the sun and took the peanut butter and jelly packets and pita bread she handed him. It was another beautiful day, and he was doing exactly what he loved to do. And with someone who had surprised him with how good company she was. If they didn't have the remote but still realistic possibility of someone chasing them, it would be close to perfect.

The sun was warm, and the breeze rustling through the trees surrounded them with a sound more restful than any relaxation app. The only sign of another human was the small plane flying overhead.

"How's the arm?"

"Sore." She smiled. "Like most of me. But it's doable. I'll take more ibuprofen after I eat."

"Up for another four or five miles before camp tonight? I know the ground is rockier over here. Not as many trails, which is the point. I think we'll come at the trailhead tomorrow from a different route. We can scope it out, make sure no one is waiting for us."

"Other than Raul."

He nodded. "Other than Raul. Though we should beat him there, if I've planned it right."

"I can make it." She touched his arm, stilling him. "Thanks for doing this. I know you didn't want to, and I've been far more trouble than you bargained for." She gave him a wry grin. "At least I got shot instead of you."

He froze. "Don't ever say that." Steel shot through his words. "I mean it, Ella. It's my job to protect you. I wish I had been shot instead of you." Heat flashed through him, and he took a breath to make it subside.

Her voice was soft. "I'm sorry. I didn't mean anything other than—"

"I know."

Silence draped over them like a heavy blanket. He wished he hadn't responded so strongly. He'd broken the companionable mood they'd had. Figures. Give him a mission and he could accomplish it. People, he wasn't as good with.

He strove for a lighter tone. "Besides, I owe you for bailing me out in high school."

She laughed like he hoped she would. "Wow, a twelve-year-old debt. I think there's a statute of limitations or something on that."

He shrugged. "It meant a lot to me. I was kind of a jerk back then. Had a huge chip on my shoulder. But you were always nice to me." He glanced at her.

Her cheeks tinged a pretty pink. He was embarrassing her? Huh. "I wouldn't have passed English if you hadn't helped me with that paper. And then I wouldn't have graduated and wouldn't have been able to start basic training. So I really owe you a lot."

She took a swig of water and then wiggled her empty bottle. "Charles Dickens isn't the easiest of reading, even if *A Tale of Two Cities* has a fantastic theme and isn't as long as *David Copperfield.*"

"The only reason I even know what you're talking about is that you explained it all to me that day in the library. I could get behind Sydney's heroism and wanting to make amends for his life. That paper was the highest grade I'd ever gotten in English. My teacher even questioned if I'd cheated, but there were enough spelling errors that proved it was me." He chuckled.

"'It's a far, far better thing I do, than I have ever done…'" she quoted and smiled. "The thing is, you got it. You understood what Dickens was saying. You just needed someone to put it in real English for you."

"Which is why you're a teacher." He took her water bottle and filled both of theirs from the clean water container and topped the other side off from the spring. He handed her her bottle then rejoined her on the log. They could sit here a bit longer while the water filtered.

"Why did you help me that day? I don't think I was very nice to you."

She leaned back on her good arm and looked up. "I never

bought the bad-boy act. You didn't actually do anything bad. You weren't mean to anyone. You weren't a bully. You just had a 'don't mess with me' attitude. Even then, somehow I knew that was a protective front. So I always smiled at you and said hi whenever I saw you. When you had your head in your hands that day in the library with *Tale of Two Cities* out before you, I figured it was a chance to help you." The pink was back in her cheeks. "Plus, there were a couple of girls in the library that day that I had a history with. I figured if I was seen with you, it might help my social standing. So I had a bit of an ulterior motive too."

Really? He had no idea he could improve anyone's social standing. But why was she blushing? Even though they were taking a nice stroll down memory lane, he didn't feel like he could ask her. It would likely make her more embarrassed. Still, it was an interesting piece of information he filed away.

She shrugged. "Anyhow, I was glad to help. Guess it was the teacher in me showing up already. And now you've helped me. In a much bigger way."

"Nah. I just told you. You saved my career."

"And you saved my life." She put her hand on his arm and didn't move it. It burned like a firebrand through his shirt. Her gaze met his and didn't waver.

He held his breath, not wanting to break the moment. What would it be like to kiss her? His eyes darted down to her mouth, imagining the feel of her lips under his. He leaned toward her.

She stood. "Uh, I'd better go find a tree and some privacy before we hit the road again." Her faced deepened its shade of red as she stumbled away.

He scrubbed a hand over his face. What was he thinking? Yep, he'd blown it again.

Cursing his clumsiness, he emptied the clean water into the storage bladder and strapped everything back into his pack, so he'd be ready to go when Ella returned.

He had to keep his mind on the mission: keeping both of them safe and alive.

ELLA PICKED HER WAY THROUGH THE ROCKS, CAREFUL NOT to slip on pine needles or a pine cone, but not really thinking about where she was going other than away. Why had she pulled back when he clearly wanted to kiss her? It scared her. Her emotions, the desire she saw in Reese's eyes. Her heart was already running away. He was going to leave. The kiss that she knew would be wonderful would just break her heart more thoroughly.

She stopped. She'd better get her bearings. The last thing she needed was to get lost by wandering blindly through the woods. Scanning the area, she made note of where she'd come from while she found a good spot for some privacy. That made her laugh. All she had around her was privacy.

She took care of her personal needs and then leaned against a ponderosa pine, savoring its vanilla-butterscotch smell while she got her bearings. She had to go back to camp after what had just happened. The last thing she wanted was for things to be awkward between her and Reese. She shouldn't have panicked. Too many feelings had coursed through her, and she did not think quickly on her feet.

As a freshman, she'd spent an embarrassing number of hours thinking about that exact scenario. But now? Well, she'd be lying to herself if she hadn't thought of it once or twice since he'd returned. Especially yesterday when he'd been so attentive to her.

So why had she run off like a scared rabbit?

Because she wasn't one of those girls who went around kissing guys when it didn't mean anything. When she kissed someone—the last person had been Lucas, which gave her a shudder—it meant something.

Reese probably kissed women all the time. With his devastating good looks—the dark, brooding type—he'd have no problem getting any woman he wanted. Why would he want her? She hadn't rescued him. She hardly thought her help on his paper twelve years ago counted. Though it was sweet he thought she'd made such a difference to him.

She went on this trip to prove to herself she wasn't afraid of adventure, that she could move out of her comfort zone. Look at what all she'd been through. What if a relationship with Reese wasn't out of the question? What if she should take a risk? He wasn't planning on sticking around. But San Diego wasn't the end of the earth. It was even in the same state.

Amanda had told her to be open to the possibilities. Reese was a possibility.

She had better get back before Reese worried and came looking for her. Heading back that way, she heard a rustling in the bushes, something larger than a squirrel. She paused, listening.

There it was again, much bigger than a squirrel. She edged back toward camp but kept her eyes on the area where the noise had come from. Had their pursuers found them? Adrenaline shot through her veins, and she resisted the urge to run and draw attention to herself.

A tawny-brown flash in the bushes almost made her knees collapse. A mountain lion stared at her from between the branches of an incense cedar.

She had to get out of here. Every instinct screamed *run!* But she knew that was the worst thing she could do. Continuing to move toward camp, she raised her arms out to the side. "Go on! Get out of here! I don't want anything from you."

The mountain lion's ears twitched, and it took a step toward Ella.

Ella glanced around for any kind of weapon—a stick, a rock. She didn't want to bend down and make herself smaller. "Go on! I'm not going to hurt you. And I really don't want you to hurt me." She kicked at some rocks and sticks, making as much noise as possible. Maybe it was a mama with cubs nearby.

A few loose stones sat on a nearby boulder, and she grabbed them. Heaving as hard as possible, she threw them toward the mountain lion. The rocks crashed into the bushes near it, and it flinched.

Ella took more steps back. "Get!" Another rock landed near the cat, and it backed up a step.

Noise came from behind Ella, and she whirled, crazily trying to spot another animal that had come up behind her.

But it was Reese. He chucked a rock that nailed the cat in the side, and it bounded off.

"You okay?" Reese touched her arm.

And that was all it took. She flung herself into his embrace, letting him hold her up while her knees wanted to collapse under her. His solid strength was safety. The soft flannel of his shirt was under her cheek. He smelled of the outdoors and something that was uniquely him. She could stay here forever.

After a minute—embarrassed—she stepped back, pushing her hair out of her eyes, feeling the heat in her cheeks. "Thanks. That was terrifying."

"You had it handled." His hand still remained on her arm, a lifeline of warmth and comfort.

"Didn't feel like it." The mixture of adrenaline and embarrassment made for an unstable mix, and she scrambled for equilibrium. She concentrated on breathing deeply and calmly.

He laughed. "Yeah, it never does. But the ending was okay, and that's all that matters."

She thought about his words as they returned to where they'd left their packs.

He handed her some ibuprofen and her water bottle.

"Thanks." She took the pills and water from him, but there was something more in that simple word. Something had shifted between them.

He helped her on with her pack, and they started off again.

The silence stretched between them as they picked their way over a nonexistent trail, but not in an uncomfortable way. Ella snuck glances at Reese.

They moved into an area where the trees thinned and then disappeared. This was where the fire had come through last summer.

"Be careful. Keeps your eyes open. This is a restricted area. The burned trees are dangerous because they could fall at any time. We'll skirt the edge of it and stay as far from the remaining trees as we can. But we have to go through here to get to the trailhead. Otherwise we'd backtrack half a day to go around it."

The ground was blackened and trees leveled in all directions; in some places the ground was a stark white from the fire burning so hot. It was like a moonscape, otherworldly. A small stand of pines huddled together on the ridge dyed pink. Must have been a place where Phos-Chek had been dropped to slow the fire down.

Those trees reminded her a bit of her own life, huddled in a protected safety zone of known quantities. Her work, family, friends, town. She hardly ever left that zone. Reese represented something totally different. Freedom, adventure. And yes, the chance of getting burned.

Maybe getting shot at and living to tell about it and confronting a mountain lion had emboldened her, but nothing about this trip had been expected. Maybe she should grab this window of opportunity and take a chance.

She studied Reese as he walked a half step ahead of her. He'd retreated to trail-guide mode. Had she hurt him by her rejection, by running away when he potentially tried to kiss her?

Caught up in her own feelings and emotions, she just now thought about how her actions impacted him. She didn't want him to feel rejected, because that was not her intention at all. But how to say that?

She took a breath. Might as well jump in and see what happened. This was an adventure after all, right?

"I have to admit the reason I helped you back in high school was because I had a crush on you." The words tumbled out before she could stop or consider them.

Reese's head whipped around, and his step faltered. "What?" Confusion and a flicker of vulnerability crossed his face.

She lifted her shoulders a bit, as much as the pack allowed. "I had a crush on you. That's why I helped you. It was a chance to spend time with you. I didn't think you'd notice me any other way."

His gaze roamed her face for a moment. "I noticed you."

Now it was her turn to be stunned. "You did?"

"Yeah." He stopped walking, giving all of his attention to her. "But a girl like you, so sweet and kind, would never give a guy like me the time of day. Until you helped me with my paper. I couldn't believe it."

This was not what she had expected to hear. She hadn't expected her own soul-bearing revelation to be met with another one from him. "How did we not know that back then?"

He chuckled. "We were dumb, scared kids. Vulnerability is the kiss of death in high school."

"Yeah, you're right about that." It took awhile for this new information to sink in. Reese had liked her in high school. Huh. This trip had been more than she'd bargained for in so many ways.

And it was like a door had opened between them. Suddenly, it was out in the open, and they weren't dancing around it anymore. She was almost a bit giddy with the freedom of it.

"I almost didn't help you," she said.

"Really? I'm still surprised you did. Crush or no crush." He bumped her shoulder with his, a grin in his voice.

She smiled. "Well, I'd been burned before, thinking that I could win someone's friendship by helping them in school. There were these girls, you probably don't remember them because they were freshmen. But they had seemed to befriend me. I spent a lot of time at one or another of their houses helping them with their homework and papers. Then one night I stopped by Mia's house. I'd left my notebook there, and I needed it for a paper I was working on that weekend. Everyone else was already there. She was hosting a party, and I had most definitely not been invited. It was so obvious that they only wanted me around to help them with their schoolwork."

She glanced up. "So you can see why I was a little afraid that would happen again with you."

"I was just grateful that someone as smart as you would spend time helping a doofus like me."

She smacked his arm. "You aren't."

"Well, I'm surprised you helped me. And still help people."

Their conversation moved more freely now as they picked their way through the edge of the burn scar, talking about high school memories and what he remembered of his first stay in Holcomb Springs. She asked him a few questions about his time in the Army, but he so quickly shut down that she avoided that subject. She thought about Cory's comment about Reese being responsible for the death of his fellow soldiers. That didn't make any sense, but she didn't think Reese was open to discussing it. But she didn't like thinking that people were talking about Reese behind his back in a negative way.

The sun grew lower in the sky, and Reese began looking for a place for them to camp. No matter how close she'd thought they'd gotten by admitting their attraction to each other, there were still parts of Reese that were completely inaccessible to her. That was understandable; they were only rekindling their friendship. Or actually, building a new one. Would he ever open up to her?

Just because they had a mutual attraction and a budding friendship didn't mean anything would come of it. He was planning to head off the mountain. She'd best remember that if she didn't want her foolish heart to get broken.

CHAPTER
TWELVE

There was a quick knock at Shannon's office door, and she looked up from her computer as Donna stuck her head in. "Lucas Slater is here to see you. Do you have time?"

Shannon frowned. "What does he want?"

"He says he has information that Ella Sommer might be missing." Donna's eyebrows rose. She didn't miss much and didn't hesitate to let Shannon know what she thought on a topic or about a person. It wouldn't surprise Shannon at all to find out that Donna was writing detective novels or police procedurals on the side. She was nosy and opinionated. And usually right.

"Send him in."

Donna ducked out and Lucas entered. "Hi, Sheriff."

She motioned to a chair in front of her desk, but she didn't get up. "Lucas. What can I do for you?"

He took a seat. "I'm worried about Ella Sommer. She's missing."

"What makes you think that?" Shannon knew about the history between Ella and Lucas. And she was glad they broke up. Not that it was any of her business, but she thought Ella deserved better. Lucas wasn't a bad guy. Just not worthy of Ella.

"I returned the kayaks I rented to the outfitters shop and asked Raul about Ella's trip. When I picked up the kayaks, Reese talked like they were still going on their three-day wilderness trip. I didn't think that trip was ever a serious idea. Ella's not an outdoorsy girl. She's more of a bookworm. Then I'd heard that Reese's trip had been canceled because a bunch of people had gotten food poisoning and that Reese and Ella had gone with Cory on a day trip but hadn't come back. So she should have been back yesterday. When I asked Raul about it today, he said they were still out there on the three-day trip. That makes zero sense to me. I don't trust Reese, and I think Raul's covering for him. Someone needs to go look for Ella."

Did Lucas think she really had no idea of what was going on in her town? She tapped a pen on her desk, considering how much to tell him. "Have you thought about going out to look for her?"

"Me? No. Who knows where they could be? I don't have that kind of experience in the woods. But search and rescue should go after them."

"What makes you think they didn't just continue on the three-day trip as planned, even though they started out with Cory's group?" She studied Lucas, watching for a reaction.

His mouth dropped open a bit. "That's just not like Ella."

"But didn't she tell you that's what she was doing over spring break?"

"Yeah, but she didn't mean it. It's just not like her. If anything, Reese talked her into it. He even told me she was a big help on his group hikes, something I know is a lie."

Shannon leaned forward. "Let me get this straight. Ella told you she was going on a three-day trip over spring break. Reese told you the same thing. And so did Raul. Why would all three of them lie to you? What's the point?"

Lucas's gaze darted around, and he sputtered a bit. "I don't know. I just don't like it."

"Maybe you just don't like the idea of Ella spending time with Reese." Shannon kept her tone soft and sympathetic.

Lucas shook his head. "That's not it. I just care about Ella's safety. You know Reese was responsible for the death of two of his men. He's not trustworthy, and I don't want Ella in danger because of him."

Steel shot through Shannon's veins. "I get this is a small town, but I don't tolerate gossip that impugns someone's character. Reese served his country honorably and was wounded to boot." She wanted to add, *which was more than I could say for you*. But she didn't.

Instead she stood. "Reese and Ella are due back tomorrow. If they don't return on time, then we'll consider if there's a problem. In the meantime, keep your gossip to yourself. Please close the door on your way out." She sat and returned to studying her monitor until she heard the door click shut.

The one thing she hated most in this town was the gossip, though sometimes she had to admit she found it useful. But most of the time it was just plain hurtful. In this case, it was obvious that Lucas didn't like the idea of Ella spending time with Reese, and he was using whatever gossip he heard to cast Reese in a bad light.

But after her conversation with Raul today, she had to admit she had her concerns too. Not about Reese being a danger to Ella but about both of them being in danger, likely from Beckett Lorde or his henchmen. She just prayed they showed up at the rendezvous site tomorrow.

* * *

REESE AND ELLA WALKED IN SILENCE, BUT NOT AN uncomfortable one. He let his mind click through everything he'd learned about Ella today while searching for a spot he and Raul had camped at previously. Why was she interested in his future plans? Was it possible that a woman like her could be interested in a man like him? Maybe that was why he'd tried to kiss her. He wasn't sure what had come over him, didn't even know he was going to do it until she jerked away.

When he heard her shouting and saw that mountain lion, his heart nearly stopped. It could have been a mama protecting her cubs, which meant Ella was in more danger than she knew. He would have done anything to keep her safe. And that realization, even stronger than his earlier desire to kiss her, thrummed in his chest. He would do anything for her.

He was never going to have another opportunity like this to be with her. He might as well make the most of it. Keeping them alive was his primary mission. But even if at the end of the trip they just ended up being friends, that was a good secondary mission. He didn't have many friends.

He didn't want to think about the future. Time enough to think about that later. Now he had to concentrate on the present.

The area he stopped and surveyed didn't look good. The fire had gone through here, and there were too many snags to be safe. Instead they would have to move on to a rockier, more exposed site. He didn't like it, even if it was remote. But they were running out of daylight and options. He started walking again to the other site. This was as good as it was going to get.

For their second night, they worked well as a team, almost like they'd been doing this together for a lot longer. Ella was a quick learner. She watched, and he could tell she was trying to understand the reasoning behind what he was doing. She was always learning. He admired that about her.

He admired a lot of things about her, truth be told.

They found a spot far enough away from the tents for their cook site and set about to prepare dinner. He noticed the mac and cheese dinner and bypassed it for pasta primavera.

They found a log to sit on and ate their rehydrated food. They'd been doing a lot of sharing, so he took a risk.

"Why don't you like mac and cheese? I thought everyone

did. You don't have a milk allergy." They had a form that asked about food and other allergies that campers filled out when they signed up for the trip.

She was quiet for a long minute, pushing her food around in the bowl.

Had he overstepped? Once again, he'd messed up.

She finally let out a breath. "It might sound… I don't know." She met his gaze. "My dad left us when I was ten. He pretended to be interested in us after he left, but he gave up pretty easily. But there was one particular time when we—Evan, my brother, and I—still thought that he loved us. We were up early and had our backpacks by the door. We almost didn't want to eat breakfast, but Mom insisted we would need the sustenance. She made us scrambled eggs. It was the last thing we had in the house because Mom was going to go shopping while we were gone.

"We ate and ping ponged between the kitchen table and the front window, waiting for Dad to show up. We hadn't seen him much since he'd moved out. But today he was supposed to be taking us to Disneyland. He'd sat with both of us on our couch and explained that while he and Mom didn't love each other anymore, they both still loved Evan and me and nothing would change.

"When our breakfast was gone, along with the last of the orange juice, Dad still hadn't come. I kept looking at the phone sitting there on its charging base in the kitchen. It didn't ring. I didn't know if that was a good thing or a bad thing." She paused and looked off into the woods before continuing.

This was not what Reese had expected. But he didn't say anything, didn't want to interrupt. He had a feeling from the rusty way she told the story, the rawness of it, that she hadn't shared it with many people.

"Mom let us watch a movie. We'd gone through *The Prince of Egypt* and started on *The Parent Trap* reboot with Lindsay Lohan. Still no Dad. We were getting concerned because by the time he showed up and we'd get to Disneyland, it would be afternoon. We wouldn't have time to ride all the rides. It cost a lot of money, so we usually made a whole day of it. It didn't make sense to just go for part of the day.

"Mom didn't know I was watching, but I saw her pick up the phone, dial, listen, and then put it down again. She forced a smile and said, 'I'm sure something came up for your dad and he hasn't been able to call.' But when *The Parent Trap* was over, I ran up to my room and flopped on my bed, crying. It was all ruined. Everything was ruined. At some point, I cried myself to sleep. When Mom woke me, my room was dark."

Ella gave a short laugh. "Mom said, 'Hey, you must be hungry. I made some mac and cheese. I haven't had time to go to the store yet, and it's all that's left in the house.' I sat up and wiped my face and asked, 'Did Dad ever call?' Mom shook her head.

"I followed her to the kitchen and slipped into my chair next to Evan. He was flipping through a comic book, one I had seen him stash in his bag. I grabbed the bowl of boxed mac and cheese that Mom slid in front of me and took a few bites. They lodged in my throat, but I choked them down. I didn't want Mom to worry about me, and food wasn't something to waste.

"Mom let us stay up and watch TV, but even when I went to bed, the mac and cheese sat in my stomach like a lump. I've never been able to even stand the smell of it." A tear glistened on her cheek in the waning light, and it lingered a moment before she swiped it away. "On the days they serve it in the cafeteria at school, I can't even go in there."

"What did your dad say about not showing up?" Reese kept his voice calm and even.

Ella handed him her bowl as they began to clean up. "He claimed it was a misunderstanding, that he hadn't committed to taking us to Disneyland—just threw it out there as a possibility —but that something came up." She shook her head. "It was such a lie, and we all knew it. I never trusted him again. And I don't think Evan did either."

"I'm sorry you had to go through that, Ella. I can't imagine what that was like. My folks and I don't agree on a lot of things, some very important things. But I can't imagine either one of them walking out of my life. Do you ever talk to him?"

"Not much. He remarried soon after that and had another family. He pretty much forgot about Evan and me." She took a breath. "The thing is, deep down I wasn't that surprised. I think part of me knew he was going to abandon us." She met Reese's gaze. "I've never told anyone this, but I knew he was going to leave my mom before she did."

"How?" That had to be awful.

"I heard him on the phone. He didn't hear me come in from school. I was happy to see that his car was in the driveway, so I came inside and went back to their room. I heard his voice and knew he was on the phone, so I was quiet, not wanting to interrupt, listening for him to finish. At first I thought he was talking to Mom because he called her 'sweetie.' But then the rest of what he was saying didn't make sense. He talked about leaving, packing up, telling her soon, and divorce papers.

"I ran into my room and closed the door, his words flying around my brain as I tried to make sense of them. I felt sick. But I didn't want to say anything to him or Mom. What if I'd misunderstood? I watched him that night. He gave Mom a kiss on the cheek and everything was normal at dinner. So I figured I'd misunderstood. Until he sat us down and told us about leaving. Then I wondered if I could have done something, if I could have stopped him somehow. You know how kids think.

"I guess I hoped the trip to Disneyland would prove that he did still want us in his life. But I think I knew deep down inside that he was capable of lying to all of us."

"That's a heavy burden for a kid to bear. And you never told your mom?" Reese packed the food and dishes back in the bear canister.

"No. What would be the point? I didn't want to hurt her any more than she already was."

"You shouldn't have had to carry that alone."

"No. I shouldn't." She gave him a soft smile. "But now you know, so I'm not."

"I'm glad you told me." He found a good spot for the bear canister. He reached for her hand as they headed back to the tents, wanting to pull her close and make everything better, but not sure he could.

In fact, he was nearly certain that he would only make things worse for her.

Ella's hand felt like it was perfectly at home in Reese's. She hadn't meant to tell him all that. Not even Amanda knew the whole story. It wasn't even the logical next step after admitting to her crush on him. But something about the moment, his soft questions and quiet-but-intense listening just made the story pour out.

And oddly enough, she felt lighter.

Their tents appeared. "Let's check out your arm and see how it's doing. We at least need to change the bandage." Reese pointed her to a log, and she sat while he grabbed the first-aid kit from her pack.

She slipped her arm out of her jacket and pulled it out of the sleeve of her shirt. It was definitely still sore. Both of their head-lamps aimed at the spot. No blood seeped through the bandage.

He peeled off the gauze. "Looks good. No signs of infection."

As he worked on her arm, her body hummed at his touch. It seemed to mean so much more than it had before. Could she really risk her heart with him? There were so many reasons why this wouldn't work.

But all she needed was one for why it would. In the words of Helen Keller: "Life is either a daring adventure or nothing at all." And Helen Keller was a woman who had every reason to stay inside the safety of her world.

Even if all she and Reese had were memories from this trip, that was more than she'd had in a long time. And tonight was their last night.

He treated her arm with antibiotic ointment and covered it up again with gauze.

The shadows were long and thick, the stars beginning to sprinkle the sky. She didn't want to return to the deep topic of her past, but their conversation before that about high school raised a number of questions, even though she still couldn't quite wrap her mind around the idea that he'd been interested in her in high school. She tried to remember who he'd dated back then.

"Who did you take to prom? I can't remember."

"That's because I didn't go to prom." He held the arm of her jacket as she struggled back into both of her sleeves.

"You didn't?"

"No."

"Why not? Everyone goes to prom. Especially their senior year." She flicked off her headlamp, preferring to let her eyes adjust to the growing starlight.

"Not everyone, Ella." He met her gaze. "Why are you so interested?"

She shrugged. "Just wanted to figure out who to picture you with."

He laughed. "It was a long time ago."

"I know. But our discussion today got me to thinking about it. Why didn't you go?"

He was silent for a moment but didn't move away from her. "I wanted to ask you, actually. But I knew I was leaving right after graduation. No point in starting anything." He looked away and switched off his headlamp before looking at her again. "You're not the kind of woman I could be casual with. You deserve more than that. Even in high school, you were serious, and you deserved to be treated well. I hate what your dad did to you." His gaze met hers in the quickly fading light.

He wanted to ask her to prom? Wow. That thought had never occurred to her. She studied his face, wishing she could read him better. She held his gaze, determined to let him kiss her. She didn't move.

But Reese was the one to look away. "It was a long time ago."

"Ha! It's never too late to go to prom." She tugged out her phone and turned it on. Since she'd only been using it to take pictures and keeping it off, it still had battery left. She scrolled through her music, hoping she had the song she was looking for on her phone. Yes, there it was. She tapped "Over My Head" by the Fray, and the sound poured out the speaker, a little jarring in the quiet night forest. It had been one of the hot songs that year. She loved the whole album.

She stood and held out her hand to him.

He looked up at her, a smile touching the corners of his mouth. "What did you have in mind?"

"A dance. Just because we didn't dance at prom doesn't mean we can't dance now."

He got to his feet and took her hand then tucked her close to him, slipping his arm around her waist.

She laid her head against his chest as they swayed to the music, his scent comforting and intimate.

Many proms might have claimed to be an evening under the stars, but this one actually was. The moon wouldn't rise until later tonight, leaving the stars to shine down on them in all their glory. The music surrounded them. This was much better than dancing with Chris West who Ella had attended prom with her junior year or Ian Cruz who she'd gone with her senior year. Both of her dates were just friends who only wanted a date to prom, not to actually have a relationship with Ella. And they'd had fun, but there had been no slow dances. That was the time for chatting with friends and studiously avoiding their dates.

She laughed, and Reese looked down at her. "What's so funny?"

"I was just thinking this was the best prom ever."

His chuckle rumbled through her. "Well, it's my only prom, so I have nothing to compare it to, but I'd say it's pretty great."

The song ended and segued into the next one on the album, "How to Save a Life."

Reese tugged her close, kissed her cheek, and whispered, "Thanks for the dance," before stepping back. He didn't let go of her hand, though, and she followed him as he sat on the log.

She switched off her phone and stuck it in her pocket, and they sat in silence for a moment, letting the echoes of the dance wash over them while they studied the stars.

"Why did you have the bad-bad boy attitude in high school when you really weren't?" Ella figured if she'd just bared her soul, he could too. And he'd gone for the prom dance idea so…

Reese was quiet for a minute then rolled his shoulders.

But he didn't say anything. And Ella regretted asking. Why hadn't she just left the sweetness of their dance alone?

CHAPTER
THIRTEEN

Reese thought about changing the subject or ignoring her question. But she'd been vulnerable with him. And if he was ever going to have a chance with her—and he wanted one—he was going to have to open up. It was a risk, but so was every mission worth achieving. Ella was trustworthy, and she was a risk worth taking. Even if it hurt. Even if it killed him.

He stared up at the stars as if they could guide his heart the way they did the paths of ancient explorers. He was certainly treading into unknown territory.

"My parents are pacifists. I don't know if you know that."

She made a sympathetic noise, but he didn't meet her gaze. It was easier telling it to the stars and the trees.

"When I was a kid, I was small for my age, didn't get my growth spurt until well into high school. There was a boy in fifth grade—Darrin—who bullied me mercilessly. He was the biggest kid in our class, and he enjoyed his size. I'd tell my parents, and they'd tell me to use my words, that violence only beget violence." He could hear the cynicism in his voice.

"One day I was walking home from school, hurrying as fast as I could hoping Darrin wouldn't catch up to me. I constantly wished I was taller or bigger so that he wouldn't mess with me.

Mostly I just wanted to get on my street before Darrin caught up with me. Maybe he'd find someone else to mess with that day. But sure enough, I heard the pounding of sneakers on the pavement behind me. I turned, and Darrin and his buddies were bearing down on me."

He let out a breath that felt like it held years of pent up frustration and glanced at Ella. Even in the faint starlight, he could see her soft, open gaze on him. It was encouragement enough to keep going.

"I resisted the urge to run. Maybe if I didn't, they wouldn't chase me. No such luck. A smack hit the back of my head and caused me to stumble. I thought about what my parents had told me, about using my words to state what I wanted. So I said, 'Stop it, Darrin. I don't like that. Please don't do it again.'

"This just egged him on. 'What? This?' Darrin smacked me again. So I tried one more time. 'I said stop. If you don't stop, I'll have to report you to the teacher.' Darrin's friend Lucas—yeah, there's a reason I don't like your ex-fiancé's name—called me a tattletale, and Darrin said I was a crybaby. 'You can't handle anything. Have to go running to Mommy.'"

The words still punched Reese in the chest, old feelings resurrecting. He was that boy again, trying to block out the words, blinking back the tears that threatened, knowing that would just make everything worse, making Darrin's accusation of being a crybaby true. "I just kept putting one foot in front of the other. I just had to make it to my street. Then I had a chance of running home before they caught me. But Lucas blocked my path, and I bumped into him. I asked him to let me pass and tried to go around him, but Darrin grabbed my arm from behind and spun me around."

Ella's hand slid over and wrapped around his.

He squeezed it, grateful for the warmth. "I knew where this was going, but I tried the last threat I knew. 'I'm reporting you to the teacher tomorrow, and you'll get detention.' Darrin said,

'Kinda hard to talk with a broken jaw' and took a swing at me. I ducked, but it caught the tip of my nose.

"My face burned and turned warm. Blood dripped from my nose. Even though I expected it, I was shocked he actually hit me. I'd never had that happen in my life. Everything in me wanted to strike back, but my parents forbade it. They abhorred violence of any kind, said that it never solved anything, just made the situation worse. I'd asked for karate or boxing lessons when Darrin first started hassling me, but my parents were adamant in their refusal."

Reese hadn't told anyone the whole story other than his parents, and the intensity of the long-buried emotions surprised him. "While I was still in shock that he hit me, he slammed me with another punch, this one catching me under the eye, and I spun and lost my balance. A well-placed foot by Lucas caused me to trip. When I put out my arm to break my fall, I was rewarded with a pop and searing pain in my forearm. I remember curling into a ball on the ground, barely able to catch my breath and hoping they wouldn't do anything else.

"Darrin nudged Lucas and laughed, saying, 'That'll teach you. You say a word and you'll get worse.' They ran off. When I could catch my breath, I gingerly held my arm against my side and headed home, grateful Darrin and Lucas had left me alone but hoping I could make it home.

"Mom gasped when I walked through the door. She rushed me to the emergency room where I was given a cast. I liked the idea of having people sign it, but I didn't want to say how it happened. I made up some story about breaking my arm falling off a neighbor's trampoline, since that's what had happened to a kid in our class the previous year.

"When we got home from the emergency room, I asked Mom if I could have those karate lessons as soon as my cast got off, thinking surely they'd see the need for them now. But she was still adamantly against them. Instead, she was going to talk to the principal. Darrin got a couple of days' suspension; Lucas got nothing. Mom drove me to and from school after that, but there were only a few days left in the school year."

He leaned back and tugged Ella's hand closer to him. "I missed swimming the first part of that summer. But I did learn one thing."

"What was that?" Ella's voice was a quiet whisper beside him in the now full dark.

"I knew Darrin would pick up where we left off when school started again. Maybe I couldn't fight him, but I could outrun him. Mom couldn't object to that. So as soon as the cast came off, I asked to join a local track club. I found out I liked running. And while Darrin was built like a football player, he couldn't run. After unsuccessfully chasing me a few times in sixth grade, he turned his attention to someone else."

"And you still run."

He nodded, surprised at first that she knew then remembering it was a small town. "Yeah. It's saved my sanity." He let out another deep breath, feeling a piece of his past slip away. "But that's why I came into high school with a chip on my shoulder. My parents had moved us up here once Raul and Rachel were out of the house. By that time I was taller and fast and figured a good offense was the best defense. If I acted tough, no one would mess with me."

"And no one did."

"Nope." But he hadn't made many friends either. "By the end of high school, the military was looking like a good choice for me. I didn't realize it at the time, but I was angry at my parents' pacifist ways. I'd been hurt by them. I guess going into the military was the most opposite thing I could think of from what they believed. They were pretty upset with me. We had a lot of arguments. They never stopped speaking to me or anything like that, but things have always been strained. Then I got my TBI and a medical discharge. I figured maybe it was time to come home and mend some fences. My parents are older. I was an unexpected, late-in-life surprise. So helping Raul is one way I can try to make things better between us."

The silence fell soft between them.

Then it was shattered by the snap of breaking branches.

ELLA HARDLY KNEW WHAT WAS HAPPENING WHEN REESE grabbed her hand and yanked her to her feet. "Wha—?"

"Shh. Trust me." His voice was barely above a whisper. She hoped he could see better than she could as he dragged her through the campsite.

He snagged up his pack, and they kept on going past the tents and up into the rockier part of the slope, keeping to the granite slabs and bare ground.

She'd heard something in the bushes and thought perhaps the mountain lion was back. Or maybe a bear. But didn't animals settle down at night? Then again, it wasn't as if they had a fire to warn them off.

But then she saw the beam of a flashlight. And knew it was a human predator after them. What were the odds that it was some poor hiker bumbling around in the woods in the dark?

She concentrated on keeping her feet under her and staying quiet as Reese tugged her along. Her heart pounded, and she actively pushed the fear away, trusting that Reese knew what he was doing. Of course he did. And he was their only hope of getting out of this alive.

He skirted them around a copse of trees before hunkering down behind some scrub brush. His voice was in her ear, sending tingles down her spine and into the confusing mix of emotions running through her.

"I think we lost them for now."

"Were those the guys who were after us before?" She put her hand on his shoulder to lean close to him. The sense of safety he provided was almost overwhelming.

"Can't imagine who else it would be."

"What do we do?"

"Wait. They won't find us here. In the morning we can get to the trailhead and contact the sheriff."

"We don't have tents or sleeping bags."

He shifted slightly, quietly opening his pack, pausing between movements. He pulled out something soft and handed it to her. A fleece. She eased off her jacket and pulled it on, then put her jacket over it. Based on the slight rustling, he was doing something similar.

He moved, putting his back against the large pine. "Come here." He pulled her between his legs, against his chest and wrapped his arms around her. "I have an emergency blanket, but it crinkles when you move. We'll have to be very still."

She nodded, not sure if the pounding in her chest was from being chased or from being held by him. She had gloves in her jacket pocket, so she eased those on. She wished she had her knit cap that was back in her pack, but her jacket had a hood.

Reese seemed to read her mind as he eased her hood out and over her head. He moved his arms around her, slowly opening the emergency blanket, each crack sounding as loud as a gunshot.

She was certain they'd be found out. But there was nothing to be done about it. It would get close to freezing tonight, and they'd need all the warmth they could get. What she wouldn't give for her sleeping bag. But she was grateful Reese had grabbed his pack or they'd have nothing at all.

When he'd gotten the blanket over them, he tightened his arms around hers crossed over her middle. His head rested on her shoulder. "If they find us, I want you to run toward the top of that hill that's just past these trees. You can hide in the rocks up there. Or head down the other side. If you head toward the lake, you'll hit the trailhead and Raul will be there." He paused. "Whatever you do, don't wait for me. Understand?"

She nodded, but her throat tightened. The thought of

leaving Reese behind in the hands of those men who had done what they'd done to Dalton Brandt… *Please, God, no. Don't let it come to that. Let us get out of here safely.*

REESE HOPED ELLA COULDN'T FEEL HIS HEART POUNDING as she leaned up against his chest. And he hoped he was doing the right thing. He'd been questioning his judgment ever since his decision had gotten two of his men killed. He'd never forgive himself if something happened to Ella because of his bad choice. He knew what these illegal growers were capable of. He'd seen what they'd done to Brandt.

While he'd never said anything to Ella, he'd been keeping an eye on their tail, making sure they weren't being followed and picking paths that wouldn't leave as much of a trail. He wasn't sure how wilderness savvy these dudes were but was banking on the fact that they were more muscle than anything.

The only way he could figure how they'd been found was that small plane earlier today. He'd thought maybe someone was just sightseeing, given the plane was circling around and flying across the valley. But they could have been looking for Ella and him. He didn't think these guys were that lucky to find them, since he'd purposely stayed away from common campsites and trails.

He'd deliberately dashed out of their previous camp in the opposite direction and then circled back, hoping that if those goons heard them, they'd think he and Ella were headed to another trailhead. Deciding to hunker down here was the safe bet. Wandering around in the dark was just asking for one of them to end up with a sprained ankle or worse. And not being able to move quickly would be their biggest liability. Those guys would literally have to stumble over them to find them here. Once the sun came up, it would be a different story. But they weren't too far from the trailhead. He still thought his plan to approach from the north would be unexpected.

His mind spun. After everything he and Ella had shared tonight, she was much more than a client he felt responsible for. His heart was intwined with hers, for better or worse.

He wasn't going to sleep; he was on watch. He'd done this enough times that he knew what to do. But this was the first time his heart had been involved. He just hoped he was capable of it this time.

CHAPTER
FOURTEEN

As the sky lightened before dawn, Ella opened her eyes. She'd dozed a bit during the night, feeling surprisingly safe in Reese's arms. He'd shifted a few times during the night, but every time she moved, he whispered in her ear, asking if she was okay, if she was warm enough. She didn't think he'd slept at all.

Right now, she'd do anything for a hot shower and a cup of coffee. But both would have to wait. She turned her head to check on Reese.

His gaze was already steady on her. "Ready to move?"

She nodded.

"Do just what I say." He carefully lifted the emergency blanket, and the cold air rushed in. He directed her how to move to avoid making noise. He got to his feet after her and slid a few downed branches over the emergency blanket, leaving it where it lay. It would be too noisy to try to pack it back up.

He pulled out a couple of energy bars from his pack and handed her one. Then he hoisted the pack on his back and held out his hand to her, pulling her close. "Remember what I said last night. If anything happens, run and don't look back."

The thought made her sick to her stomach, but she nodded.

The woods had always been a sanctuary for her, a place where she made good memories, where she had felt like she belonged with her mom, brother, and friends.

But now it had morphed into a place of hostility, with unseen threats and a real threat of danger. Would she ever look at these woods again with that previous sense of peace and relaxation? She didn't think so.

With her hand firmly in his, they moved out, hugging the still-deep shadows.

She couldn't get a read on his mood. He was focused and back in trail-guide mode. Which she was grateful for. But yesterday she'd made all the first moves, telling him she had a crush on him, giving him a "prom," telling him about her dad. Today she felt a bit foolish. Had she just let this experience go to her head like some people did on vacations or summer flings? Those things never lasted in the real world. And she had a sinking feeling that whatever this was between her and Reese wouldn't last in the real world either.

In a few hours, she'd know for sure. One way or another.

If they made it to safety.

Reese kept them moving. The familiar whoosh of adrenaline through his veins got him focused on the goal and keenly attuned to the area around them. He could see the end in sight. They just had to get there.

The problem was that to make the approach the way he wanted, they'd be exposed for a bit as they climbed the ridge. But if they got to the ridge, they could reach Raul by radio. Most likely. They'd have help and another set of eyes. Safety was within reach. They just had to get to the ridge.

He stopped at the bottom of the slope, offering her water from the bladder and doing reconnaissance. He'd heard or seen nothing that made him think the guys were after them or even knew what direction they were headed. But he'd been taking calculated risks this whole trip, and one of them somewhere along the line hadn't paid off. And it only took one break in the chain of events to cause a catastrophe. The sooner they got out of this wilderness the better.

There was also a chance that their pursuers had staked out the lakeside trailhead too. Maybe all of them along this part of the valley, figuring he and Ella would come out somewhere. Did they have that kind of manpower? Could they remain inconspicuous? All questions he didn't have the answers to.

All he could do was get them to the top of this mountain to see what was going on. If it wasn't safe, he could at least radio Raul and get help.

"Stay here." He dropped his pack and headed out of the shade of the trees into the sun, finally feeling a bit of warmth after being chilled to the bone last night. Moving had gotten them warm this morning though.

He kept to the edges of the trees then scouted out the area. It had enough cover for the most part. A lot of boulders dotted the side of the slope and some scrubby brush with a few trees. There was one unavoidably exposed area; they'd have to be careful there. He reviewed the plan. It was really the only one they had.

Without supplies, spending another night in the cold was going to be a problem. He had to leave the emergency blanket behind. It was just too noisy to pack up. Putting the branches on it would keep it from blowing away and making noise. And maybe even camouflage it a bit. But it was another calculated risk. And those were piling up. Reese couldn't help but feel that he was pressing his luck. Or God's patience with him.

He took a deep breath. *Lord, protect Ella. Guide my decisions. I'm doing what I think is best, but you know the whole situation. Please don't let me stumble into something dangerous. If I'm making a bad decision, let me know. Stop me. Protect us and get us safely home. Thank you for your protection so far.*

What they'd been through could have been so much worse.

Ella had only been grazed by the bullet. He'd chased off the mountain lion. They'd spotted their pursuers and gotten away. Looking back, he could see God's hand on them. But this time he didn't want to rely on his own knowledge and understanding. He wanted guidance. He waited, listening. When another plan didn't present itself and peace washed over him, he took that as confirmation.

With a final whispered *thanks*, he headed back to where he'd left Ella.

Her eyes were wide and intent on him with trust and only a bit of fear. He hoped he was worthy of that trust. He pulled her close. "It looks good. Let's go."

He took her hand, and they set a quick pace toward the slope, making their own trail between boulders and trees. When they had to scramble, he let go of her hand and led the way.

They paused behind a large slab of granite before crossing the wide-open expanse. He scanned the area once more, watching and waiting for movement from every direction, even overhead. If their pursuers had sent a plane up yesterday, there was a good chance they'd do that again today. And he had to consider that possibility.

A red-tailed hawk soared overhead on the warming air. Blue jays chattered in nearby trees. Just a normal day in the forest. The contrast was startling. Would he ever be able to look at the wilderness the same way again?

When nothing changed after long minutes, Reese knew it was time to act. The longer they waited, the bigger the chance of their discovery.

"Ready?" He reached for Ella's hand. He didn't need to, but he'd grown accustomed to hers nestled in his and the connection it gave them.

Her soft brown eyes met his. He saw so much trust there he had to swallow down the emotion it raised. He only hoped he was worthy of it.

She nodded.

Swiveling his head from downslope to across where they were going, he moved them at a fast clip across the side of the mountain. Not the easiest going, since finding a solid foothold on the slope wasn't easy. They were about halfway across the open space when there was a sharp tug on his hand.

Ella went down.

Reese dropped to his knees next to her, scanning the area. "What happened?"

She shook her head. "Just rolled my ankle on a rock and lost my balance. I think it's okay though."

He glanced around again. She could be telling the truth, or she could be in shock and not feeling any pain. He got to his feet. "Let me help you up." He lifted under her arms and stood her on her feet. "Okay?"

She held on to him for a moment, considering. "Yeah. It's a little sore, but it can bear weight."

He took her hand on the side of her sore ankle. "Let's get out of this area." He hated how exposed he felt. It was an all too familiar feeling from his tour in Afghanistan. And the memories of how the last one had ended…

They hustled across the slope, Ella's slight limp barely noticeable. And not a word of complaint from her.

Once they got into cover again, the tension eased from his shoulders. He stopped and checked the way they had come and down into the valley. No sign of anyone or anything. So they would keep going.

They finished the climb up to the ridge with no other mishaps. At the top, he picked out a good spot to rest, a collection of granite boulders to rest behind, but he could look out across the valley. They'd left their water bottles back at camp, but they took turns drinking from the spout on the water bladder strapped to his pack. The bear canister with their food was back in camp too. He only had a few power bars and some trail mix in his pack. He handed those to Ella while he dug out the radio.

"How's the ankle?"

Ella twisted her boot around. "Not too bad. Just a little sore. It'll be fine." She snacked on the trail mix.

He turned the radio on and tested the batteries. Still good. He flipped through the channels but didn't hear anything other than static. It was still early yet.

He ate a power bar and drank water, enjoying the last few minutes of peace in the wilderness. It was hard to believe that shortly his time with Ella would be over. They would be safe. But they wouldn't have the closeness they'd developed alone together. Would they go back to their daily lives as if nothing had happened? His chest squeezed at the thought.

No, he wasn't going to let that happen.

He stashed his and Ella's wrappers in his pack then moved around the boulder. The lake spread out in the distance, the dirt trailhead parking lot a slightly closer smudge. The sun sparkled on the lake. They'd had fantastic weather. *Thank you, Lord.* Bad weather was a complication they hadn't needed.

"Come here." He motioned Ella to his side.

She scooted over and joined him. "Beautiful. It's so wide open. It's like you can see forever from up here. Those houses dotted around the lake look like dollhouses. And I know some of them are mansions."

"A different perspective of things." And that's what this time away with Ella had given him. A different perspective. One he'd needed.

He slipped his arm around her shoulder and met her sweet gaze. "Ella, I know it's been a rough few days, but I wouldn't trade this time with you for anything." He traced a finger down her cheek, gently touching the scrape where the bark had caught her. His thumb found her chin, and his hand curled around her neck. He flicked his gaze up to meet hers, to see the welcoming look there, before lowering his mouth to hers.

Soft and sweet, her response to his kiss sent blood rushing to his head, blocking out everything else but the two of them, together, with a wide open view of their future.

Her fingers curled into his jacket, pulling him closer, just about making him lose his mind and forget where they were.

Reluctantly, he pulled back. He ran his fingers through a section of her hair. "We should do that more often."

Her contented smile turned him inside out. "We should."

"Ready to head home?"

She looked around the area, taking it all in. "Yeah. I am. But this has been amazing." She patted his jacket over his heart. "You have been amazing. Thank you."

He gave her one more quick kiss then got to his feet, holding out his hand to pull her up next to him.

A puff of dust drifted over the trailhead parking lot in the distance. Must be Raul. He lifted the radio. "Raul, it's Reese. Do you copy?"

He waited a long beat before repeating it.

Still no answer.

Then some static and "Reese, is that you?"

"Yeah, brother. We're ready to come home."

Raul's laugh came through the radio. "Glad to hear it. I was worried. I imagine you have a story to tell. What's your ETA?"

"Close to an hour. We're on the ridge. I can just make out the van." Raul's words about having a story to tell was his way of indicating he'd heard something of their trouble. Probably from Cory. Who knew what he said? But he was glad Raul had a heads-up because Reese didn't want to tell him anything important over this open radio.

Another plume of dust appeared. A vehicle was coming toward the trailhead lot, but the trees blocked it. Was it a four-wheeler? Looked like a side-by-side Polaris. Not uncommon around here.

The hair on the back of Reese's neck stood up. "Raul, watch yourself. These guys aren't playing."

"Copy that."

Reese focused on the lot, hating that he was so far away,

unable to get a good read on the situation or do anything even if he could.

"I—" Raul's voice cut off on the radio just as the sharp crack of gunfire reached them.

Ella gasped and squeezed Reese's hand.

The van lurched forward and wove crazily around the lot. The Polaris passenger clearly had a weapon raised in his hand. The van swerved toward the Polaris as more gunfire rang out. Then the van disappeared into the trees.

"Raul!" Reese shouted into the radio, but there was no response. "Raul!"

He grabbed Ella's hand and took off down the hill, dodging rocks and trees. He was so stupid. Why hadn't he considered the bad guys would go after Raul? But Raul didn't know anything. Maybe the bad guys thought he did. Or maybe they'd just followed him to the trailhead, assuming he would be there to pick up Reese and Ella. It wasn't like that was a secret. The Outfitter's trips and trails were well known.

Lord, please keep Raul safe. Keep us safe.

His plan had been literally shot up.

And there was no Plan B.

CHAPTER
FIFTEEN

Shannon pulled her department SUV into the lakeside trailhead lot. McCann and Roberto Salinas were already there. A Holcomb Springs Outfitters van was slung across the road and into a tree. Bullet holes pock-marked the side. Her stomach clenched. Raul had been well enough to make the 911 call. She'd been at her desk reviewing reports when she'd heard the call. And she didn't think it was a random shooting. It had to do with whatever trouble Reese and Ella were in.

The forest service would be here any moment. Technically it was their jurisdiction, but they were spread thin and both departments provided support for the other.

While she'd had her doubts before that Ella and Reese were in actual trouble, she was certain of it now. She slipped out of her unit and over to the van. The driver's side door was open.

Raul sat in the driver's seat talking to Jonas. She didn't see any blood. Positive sign.

"Hey, Sheriff." Raul had his hand wrapped around his knee.

The fire department should be here to check him out as soon as she cleared them to come in. She turned to McCann. "Any sign of the shooters still around?"

He shook his head. "Salinas and Chang are checking the area out, but Raul said they were in a side-by-side and took off after a short search of the woods for him."

She nodded and radioed for the fire department to come in. "What happened?" she asked Raul.

A forestry department truck pulled up, and Walt Longrin got out and headed over.

"Good timing." Shannon shook his hand. "This is Raul Vega. He was about to tell us what happened."

Raul told them about arriving to pick up Reese and Ella, hearing Reese call in on the radio and warning him. "It gave me enough time to duck under the dashboard and drive. I headed toward those guys on the side-by-side knowing I had to make a dash into the woods. They would have caught me on the road with that Polaris. But I figured I could get a good enough head start and beat them in the woods. They weren't expecting me to head towards them, and that threw them off their game. I was able to get over here and use the van as cover while I ran into the woods and hid."

The fire department pulled up, and paramedic Marco Valdez hopped out. McCann filled in the firefighters while Marco studied Raul's knee, easing his jeans up over it.

"It's my bad knee." Raul winced at Marco's prodding. "Hopefully I just sprained it running through the woods and didn't undo all the surgeon's hard work. I haven't run in six months."

"Where did you hide?" Walt Longrin asked.

Raul pointed out the windshield through the woods to a rock outcropping. "I was able to make it to those rocks. By the time they got turned around and out of their Polaris, I was all the way through the woods and up in those rocks. I texted Jonas here and watched those guys wander around searching for me, but they gave up pretty quick. I wasn't their target." He met Shannon's gaze. "They're after Reese. I was just the bait. I don't know why, but he knows he's in danger. He warned me. If he hadn't…" Raul shook his head and turned his attention to the ice pack Marco put on his knee.

"Do you know where Reese was when he radioed you?" Shannon asked.

"Not for sure. Typically he would be heading in from the main trail." Raul jerked a thumb over his shoulder. "But he said he was on the ridge and could just make out the van and was about an hour away."

"Where's the radio? Have you tried reaching him?" Walt asked.

Raul scanned the inside of the van. "I must have dropped it when those guys showed up. It's got to be here somewhere."

Walt went around to the other side and opened the door, searching until he found the radio. He tried a few times to reach Reese with no answer.

"Thanks, Raul." Shannon squeezed his shoulder then motioned to McCann and Walt to step over to her vehicle. "Anything to add to that?" she asked McCann.

"Salinas tracked the Polaris down the forest service road until it hit a crossroads and the tracks got lost with all the others out there. They could be headed in any direction. Do they know where Reese and Ella are? And can we get to them before these guys do? And who are these guys anyway? Those are the big questions I have."

"Reese told Raul he was on the ridge. Let's grab some binoculars and see what we can see."

"Good idea." Walt headed to his truck.

She headed to the back of her unit and grabbed the glasses out of the rear, handing a pair to McCann, reminded of how she'd done something similar with Tony a week ago. Her mind flitted briefly to their coffee time yesterday and his offer of help. She yanked her thoughts back to the present. She couldn't afford any distractions.

Gesturing down toward the trailhead, she and McCann took off in that direction. Walt Longrin caught up with them.

"Knowing Reese, if he saw or heard the gunshots, he'd head in this direction to help his brother. Even if he knew it was futile."

McCann nodded. "Yep. That's probably what they were betting on. Or thinking they could take Raul hostage. But he's also smart enough not to walk into a trap. And he has Ella with him, so he'll be doubly cautious."

"Which puts us where?" They'd reached a spot with a clear view of the ridge. She lifted the binoculars and began scanning. "Do we wait and see if he shows up here in an hour?" She checked her watch. "Or less."

McCann lifted his own glasses. "Or can he get here from there without being intercepted? Those guys who are after him know he was headed here. It's narrowed down their search perimeter."

Walt was quiet. He didn't say much, but he was a deep thinker. When he spoke, Shannon had learned to listen. If any of them would spot something, it would likely be him.

They scanned the area in quiet for a moment then Shannon lowered her binoculars. "See anything?"

"Negative." But it was a long moment before Walt took the glasses from his eyes.

"Me neither."

Walt turned to Shannon. "Let's keep some folks here in case Reese and Ella do show up. Someone can keep trying to get Reese on Raul's radio. Then let's get search and rescue up. We'll need some four-wheelers and some experienced folks to see if they can find Reese and Ella, or at least their trail."

Shannon nodded and pulled up her radio and issued instructions.

Walt did the same.

"I have an idea. Be right back." McCann jogged over to his SUV and rustled around in the back before returning. He held up a small mirror. "I'll try to signal them." He aligned the mirror with the sun and pointed the reflective flash toward the ridge.

After holstering her radio, she took one last look around the area, seeing if McCann's efforts were producing any results. They waited long moments, the traffic on their radios breaking what would be a peaceful scene of warm sun and a light breeze rustling the pine branches. Once again she was thankful she didn't work in a big city.

A piece of paper skittered across the dirt parking lot. Why didn't people pick up after themselves? People enjoyed the beauty of nature but weren't overly concerned with keeping it that way. She headed toward it. The trash can wasn't even that far way. Snatching it up, she headed toward the bin when the logo on the paper caught her eye.

Belle Lumber. The heavy paper had puncture holes in the corners and a printed number. This was a tag that was stapled to lumber orders.

She changed direction and headed toward Walt and McCann. "Look at this." She waved the paper she grasped by the edges.

Walt studied it without touching it. "You think Lorde is behind this?"

"I wouldn't be surprised. You know I think he's got money laundering going on and that he's behind the illegal grows. He's got all the resources to make it work. He'd be able to hire muscle to go after Reese and Ella."

Walt rubbed his neck. "I don't disagree with you, but we haven't been able to make anything stick. This isn't convincing proof."

"But it is something."

They headed back to their units, and Shannon retrieved an evidence bag and slipped the tag inside.

Now the question was should she make another trip to see Lorde?

Ella could barely catch her breath. She concentrated on breathing in and out and keeping her feet under her. While she wished she had the supplies in her pack, she was grateful not to be juggling its weight right now. Reese held her hand in an iron grip, but his singular focus made her wonder if he even remembered he was dragging her along.

He slowed their steps and pulled her behind a stand of trees. *Thank you, Lord.*

Reese scanned the area while pulling out the water bladder. It was pretty depleted. But she imagined water sources might be a place their pursuers would look for them. He handed it to her.

She gulped the water and made sure to save enough for him. She passed it to him and finally caught her breath.

Reese drank and then put the water bladder away. The silence fell heavy on them, the peacefulness of most of their trip shattered by the gunshots.

"Do you think Raul is okay?" She had to know; she knew he was thinking it.

Reese's face hardened, and he gave a short nod. "He's a smart guy. I gave him a heads-up." But the way he wouldn't meet her gaze made her wonder about his own belief in his words.

"Can you reach him on the radio?"

He shook his head. "I turned it off. Too risky. If I call Raul and those guys are nearby, it could give away his position. They might even have been listening to our earlier call. And given that we had people chasing us last night and waiting for us today, I don't want to do anything to give away our position. While I'd like to make sure he's okay, there's nothing he can do to help us out here. We're on our own."

Ella let those words sink in. She'd set her heart on being out of this mess today and back home in her warm bed tonight. They had no beds. No tents, no sleeping bags, and now no emergency shelter. "What do we do?"

He leaned his head back against the tree. "They knew we were coming. It wasn't too hard to guess. With enough manpower, they can stake out the trailheads and just wait for us to show up. Which tells me that grow is a much bigger operation than a couple of goons squatting on government land. Which means if it was a plane that spotted us yesterday, that's part of it too. Someone with money is funding this thing."

He let out a sigh. "The best option would be to hike out the backside of the mountain down into the high desert. But we can't do that in one day, and we don't have supplies to stay here overnight. We have to think outside the box. If we trail blaze across the side of the mountain, we can eventually get around to the residential side of the lake." He grinned at her. "You know everyone. Surely someone will take us in until help arrives."

She smiled back; she couldn't help it. Before she could say anything, a flash of light caught her attention. She turned, but Reese was already moving for a better view. It was reflection off something. But in a regular pattern, which meant it was a deliberate signal.

"I can't get a clear view of the trailhead anymore, but I think someone down there is using a signal mirror."

"For us?" Hope sprung in her chest. Maybe this would be over soon.

"Probably. But are they friend or foe? That is the question. We could walk right into a trap. And once down there and visible, there aren't good options."

"What if Raul was able to get help?"

Reese was quiet a long moment. "It's a possibility. We just don't know for sure. And the downside is too great to risk it."

Hope deflated like a balloon.

They stood in the stillness. Her stomach rumbled. They were out of food. She wanted more than anything to head straight down to that trailhead and be done with it. But Reese was right. They had no idea what was going on down there.

And they were running out of time. They had to get moving.

"Let's do it." She turned to face Reese.

His gaze was steady on hers. "I'm so sorry, Ella. This is all my fault. If I hadn't wanted to drag you away from Cory and show you that waterfall, we'd never be in this mess."

"Are you kidding? We could play this game all day. It's my fault for insisting on this trip when you wanted to cancel it." She touched his face, rough with three days of stubble. "We've been down this road before. It's not our fault. It's those stupid guys who are after us. And you have done a fantastic job of keeping us safe. And you'll keep doing it. So get your map out and let's make a plan."

He studied her a long moment, his gaze soft and vulnerable. Then he pulled her close and kissed her with passion and intensity, a short and powerful kiss like a lit fuse that was snuffed out and over all too soon when he pulled back. "You're…amazing."

Ella's head spun, and she was thankful she had the tree for support, because that kiss was knee weakening for sure.

He let go of her and reached into his pack for the map. They studied it as he traced out a way for them to wrap around to the lake and the houses that lined the shore. Hiking along the side of a mountain without a trail wasn't going to be easy. And she was already tired and hungry. But she was ready for this to be over. And the only way for that to happen was to get around this mountain.

Reese put the map away and they started out, making their way around loose rocks, trees, and pine duff. Much like what they'd been doing the past two days, but this time the steep angle of the slope made it more difficult.

She kept her eyes on where she was going. She was thankful for Reese. She couldn't have done any of this without him.

"How'd you get so good at this outdoors stuff? You mentioned you did some of it with Raul when he was home from college. How did you both get interested in it?"

Reese glanced back at her before answering. "My dad and Raul liked to fish and camp. I was thrilled when I was considered old enough to go with them. One time when I was in fifth grade, right before that bullying incident, Raul was home for college on spring break. I can't remember why he wasn't with his friends, but he and dad planned a fishing trip, and they brought me along."

He paused a minute and dug around in a pocket of his hiking pants, pulling out his wallet and then a slightly crumpled photograph. He handed it to her.

A young Reese, flanked by Raul and their dad, was holding up a fish as big as his head. His toothy grin stretched across his face with pride. Raul and their dad also were beaming with pride, their arms wrapped around his shoulders. It was a perfect father-and-sons moment; she could see why he carried the photo with him.

She handed it back, and he tucked it away before heading out again.

"What I loved most about that day was that they treated me as one of the guys, not the pesky little boy they were allowing to tag along. I got to bait my own hook and haul in my own fish. After that, I felt accepted. And by the time I was in junior high and high school, Raul and I were out here on our own for weekend trips and longer. It was like this… this space away from the world. Here I was competent and capable and not bullied by anyone. It was almost shocking when I'd go back to school and be in that environment. It was like I was two different people."

Ella nodded. "So I got to see the real you in the library that day. That's what I'd always thought. That the Reese I had a conversation with about *Tale of Two Cities* was the real Reese. Everyone in high school is pretending to be someone else anyway."

"Yeah."

They hiked on in silence for a bit, Reese offering his hand now and again to help her over a larger boulder. It was hard to believe they were in danger for long stretches of time. Instead, it felt like the world consisted of her and Reese. One way or another, that would come to an end sooner or later.

But she couldn't help but want to hold on to this space, this thing they'd created between them. The question was, how would it survive the real world?

CHAPTER
SIXTEEN

Shannon and Walt used the back of her SUV as a staging area, laying out maps and discussing search patterns and likely places to look for Reese and Ella.

Raul had gotten a hold of Cory and canceled the day trip he was supposed to lead so Cory could be available for SAR. He hated to disappoint customers, but his brother and Ella were in danger. That took precedence. An ice pack was Ace wrapped to his knee. He had refused to go to the urgent care clinic for treatment and instead wanted to be part of the search. "A few disappointed customers don't matter."

Shannon appreciated his input. He was the next best thing to having access to Reese himself.

The search and rescue folks began showing up, Cory among the first of them.

"Hey, Sheriff. Walt." Cory nodded to both of them then leaned over the map. "Where were they last seen?"

She pointed to a spot on the map. A Dodge Ram truck pulled up and Tony Stafford got out. Her heart did a little flip, and she pushed it down. "Pastor, what brings you out here?"

Tony smiled at her as he strode in her direction. "I came to help."

Her return smile was genuine. "Thanks."

The SAR rig pulled up and Marco Valdez and McCann climbed out. She'd sent McCann back to get equipped to go on the search. If they came across the bad guys, she wanted one of them armed and able to perform an arrest. Walt couldn't spare any sworn officers. McCann was good in the woods, which had surprised her considering he'd transferred up here from Laguna Vista several years before. She had initially pegged him for a city guy.

"All right. Listen up." Walt waited for everyone to quiet down and gather around. He pointed to the map and told them what they knew. "McCann, Valdez, Cory. I want you three to head out to where Raul thinks they might be up on this ridge. Watch your backs for bad players. Comms will likely be intermittent or nonexistent, which is why I'm sending you three out. You can handle whatever happens on the fly."

The three men did a final check of their gear and headed out. Another forestry truck pulled up with a trailer of four-wheelers and a side-by-side. Walt met with them then sent them down the trails that Reese and Ella should have been on. Just in case. Raul went with them since he could ride in the side-by-side.

She turned to find Tony standing there, watching her. "You okay?" He reached out for her shoulder. Just a brief touch, but enough to shoot fire through her. He provided a bubble of calm now that everyone was off on their assignments. She had the hardest role. Waiting for news.

"Yeah. It's my job. Just hate it when people get hurt. Or potentially could get hurt. I feel like I should somehow be able to keep everyone safe."

He didn't say anything. He didn't have to. She knew it was ridiculous and unreasonable. But it didn't change the way she felt. This town and its people were her responsibility.

Footsteps approached, and she broke eye contact with Tony.

Walt walked up. "Hey, Pastor. Sheriff, I've got another incident to handle. Illegal campfire. Can you hold down the fort while I take care of that? I'll be back. In the meantime, I'll monitor the channel."

"Sure. It's just waiting for news at this point."

"I'll stay in touch." Walt nodded and headed off.

She turned back to Tony. "Thanks."

He reached for her hand. It was only the two of them, so she ate up the contact and assurance. "You've got a great team. They're highly skilled, and you're a good leader. Reese and Ella have the best people looking for them." His gaze softened. "Let me pray for all of this." His voice lifted all of her concerns to their heavenly Father, care for Reese and Ella, for the searchers, that the campfire wouldn't get out of control and create more danger. And that Shannon would have peace and wisdom.

Tears pricked her eyes, and she blinked them away. His tenderness and concern was almost more than she could manage. When he finally said *amen*, she squeezed his hand, unable to speak for a moment. So this was what it was like to have someone on your side, supporting you. It had been so few and far between in her life that she was used to doing it all alone.

She savored it for a moment then shook herself back to reality, releasing his hand. Tony was the town's pastor. He cared for people. It was part of his job.

Better not get too reliant on it.

<hr>

Cory followed Marco and Jonas up the side of the mountain, scanning the area for any trace of Reese and Ella. If the sheriff hadn't put him on this team, he would have insisted. He wasn't sure how things were going to go down, but he had to be there when Reese and Ella were found. They'd been climbing for several hours now, a task made more difficult by the lack of a trail and the steep slope. Unless Reese and Ella were staying put, the best the SAR could hope for was to find their trail.

He was the only one who knew Reese and Ella were low on supplies, that they didn't have their tents or sleeping bags. Or Ella's pack. Or the bear canister of food. Reese would have planned for emergencies, but they had to be running low. Reese wasn't the type to panic, but he'd be forced to make some tough decisions. And Cory wanted to be there when that happened.

Jonas's radio crackled, startling Cory out of his thoughts. He was surprised they still had service up here.

They halted. Cory used the opportunity to take a drink as he concentrated on what was coming over the radio.

The feed kept cutting in and out, even on the stronger police radio Jonas carried. It sounded like there was another team out searching, feds on four-wheelers heading down the main trails where they could make good time and search off the well-traveled roads that Reese and Ella should have been on.

The second search team was not good news. It was no secret where Reese and Ella had last been seen—with his hiking group when they stopped for lunch. Raul had interviewed all the participants on that hike, so he knew about the waterfall and the gunshots.

The boss was in damage-control mode, but his hired goons were mostly muscle, not experienced outdoorsmen. If it weren't for the boss's money and the numbers of men he could call up, they would never have even gotten a lead on Reese and Ella. They needed Cory's input on everything—where Reese and Ella had likely headed, which trailhead they'd come back on, and when they were due.

Which was why it was imperative that Cory be on the SAR team going after them.

He concentrated on listening to the radio call, trying to understand what had cut out. But he heard one thing clearly. They had found a dead body.

He stepped behind a tree on the pretense of taking care of personal business and typed out a quick text. No idea if or when it'd go through. The boss wanted to be kept in the loop. But Cory could handle things.

He came back around the tree to find Jonas's eyes on him, narrowed. "You have service up here?"

Cory shrugged. "Not sure. But I have a date tonight. Wanted to let her know I wasn't going to make it."

Jonas studied him. The guy read people for a living. Cory kept it cool and neutral.

"Seen any signs that give you an idea of where they were headed?" Jonas asked.

While Cory got the feeling this was a test, he had to keep Jonas off their trail. Or at least delayed. "Hard to say. But this is a difficult way to travel. Seems like they might have headed for an easier route."

"So you didn't see Reese's boot print back there?"

"Must have missed it."

Jonas cut his gaze to Marco. "Ready to move out?"

Marco recapped his water. "Yep."

Jonas might be armed. But Cory was too. Worse came to worse, he'd take care of things himself.

CHAPTER
SEVENTEEN

Reese knew Ella had to be tired and hungry, but she hadn't said a word. His view of her had changed completely on this trip. What would things be like when they got back home? He didn't know. What he did know was that she was worth fighting for.

They came across a small stream that was more melted-snow runoff than anything. But it was a good spot to refill their water and rest a moment. They had no food left, and he was hungry. But they could go without food. They couldn't go without water.

He slipped off his pack. "Let's rest here a moment while we refill the water bladder." He dug around until he found it.

Ella found a log in the sun and sat, lifting her face and closing her eyes. Even after three days in the woods, she was beautiful. The sun caught her brown hair, shooting red streaks through it. He thought of how it felt sliding through his fingers.

He turned his attention back to the filtration system, getting enough water into the top part. "You okay?"

She nodded but kept her eyes closed, face in the sun.

Once the top part was full, he hung the system from a branch and waited for the water to filter. He joined Ella on the log. The sun did feel good, warming his chilled bones.

She turned and smiled at him. "Thanks for the break."

He touched her cheek. "Arm okay?"

"Yeah. My legs hurt more now, I think. You should promote this as a super workout." She leaned her head on his shoulder.

He slipped his arm around her. How long could they stay here, just like this? Probably not any longer than the water took to filter.

"So it's your turn. I told you about my childhood. What are your good memories?"

She let out a long breath. Then smiled. "Fifth grade. That seems to be a pivotal year. One of the reasons I teach it. That's the year we learn about American history. When I was in fifth grade, we put on a play about the signing of the Declaration of Independence, kind of like the movie *1776*, if you've ever seen that. Now that I'm a teacher, I have my class put on a play about the gold rush in this area as part of the end-of-the-year project.

"Anyway, I had gotten the part of Abigail Adams. Before the play started, I remember peeking around the curtains on the wings of the stage looking into the audience. I was hoping my dad would be there. This was before he left us, but he'd been busy at work and not home much. Now I know why and what he was really busy with, but back then I didn't."

She stretched her legs out and shifted on the log, snuggling a bit closer to him. "Even before opening night, I'd had the best time being in the play. It had been fun rehearsing and being part of a big group with my friends, all trying to work toward the same project. And I was even pretty good at it. I knew I'd miss it when it was over. The only thing that would make it more perfect was if Dad would show up.

"So I was peeking out while the house lights were still on. He'd promised he'd be back in time for my play. I scanned the lines of folding chairs until I spotted Mom and Evan sitting about seven rows back. But no Dad. My heart sank. I searched the people milling down the aisles and in the back of the cafeteria. The lights flashed twice. Two minutes until we would begin."

He could just picture her. And he couldn't wait to see the play her class put on this year. She was born to be a teacher.

"Mrs. Goins came up behind me and stage whispered, 'Ella, get to your place.' I nodded and gave the room one last look. Just then the cafeteria door opened and my dad slipped in. He spotted Mom and Evan and headed for them. I was so excited. I was able to sneak back to my spot with the rest of the cast. All of our hard work paid off that night. I put on my best performance ever, like I was doing it just for my dad. I felt so special and accomplished.

"After the play, he gave me a carnation—like I was a real actress getting flowers—and we took a family picture. It was the last one we had. He took all of us out for ice cream. It was the most perfect night ever." She was silent for a moment, then lifted her head and looked at him. "I kept the picture on the dresser in my room for a long time. I still take it out occasionally. But for a long time, I couldn't look at it. It was too hard, given his later betrayal. I would always wonder why we couldn't just stay the way we all were that night."

Reese tucked her hair behind her ear. "I don't know. The older I get, the more I just don't understand a lot of things about why people do what they do. But I'm glad you had such a great experience. Is Mrs. Goins why you became a teacher?"

"I think so. The advantage of still living in the town you grew up in. I could talk to her any time after school, even when I was in high school. She retired right before I became a teacher, but she'd still invite me over to talk about lesson plans and give advice."

Reese shot a glance at the water system. It was nearly done. He didn't want to leave this spot. But they had to. He kissed her forehead then pulled out the map. "Time to head out, but look at this." He pointed to a spot on the map. "We're not too far away. This is almost over."

She wrapped her arms around his neck, nearly crushing the map between them. "Thank you, Reese." Her voice in his ear sent sparks ricocheting around his body. "For everything."

He held her tight. It wasn't over yet.

TONY SAT WITH SHANNON IN THE CAB OF HER SUV WITH the heat on. They'd settled into a comfortable familiarity he was enjoying, despite the circumstances. Despite a few of his missteps, he thought they might have found a groove they could build on. It was a busy week at church, but this was a good test of if they could make something work with the craziness of both of their schedules.

Shannon shook her head. "I don't like the report of the dead body at all." She'd called in the coroner and had them cordon off the area. "It's likely Brandt. Hopefully it's him, sad to say. If it's someone else, someone I'm not even aware of, then that's a whole other problem." She ran a hand across her head and down to the back of her neck, underneath where her hair was knotted into a bun. A few pieces had slipped out, giving her a slightly less polished air, more vulnerable.

It was all he could do not to reach over and tuck them behind her ear.

"It's going to be a long night. I'll text Donna to order food and have it delivered out here for the team. I missed lunch."

"I didn't even think to ask. I should have brought you something." Tony mentally filed that bit away.

Shannon shook the bag of peanut M&Ms. "My reserves." She smiled then gave a short laugh. "Donna texted back. This is interesting." She read the text out loud.

Beckett Lorde called for you. Said he had resources to offer for your search. He could put up his plane. Just let him know. He was happy to help.

"Donna's not a fan of Lorde any more than I am." She shot a quick text back. "Thanks but no thanks." She turned to Tony. "I found a Belle Lumber tag in the lot earlier. It could mean anything. Lorde is good at covering his tracks, and he knows it. But I don't trust him."

Her phone buzzed again. "Zach. He wants to go to Isaiah's house." She leaned her head against the head rest. "My busiest times usually correspond with Zach's school vacations, so his dad usually takes him. I don't even care what the real reason is. It bothers me more that Dan doesn't find it convenient to spend time with Zach. And it means he's spending spring break at home playing video games. Which was why it was so great you took him Monday. But he hasn't seen any of his friends. And he's not happy about it."

"So you'll let him go over to Isaiah's? That's the Schillers, right?"

"Yeah." She waited a beat. "I get it. He was supposed to be with his dad this week. And then he was grounded the week before. I'm sure he feels like he's under house arrest. But I don't like him to be anywhere but at home or with his dad when I'm on a big case like this."

"Why?"

Her fingers clutched her phone, turning her knuckles white. There was definitely something going on under the surface. He hoped she'd trust him with it.

Her voice was tight and snappy with tension. "Because I'm his mother and I want him safe where I don't have to worry about him."

"Okay." He kept his voice calm. This wasn't about him, though her tone stung.

Her face immediately softened. "I'm sorry, Tony. I'm tired and hungry. And Zach— I know I'm overprotective. It's just the things that I see…"

"I understand." He did, intellectually. Though he'd never

know what it was like to be a parent. Still, she carried the burden of being a single parent and caring for the town. It was a lot. And she could be expected to be a little emotional and unreasonable at times.

Her phone lit up. Another text from Zach.

Her fingers hovered over the phone. She gave a short laugh. "Here's what my astute son says." She lifted the phone to show Tony.

You always get like this on a big case, like somehow it's going to infect me. I'll be fine. I'm almost 18. And you like Isaiah's parents.

He raised his eyebrows. "At the risk of incurring your wrath, he has a point." He smiled.

She grinned back. "I know. And I'm sorry for snapping." She held his gaze a moment. "What do you think?"

Her tone was more curious as to his opinion rather than asking for advice. But he'd take what he could get and tread carefully. "Is it true you like Isaiah's parents?"

She nodded.

"Then I think you should let him go. I don't have kids, so I want to be careful not to overstep." Tension touched his voice as he said the words. Every once in a while, the pain would surprise him. Maybe more this week since he'd spent some time with Zach and really liked him, wondered what it would be like to have a kid like him. "But what I see in my family counseling is parents holding on too tight and kids rebelling just to spite them. Sometimes a little loosening up and trust can go a long way."

She let out a breath. "Can't argue with that. I've seen it too. Zach has definitely been testing limits lately. But if something happened to him… I know in my head I can't keep him under my protective care forever. At some point I'll have to risk it."

"Isaiah's seems like a safe place to start."

She nodded and typed on her phone, showing him the text.

Okay. If his mom picks you up and you stay there. Don't go anywhere else.

Zach's response came back fast.

Thanks!

"If it makes you feel better, I can check on him later or bring him home if you have to stay late."

"That's sweet. Thanks. I don't know what I'd have done over the years if folks hadn't stepped up to help me." She pulled out her stash of peanut M&Ms, took a handful, and offered the bag to Tony.

He grinned at her and took some. Seemed like they'd navigated that successfully.

The radio crackled. He had to listen carefully and still couldn't make it all out. But the gist of it was two of the feds were going to secure the scene of the body until the coroner's team arrived. Raul had an idea of where else Reese and Ella might have gone, based on their past camping trips. They wanted permission to check it out.

Shannon gave it. "At this point, any ideas are welcome. The afternoon shadows are getting long, and it'll be dark sooner than any of us would like."

A personal vehicle pulled into the trailhead lot. Shannon turned her attention to it. "We don't need any hikers in this area right now. And it's a little late in the day to get started."

Lucas Slater climbed out and headed toward the SUV with purposeful strides. Interesting. He didn't strike Tony as an outdoorsy type. But he'd been surprised before.

She rolled down the window. "Lucas. What can I do for you?"

"Sheriff." Then he leaned forward and spotted Tony. "Hey, Pastor. I came to find out what you were doing to find Ella. I told you yesterday she was missing. And also to make sure you planned to arrest Reese when they got back."

Shannon raised her eyebrows. "Why would I do that?"

"Gross negligence. He never should have taken Ella on this trip and put her in danger. I don't think she actually wanted to go. I think he either tricked her into it or took her against her will. It's just not like her."

"So you've said. But everything points to her going on this trip because she wanted to. You even admitted she told you that herself. So do you have any new information to add?"

He shifted from foot to foot. "No. I just wanted to know how the search was going. If you'd started yesterday, she might have been found. If something happens to her…"

Shannon's gaze narrowed and hardened. Tony didn't think Shannon would take well to a threat and hoped Lucas had sense enough to swallow what Tony thought he was about to say.

When Lucas didn't continue, she did. "We have teams out searching for them. The best thing you can do is go home and wait for news." Didn't he have a fiancée? His respect for Lucas was plummeting rapidly. What was his game? Why was he so interested in Ella when they weren't together? Hadn't he and Ella been engaged? Did he still have feelings for her? Or was it because she was with Reese? Men could be territorial.

Tony leaned over. "Hey, Lucas. It's going to be okay. The sheriff has the best team out there. Reese knows what he's doing. If you have any information on who could be after them, that would be helpful. Any ideas?"

Lucas frowned and shook his head. "I didn't know anyone was after them. I just didn't think she was safe with Reese. You know he got his men killed in Afghanistan, right?"

Shannon shot Tony a look. Oops. He'd divulged information. True, anyone with a radio or a scanner knew or could figure out what was going on. Since it was a small town, news would travel fast. He was trying to help, but he'd put his foot in it, and Shannon wasn't pleased. And things had been going so well.

He leaned back, hands raised. "Lucas, I haven't preached on gossip for a while, but repeating information that you don't have first-hand knowledge of only creates division and not unity. If you have some concern about information you've heard about Reese, you should talk to him directly."

Lucas glanced away before turning back to them. "Sorry. I'm just worried about Ella. And I don't trust Reese. No one seems to take my concerns seriously, and now she's in trouble."

Shannon used a calming tone. "We don't know that." Her radio crackled, and she turned her attention to it.

It was the team of feds checking in. "We found their tents, sleeping bags, and bear canister with food. And one pack. But no sign of them."

"Location?" She pulled out her map, running a finger over it. She was pointing to a spot farther away from the trailhead and from where Raul had heard from them earlier. Perhaps it was a place they'd camped at earlier in their trip.

Tony's mind flipped through possibilities. None of them good. Reese and Ella were without food and shelter.

"Document and bring it in," Shannon said into the radio. "Report any blood or sign of struggle."

She turned to Tony then realized Lucas was still there. "Lucas, go home. There's nothing you can do here."

His face was pale. "Was that Ella's tent they found? What is she going to do without shelter? It'll get below freezing tonight."

"We're handling it. Reese is an experienced survivalist."

Lucas stared at them, his gaze begging them for... something. Finally, he turned and headed to his vehicle. But it was a long moment before he actually drove away.

She turned to Tony and rubbed her hand over her face. "I hope that food gets here soon. And I don't like what the feds and Raul found. Were Reese and Ella chased off by a bear or mountain lion? Or is there another person or persons after them? What would make them leave critical supplies behind?"

"I don't think we'll know for sure until Reese and Ella get back and tell us. But what you told Lucas is true. Reese is good at what he's doing."

She nodded. "If it were an animal, they would have circled back once the threat was gone. The only thing that would make Reese abandon critical gear would be a significant threat like a wildfire coming at them—which didn't happen—or someone putting their lives in danger. And given what he said to Raul on the radio, it seems he knows someone is after them."

Tony leaned back. "So let's assume two sets of pursuers. The one down here that shot at Raul and the other chasing Reese and Ella through the woods. Reese has to be better than anyone they'd send after him and Ella."

"But Ella's the weak link. She's not as experienced as Reese or as physically fit."

"True. But we can't do anything about that. So what does two groups of pursuers tell us?" His role was to support her and be a sounding board. And hopefully make up for his earlier mistake.

"That it's not some random crazy chasing them. That it's someone with an agenda. And that makes me think of Lorde."

"He did offer to help."

"Yeah." She scoffed. "To get our intel and find out what we know. If he spotted them, you can be sure he'd try to get his men there first."

"Any chance it could be anyone else? I'll admit I don't like the guy; he's hiding something. But let's not rule anything out prematurely. What's his motive?"

She shot him a glance and a wry smile. "You sound a lot like McCann. He's always cautioning me against focusing on Lorde. As to motive, I don't know. But my guess would be that Reese and Ella stumbled onto something he didn't want them to see. I've been convinced he's behind illegal grows in the national forest. Not my jurisdiction, but it affects my town. If they saw something, he'd be motivated to make sure they didn't stay alive to say what they saw. And to serve as a warning to others."

His gaze on her softened. She was under a lot of pressure, and lives were at stake. "Let's say it is Lorde. What then? You can't just march into his office and demand he stop going after Reese and Ella. Even Walt Longrin couldn't do that. There's no proof."

"Just my gut. And it's telling me they're running out of time."

CHAPTER
EIGHTEEN

Ella leaned against a tree. She was tired and hungry. Her arm burned. She suspected she'd broken the wound open again. One of the times she grabbed Reese's hands, she accidentally reached with her injured arm and felt a sharp stab. There was a warm spot under her jacket she thought was blood. But the first-aid kit was in her pack back at their camp. There was nothing they could do about it. Hopefully her two shirts, Reese's fleece, and her jacket would absorb enough of it.

Reese handed her the water bladder, and she drank and handed it back. He finished off the last of it.

She studied the trees around them. They looked the same as what they'd been traipsing through all day. "Feels like we've been in this wilderness forever. Are you sure we're not walking in circles? I've heard of that happening with people."

He stowed the water bladder. "We're not walking in circles. Come here." He climbed up a stack of boulders, holding out his hand for her to follow.

She grabbed with her good hand. When she reached the top, she saw what he was pointing at. Houses. In the distance, but real proof of civilization. "So how do we get from here to there?"

"The same way we've been doing it. We walk." He grinned at

her then scanned the area around them. "Who lives in that place?"

She squinted. He was pointing at a big, luxurious cabin, three stories with a huge front of windows facing a view of the lake. "I think that's Beckett Lorde's place."

"Huh. Could be the closest place." He started down off the rocks, helping her with her balance.

"I'm not sure if it's even his. But there are gates and security everywhere. It's been rumored to belong to all sorts of people, from Silicon Valley billionaires to Hollywood movie stars. It never looks like anyone is there, except occasionally someone will report seeing a lot of fancy cars, like someone is hosting a weekend party."

Reese pointed them back through the woods. At least now they weren't going around the side of the mountain and were headed downhill. Her legs still screamed though.

"Whose house do you think would be closest?"

"A lot of the houses on this side of the lake are vacation rentals. It's spring break, so they could be rented out. Or they could be vacant if their owners only come up in the summer. But the D'Agostinos, the owners of Bella Sorgenti, live out here. If we get to a road, I can get to their house."

"We'll want to avoid roads if we can. Makes us too visible."

Yeah. For a moment she'd forgotten there were people after them and that's why they were in this predicament.

The ground steepened and the trees thinned out. They were traversing a valley between hills that continued to get narrow and get rockier. More snow pockets sat in the shadows and rivulets of runoff made the ground damp. This probably grew into a bit of a creek with any rainfall.

Something exploded off the rock next to her, showering her with shards.

Reese grabbed her arm and pulled her down behind the nearest rock. "Keep your head down." He swore. "Looks like they've found us. We don't have much time." He met her gaze. "Do exactly as I say, okay?"

She nodded.

He gave her a hard, quick kiss and looked like he was going to say something but then turned away, scanning the area. "Stay low. We're going to head over to those rocks. Then from there we can dash into that stand of trees. I'm going to create a diversion. When I say run, go."

She nodded.

He picked up several softball-sized rocks and heaved them up the gorge into a stand of trees. "Go!"

She took off and heard the rapid *pings* of gunfire. She didn't look back. Adrenaline fueled her numb legs, and she cringed, expecting to feel a bullet slam into her at any moment.

As soon as she landed behind the rocks, Reese was nearly on top of her.

"You okay?"

She could only nod. She had no words. If she did more than follow Reese's instructions, she'd fall apart. She wouldn't let herself think about who was after them. Or what might happen if they got caught.

"We're going to move again to those trees. They'll be hard pressed to make it down that valley and shoot at us at the same time." He stared back over where they'd come from. "Go!" He gave her shoulder a shove.

She got her feet under her, stumbled a bit, and ran. Her legs felt like lead and rubbery all at the same time. She slid behind the trees, panting. She couldn't believe this was actually real. This didn't happen to people like her. She was a schoolteacher in a small town living a boring life. She should have been content with that and not wished to add some adventure. Maybe Lucas was right about her.

Reese slid in next to her, his eyes on the gorge behind them. He was so competent and skilled. She was incredibly grateful for him. If they managed to get out of here alive, it would be due to him. But no way would he be content with her life, her small town. He was made for bigger things. And she would only hold him back.

A couple curse words echoed down to them along with a tumble of loose rocks and dirt.

"We gotta go." Reese grabbed her hand and tugged her out of the trees.

She had no idea where they were running to, but the ground leveled out, trees blocking their view from their pursuers. She spotted a small road, more like a private driveway. The ground around them had deliberate contours, like it had been graded. They followed the driveway from the safety of the woods. She'd gotten disoriented, so she wasn't sure where they were headed or whose houses might be back here, but anyone would be better than what they were running from.

A crashing through the woods behind them told her their pursuers weren't far behind. And they didn't seem concerned at all with letting her and Reese know that. Of course, they were armed, and she and Reese weren't. Were they? Reese had never mentioned carrying a weapon, but he was in the military so perhaps he had one. It gave her a small flicker of hope. Reese's skills were their only advantage in this fight.

Then she saw the iron fence with spikes on the top. This was one of the expensive houses up here.

And it was a dead end.

***

GUNSHOTS SPLIT THE AIR, AND CORY JERKED UP. NO WAY Jonas and Marco wouldn't notice that. He swore. Those stupid thugs the boss had hired. Unless they'd actually gotten Reese and Ella, they were just making things worse and announcing their position. This was not going to resolve itself in the neat and tidy package the boss wanted.

McCann held up his hand. "Those sounded like they came from down that gorge. I need to check it out."

"Nah. I think they came from the other direction. The sounds just bounced off the mountains and made it sound like it was from down there." Cory had to stall, delay, or divert, which had been difficult with Jonas since he was determined to find Reese and Ella and was also a decent outdoorsman. Cory's hand might be forced.

Jonas frowned then turned to Marco. "What'd you hear?"

"They're from the gorge. Let's go."

Jonas hesitated. "I don't want to lead you guys into danger. It's not in your job description."

Marco scoffed. "I run into burning buildings for a living. I'll take my chances."

Cory couldn't let them go without him. "I'm in. But I still think you're headed the wrong way."

Jonas studied him for a minute, opened his mouth like he was going to say something, then simply said, "Let's go." He turned to Marco. "You want to bring up the rear?"

"Sure."

Jonas started out and Cory fell in behind him, not happy that Marco was behind him. He was hoping to lag a bit, create a diversion, or at least update the boss. But it seemed like Jonas suspected something, and Cory couldn't let him act on his suspicion.

He hoped when they found Reese and Ella that the hired muscle wouldn't get in the way of what he needed to do. The stakes were too high.

Donna had delivered sandwiches and drinks, and Shannon and Tony were eating theirs in her SUV. Walt Longrin had returned as well and had joined them, pulling his truck up next to hers. The food helped; she could feel it raising her blood sugar. Better than the peanut M&Ms she'd been munching on.

The sound of four-wheelers returning grew stronger, and soon the second search team was back.

Shannon and Tony hopped out of her SUV. Raul limped out of the side-by-side, and the feds brought the camping gear they'd retrieved over to Shannon's SUV. "Any signs of foul play?" She picked up the tents.

Raul opened the pack he carried and pulled out a bag of bloody bandages. "Just this. This is Ella's pack. Looks like she's hurt, but maybe not too badly. There's not a ton of them."

One of the other searchers brought over the bear canister. "This is intact. Doesn't even have any scratches. So I don't think a bear chased them off coming after their food."

A series of sharp reports split the air from a distance.

Shannon turned to Walt. "Gunfire. Have you had any reports of poaching? Anything related to those shots from Monday?"

He shook his head. "Hard to tell the way sounds bounces around here off the mountains. But it sounded like it's coming from the far side of the lake."

She lifted her radio and called McCann. After a few tries, she reached him.

"Shots came from a gorge down below us." He gave her his coordinates. "Investigating now. But we likely won't have comms once we head into the gorge."

She and Walt moved toward the map and found his coordinates. Directly below McCann's position was where some of the lakefront houses started. She could get close with her unit. She radioed her other units the approximate position as well.

The hardest part about leadership was leading, coordinating the pieces and not being in the field. She knew she couldn't do a better job than McCann, but it killed her to be sitting there eating sandwiches while her guys were out there and members of her town were in danger. But this she could do.

She looked at Walt. "I'll head out there and see what I can find. Probably will pick up McCann's team."

"Be careful and keep me posted. Thanks for dinner." He raised his sandwich in salute.

"Any time." She updated McCann then closed up her SUV and headed to the cab.

Tony opened the passenger door to climb in.

"Nope, you're staying here." She swung up into the driver's seat.

"You could use the backup, at least another set of eyes."

"You're not a sworn officer."

"But I'm a chaplain."

"Who usually shows up after the danger is over. I'll call you if I need you." Her tone was rough; she knew it. But she didn't have the brain power to think about that right now. She had a job to do. He would either understand or he wouldn't.

Tony gave her a long look then nodded and shut the door, walking away.

Shannon climbed inside and drove off, kicking herself at the slight slump she saw in Tony's shoulders. She'd made the right decision; she couldn't put him in danger. There were too many unknowns. But there had to be a better way to convey that to him. They couldn't seem but help bumping up against each other, like they were each performing a different dance.

She sped down the forest service road as fast as the ruts would allow. She had to face it; she stunk at relationships. Her son, her friends. At least her team respected her.

But she couldn't think of any of that right now. She had to focus on her job and finding Reese and Ella and getting them home safely.

The lengthening shadows might as well have been hands on a clock ticking away the time.

REESE STARED AT THE FENCE. THEY DIDN'T HAVE THE luxury of scouting out each direction, picking the best way to go. They only had one chance at this. He could hear their pursuers behind them. He shot up a quick prayer for guidance then pulled Ella along a path parallel with the fence. The vegetation had morphed into deliberate landscaping—clearly someone's private property—and he glimpsed a paved driveway through the trees. So many ways this could go wrong. No one could be home. He could put innocent people in danger. Like Raul earlier. He hoped he was okay but couldn't allow his thoughts to go there. He had to concentrate on this problem.

He pulled Ella down behind some of those bushes, wishing he'd given in to Raul's urging that he carry a weapon. He hadn't had any nightmares on this trip, which was somewhat surprising. Still, he hadn't expected this kind of danger. Not the human kind, anyway.

And that was his problem that had gotten his men killed. He hadn't anticipated the danger. *Lord, please help me not to get Ella killed too. You can take me, but please don't let her get hurt.*

He focused on the mission and got a look at the house. It was the biggest one on the lake. The one they had spotted from the top of the hill before descending the gorge. What were the odds that anyone was home? Or that they'd help them?

A gate crossed the road. There was a call box and a camera. If he wanted access, he'd have to show himself. He was willing to risk himself but not Ella. Still, they couldn't remain here. But he could be bait and draw attention away from her.

"Stay here."

"Wait. What are you doing?" Ella grabbed his hand.

"Seeing if anyone is home."

"But you'll be out in the open, exposed."

"It's a chance I'll have to take. If something happens to me, stay hidden." He gave her a wry grin. "'It's a far, far better thing I do, than I have ever done…'"

She squeezed tighter, tears welling. "Don't quote Sydney Carton to me."

"I have to go." He peeled off her fingers and darted out of the bushes and to the driveway. He pushed the button, desperately hoped this gamble had paid off. What other choice did they have?

A rustling in the bushes caused him to whip his head around and dive for cover behind a sculpted bush.

Through the gaps in the trees he could spot a man—maybe two—headed toward them.

CHAPTER
NINETEEN

Cory spotted the shooters at the bottom of the gorge just as Jonas yelled, "Stop! Sheriff's department!"

Both shooters ducked into the woods at the bottom.

Jonas took off, half running, half sliding down the rest of the way. Cory hoped he'd fall or twist an ankle. That would be justice.

He picked up his speed. He couldn't let Jonas get there before he did. Dirt filled his boots as they made their way down the steep incline. It felt like it was taking forever to reach the bottom.

A few more shots rang out just as Jonas arrived at the mouth of the gorge. He darted into the woods, headed in the direction of the gunfire.

Cory swore. The boss needed to hire better people, though they were only supposed to guard the grow not track people through the woods. But now Cory was in a difficult position. His usefulness to the boss was that he was part of the SAR team and worked for Raul's Outfitters. He was in these woods and knew what was happening in them, what people saw, and what they suspected. If he pulled his gun, his cover would be blown.

It would be a last resort. Trying to find a new supplier to feed his addiction would take too long. He needed to keep the boss happy.

He dashed into the woods after Jonas. He could see flashes of people through the trees, but not enough clearly to get a bead on what was going on.

He found Jonas stopped on the edge of what looked like a paved driveway, studying the surroundings, hand raised for silence.

Marco jogged up next to him, and Cory took a casual step back, then two, easing his hand toward his holster at his lower back. If he pegged both of them, maybe it would look like the guys after Ella had gotten Jonas and Marco too. But scrutiny as to how he was spared would be intense. He liked his life and didn't want to give it up. The boss paid good, but not that good. It was his product that kept Cory working for him.

He heard the roar of an engine in the distance and growing closer. Company was on the way. The question was, what kind?

He stepped farther back into the woods. Jonas and Marco did, too, just as an older, beat-up pickup truck zipped past them on the road. The density of the trees only gave them a quick glimpse before it was gone. Two passengers, probably male, ball caps pulled low.

Jonas jumped out into the street after it then shook his head. He picked up his radio and called it in then tilted his head toward the driveway. "Let's see where they came from."

The driveway wound back through the woods like a number of them did. Several houses back in the woods could share one. But when Cory got a peek of where this one was going he stopped in his tracks.

Things either were going better than he planned.

Or worse.

THE GATE ENGAGED AND SLID OPEN. REESE HOPED HE wasn't leading them into a trap, but he didn't have much choice. Their pursuers were getting closer, and they'd find Ella. The house might give them more cover. Or at least a place to call for help. He waved for Ella to come up.

She got to her feet and stumbled toward him, vulnerable and exposed. "Reese. What are we doing?"

He gave her what he hoped was an encouraging grin and tugged her through the opening. They hugged the landscaping as they jogged alongside the curving driveway. He spotted the pursuers between the vegetation. Had they spotted them? He pushed Ella in front of him.

He heard nothing but the gate.

The huge house came into view, looming over them with stacked-stone retaining walls and sweeping staircases leading to a wide front porch.

He glanced behind. The pursuers had spotted them and were heading for the gate.

And there on the porch, waiting for them, was Beckett Lorde.

SHANNON SPED DOWN THE TWISTING MOUNTAIN ROADS, tuned into the radio, scanning for anything that might jump out from the side of the road. But her mind spun on Beckett Lorde. He was crafty. And he was good about putting on a front of being a good citizen. He was "helpful" with Dalton Brandt. He offered to "help" today with the search. If she pushed too hard on him, she'd come off looking like she had a vendetta against him and he was the good guy. She had to tread carefully.

What was his game? She had her suspicions. Drug running, money laundering. But he was good at covering his tracks. She wouldn't be surprised if Brandt's disappearance never led back to him or went cold.

She got closer to the lake, closer to some of the more expensive homes with lake views. Interesting choice that brought Ella and Reese this way. At least, she hoped they were over here and soon to be found and that McCann wasn't chasing something else. She'd know soon enough.

Someday Lorde would slip up. And she'd be there when he did. She just hoped no one else in her town suffered before she got him.

Reese halted and pulled Ella to himself.

Lorde stood on the porch with his hands shoved in the pockets of a pair of designer jeans and wearing a cashmere sweater with the sleeves pushed up. "I have to admit, the two of you were the last people I expected to pay a call. You look a little rough. Come on in and I'll get you something to drink. I think my housekeeper even left something in the fridge I could warm up." He turned and gestured them inside.

Welcome to my web, said the spider to the fly.

Ella looked at Reese, uncertainty and relief battling in her expression. She needed a break. She needed to get off her feet, get some food and water into her. And that was one problem Reese could solve. He'd deal with the others as they came up.

He held out his hand for her, and they ascended the stairs together. The A-frame on steroids was made of logs, stone, and a lot of glass. They entered into a massive great room that soared two full stories with one end of the room flanked by a stone fireplace. He couldn't help but feel they were entering the lion's den.

Lorde gestured to a massive leather couch in front of the roaring fireplace. "Have a seat. I've got coffee on, but I can get you water or tea."

The heat burned Reese's face after being so long in the cold. Ella nearly collapsed on the couch, and he eased off his backpack and sat down next to her, not relaxing.

"Coffee would be great." Ella stripped off her gloves and held out her hands towards the warmth.

"Same for me." Reese scanned the room. There were a set of french doors leading out to a wraparound deck with a magnificent view of the lake. And a long drop down. Lorde had to have heard the gunshots.

He tugged out his phone and tapped a text to Raul, hoping he'd get it, that he was well enough to get it. He'd forced himself to concentrate on getting Ella and him out of danger and not worrying about Raul, something he had no control over. But it had remained there in the background, like a buzzing static that wouldn't leave him alone.

Lorde came over with two cups of coffee. "Sorry, not much of a signal here. But you can use the landline in the kitchen if you need to call someone. I'm sure the sheriff will be glad to hear you're safe and sound. I offered up my plane to look for you both."

Reese met his gaze, but it was inscrutable. This guy could play poker for a living. Currently it looked like they were all playing charades. "Sure. I'd like to let them know we're safe." He stood and moved toward the kitchen, keeping his gaze on Lorde, who'd perched on the arm of the sofa next to Ella.

"How did you guys get lost?" Lorde asked. "I thought Reese was the ultimate outdoorsman."

He hadn't talked to Ella about what to say, but he hoped she wouldn't mention being pursued. Information was power, and the less of it they gave away, the better. Especially since he didn't know what game Lorde was playing. Reese found the phone and lifted it.

"Uh, there was a mountain lion. I panicked, I guess. Reese helped me, but I think I got us lost and away from our gear."

Good girl. He punched in 911 and told the dispatcher who he was and where he and Ella were. She said someone would come by to pick them up. He hung up the phone and headed back to the great room.

Lorde looked up. "I can take you two wherever you need to go."

And they'd never be seen again. "Thanks, but the sheriff has someone on the way." Reese stood next to Lorde, crowding his space a bit. He didn't like how close he was to Ella.

Lorde studied him, then rose and moved toward the bank of windows.

Reese took the couch next to Ella, alert, watching for Lorde's next move. He was betting that Lorde wouldn't dirty his hands, that he hired help to do that. That as a businessman motivated by money, he'd play the odds.

But he didn't know for sure.

"Ella, it's a good thing you had Reese with you. He's good at what he does." Lorde turned from the window to face them. "Most of the time, I suppose. There was that time he got the men under him killed. So I guess you're lucky you survived."

Reese's blood boiled, and he saw red. He felt Ella's gaze on him, saw it out of the corner of his eye. And checkmate. That was Lorde's game. If he couldn't kill Reese out in the woods, he'd assassinate his character. Make whatever he said unreliable.

The kicker was, it was true. Reese had gotten his men killed. He'd made a bad call and men had died. He'd ended up with a TBI and a medical discharge from the Army. He'd wanted to tell Ella himself, but now it was too late.

Lorde gave a harsh laugh. "I do my research. I've had my eye on you for a while, Vega. I actually thought I could use you in my operations." He pursed his lips. "But I've changed my mind." He waited a beat. "Though I'll still keep my eye on you."

There was an electronic *ding,* and Lorde pulled out his phone. "Ah, looks like the sheriff is here. That was fast. She must have been in the neighborhood. I wonder why." He shoved his phone back in his pocket.

Reese shot a glance at Ella, but she had both hands wrapped around the coffee mug. Then he spotted a trickle of red down her hand. "Ella? Is your arm hurting?"

She looked at him, confusion in her eyes.

He lifted her wrist, pulling her hand from the mug, and tugging off her jacket sleeve. It was slick with blood, some of which dripped on Lorde's fine leather couch, he noted with some satisfaction. Her shirtsleeve was soaked through. Her wound must have broken open and bled badly. And she hadn't said anything. "Bring me some paper towels," he barked at Lorde, just as there was a pounding on the front door.

He scooped Ella up and carried her in that direction as Lorde opened the door.

Sheriff McIntyre stood there, hand on her belt, within easy reach of her gun, Reese noted. Her eyes widened at the sight of Ella in his arms.

"She needs medical attention. Let's leave the explanations for later. Lorde, thanks for your hospitality. Sheriff, can you grab my pack?" Reese swung out the door and past the sheriff, down the stairs to her unit.

"Happy to help anytime," Lorde said. "I'm always just a phone call away, and I have eyes and ears all over the valley. Not hard to get a message to me."

Reese ignored him and climbed into the backseat with Ella. The sheriff tossed his pack in the back and closed the door behind him, hopped up front, and sped out of the driveway. She got on the radio, but Reese's attention was on Ella.

He gave her a quick update on Ella's injuries and what they found as she sped them toward urgent care.

The sheriff glanced in the rearview mirror. "One of the search teams looking for you found the body. The coroner's up there now racing dark to search the scene and bring the body out. But they didn't find the grow. I'll let Walt know, and he can send a team back there tomorrow."

"If Lorde hasn't already moved it."

The sheriff let out a sigh. "I'm sure he already has. How did you end up at his place?"

"Dumb luck. His goons were shooting at us, and his house

was the closest. We weren't even sure it was his. But I guessed that he wouldn't actually get his hands dirty. That he let his goons do the dirty work. It was a calculated risk."

"And he comes off looking like a good guy for rescuing you. Keeping his reputation intact. He's smart. I'll give him that." She swung her unit in front of urgent care then climbed out and opened the back passenger door.

Reese gathered up Ella and carried her inside.

Her head lolled against his arms, and she looked up at him with her big brown eyes. "My hero." She smiled. Then she was whisked off onto a gurney and taken back to a treatment room.

After all the movement and planning and reacting of the past three days, he found himself suddenly alone in the waiting room. He fell into a chair and started to put his head in his hands but one was covered in blood. So was the front of his jacket. *Please, Lord. Help her.* It looked like a lot of blood. She was low on food and water, not in a strong position to handle a lot of blood loss.

He found a bathroom to wash up in and stared at himself in the mirror. He looked rough. Stubble, dark circles, dirt, blood. At least Ella was in capable hands now.

And the best thing he could do was walk away. They were too different. His life would just bring trouble into hers. He'd gotten his men killed, almost gotten her killed. And Lorde, for some reason, had given him a clear warning that he'd be watching. He couldn't put her in the crosshairs anymore.

When he exited the bathroom, Raul was there in the waiting room with the sheriff. He had an icepack Ace wrapped to his knee and was on crutches.

Relief washed through Reese. His brother wasn't too much the worse for wear. In two steps he wrapped him in a bear hug. "You're a sight for sore eyes, man."

Raul slapped him on the back. "I could say the same for you."

When they broke apart, the sheriff said, "Do you need any medical attention, Reese?"

He shook his head.

She gave a wry grin. "Yeah, just like your brother. I'd like to take you to the station to get your statement." She noticed his gaze flit down the hall. "Ella's in good hands. They've got her on an IV, and she's going to get some stitches. But they'll keep her here for a while. There's nothing else you can do."

She got that right. "Yeah, let's go."

And he walked out the doors without a backward look.

CHAPTER
TWENTY

Shannon pulled a water bottle out from her fridge in her office and handed it to Reese. Donna brought in a sandwich and chips for him. Shannon sat and leaned her arms on her desk. "How are you really?"

He shrugged and tore open the chips. "Fine. Cold, tired, hungry. Nothing I haven't been before." He lifted the bag with a small grin. "Thanks for this."

She nodded. "Eat. I'll take your statement then get you out of here as soon as I can." Raul had come with them and was sitting in the waiting area. Marissa would pick them both up when Shannon was done with Reese. And things were going to get busy.

Salinas and Chang were in the area and had picked up McCann and the others. The county had set up roadblocks on the mountain roads, but without a clear description of the vehicle, she didn't hope for much. Her men were searching in town, and Walt was dispatching some of his men now that they'd found Reese and Ella. It could be a long night.

Which meant she'd need to think about what to do about Zach. Easiest thing would be to let him spend the night at Isaiah's house. He'd be thrilled.

But first, Reese's statement, now that she'd let him get a few bites of food in him.

He told her about his original group calling off due to food poisoning, Ella and him joining Cory's day trip, and the hike up to the waterfall. He brought out the map and his phone, giving her the coordinates and images he'd taken.

She called them into Walt for his team to narrow their search. He also told about finding the body and how they'd been chased out of the area by gunfire, about Ella getting wounded.

Using the map, he retraced their journey across the valley and along the mountains, indicating where they'd been spotted, where'd they'd been when Raul was shot at, and how they'd finally ended up at Lorde's house.

"Anything give you any clues as to who was behind all of this?"

Reese shook his head. "No. But there had to be at least two groups of guys involved. One waiting at the trailhead and one chasing us. Neither of which were strong outdoors types. Either the group trailing us got real lucky in finding us, or that plane we'd seen earlier spotted us."

Shannon thought about Lorde's offer to send his plane up to look for Reese and Ella. She'd bet he'd already done it.

"That leads me to think this isn't just some potheads with an illegal grow. This is someone with some money and hired guns." Reese finished off his sandwich.

"Did Lorde say anything at his house that would make you think he knew anything?"

A flash of pain blinked through Reese's eyes before he shut it down and returned to report mode. "Just some veiled threats about doing research on me and having eyes and ears everywhere. Nothing overt, but I took it as he knew I'd seen either the body or the grow, and he was warning me there would be consequences if I said anything."

Lorde was good, she'd give him that. But he'd slip up at some point, and she'd get him. Just probably not today.

She asked a few more clarifying questions then stood. "Thanks, Reese. Now get out of here and head home." She smiled. "Raul's going stir crazy. Get some rest. If I have any questions, I'll let you know. Tomorrow you can pick up your gear that we retrieved."

"Thanks for dinner." He shook her hand then left her office, a weariness dogging his steps.

She could only imagine. She picked up her phone to text Isaiah's mom about Zach sleeping over, but there was a commotion in the bullpen. She stepped out.

McCann and Salinas had come in along with Walt, Marco, and Cory.

"Find anything?" she asked.

McCann met her gaze then it flicked to Cory. "I'd like Cory to tell us who he was contacting while we were out searching for Reese and Ella."

Cory's face hardened. "How is that any of your business?"

"One, because you were distracted on a SAR assignment." McCann dropped his pack and crossed his arms. He was dirty and probably hungry too. "Two, I found it highly coincidental that the shooters chasing Reese and Ella suddenly knew where they were. And then conveniently disappeared. The whole trip you missed signs of Reese and Ella's trail and tried to redirect us. Now, want to tell us what was going on?"

Cory scanned the room.

Shannon smirked. He wasn't that stupid to make a run for it. He wouldn't get far with Salinas, Walt, and Chang all in close proximity. Not to mention they knew where he lived. She trusted McCann's instincts, but she was surprised by Cory. He'd been a faithful member of their SAR team, worked with Raul. She wouldn't have thought he'd willingly put Reese and Ella in danger.

"It was just a woman I was seeing. No big deal. If you want more than that, you'll have to get a search warrant." Cory reached for the pack at his feet. "I gotta get home." He grinned. "Got a hot date."

McCann pointed to a chair next to his desk. "Make yourself comfortable. I need to get your statement. You're a person of interest. You're going to be here awhile. Don't worry; we'll feed you." He pinned Cory with his gaze until the man swore under his breath and moved to the chair.

Shannon met McCann's gaze and nodded. Maybe Cory would provide the link to Lorde. If he knew something. He definitely knew more than he was telling. She gestured Walt back to her office. They caught up and agreed to keep each other in the loop.

Once everything and everyone was settled, she returned her thoughts back to Zach. She typed out a text to Isaiah's mom, Amber, asking if Zach could spend the night.

The text from her came back.

Normally I wouldn't mind but I'm not home. Jordan and I are out of town.

Shannon fumed. Zach had lied to her. Again. She squeezed the back of her neck. What was she going to do with him? And how did he get over there if she was gone.

She texted Zach.

Where are you?

At Isaiah's like I told you.

Is his mom there?

There was a delay in his response.

No. I guess they went out of town. Isaiah said it was okay tho.

I didn't say it was okay. You should have told me when you found out.

She was giving him the benefit of the doubt. She suspected he and Isaiah had planned to get together because his parents were gone. But that wasn't a conversation to have over text. The problem was, she needed to be here at the station. Why couldn't Dan have stepped up and taken Zach with him like they'd planned? Then she wouldn't be scrambling last minute to figure out what to do. This tension between work and home pulled at her far too often. And even though Zach was almost eighteen, she still worried. She saw far too often what could happen to boys his age.

She looked out her office window into the bullpen. McCann was taking Cory's statement. Marco had left. Roberto Salinas and Brett Chang were going through their gear.

Then the door to the reception area opened. Tony entered with a Bella Sorgenti bag over his arm. She hurried out to help him.

"What's this?" The bag she took was warm and smelled like tomatoes and spices.

"Mrs. D'Agostino thought you all could use a hot meal tonight after the search and rescue. They donated a lasagna, salad, and bread sticks. I volunteered to bring them by." Tony followed her to the horizontal filing cabinet that they used as a counter to hold food and snacks.

There was more to the story, she was sure. But she was grateful. They offloaded their food, and everyone came over to fill plates.

"Thank you." She touched his arm. "I'm sure you had more to do with this than just being the delivery driver."

He shrugged, but his gaze was guarded. "I'll get out of your hair. Is there anything else you need before I go?"

"You're not staying for lasagna?"

"Nah, I've got to get back. Unless you need something?"

She considered it. He'd done so much already, but he was offering, and she needed help. "Would you mind terribly swinging by the Schillers' place and picking up Zach and bringing him home? I just found out Isaiah's parents aren't home, and I can't leave here yet to go get him."

"Sure, I can do that." He shoved his hands in his pockets. "I'll have him text you when he's home."

"Thanks."

He nodded and turned to leave.

Just as he got to the door, Shannon stopped him. "Hey, coffee tomorrow afternoon?"

His gaze shuttered a bit. "I'll check my calendar and let you know." Then he was out the door.

She headed to fill her own plate, but her mind replayed their interaction. Something was missing. Everything was cooled down. He was helpful—and she was grateful—but he had pulled back.

Probably because she'd snapped at him twice today, the last time ordering him out of her truck. She grimaced. Tomorrow at coffee she'd apologize again and try to explain. Though she didn't quite understand it herself.

She texted Zach that Tony was on his way to pick him up. And enjoyed the Italian food instead of thinking of what a mess her personal life was.

ELLA SAT ON THE GURNEY IN URGENT CARE. THE IV BAG was nearly empty, the warm blanket had felt amazing, and her arm was all stitched up. She was so glad Doc Tia could take care of her here and not send her to the hospital down the mountain. She was ready to get out of here as soon as someone would let her.

What was Reese doing? Probably giving his statement to the sheriff. She'd need to do that too. After all of their togetherness, it felt like a piece of her was missing not to have him next to her. She couldn't even think about what it would be like to be in her own bed tonight and wake up tomorrow and not see Reese.

She thought about what Lorde said about Reese getting his men killed. Why hadn't Reese told her what happened? They'd talked about enough subjects, and he'd had plenty of opportunity to tell her. What did it mean that he hadn't? Maybe they weren't as close as she'd thought. Maybe he was just distracting her from the danger they were in by talking about things he thought she wanted to talk about.

And what was she thinking getting her heart all tangled up with his? He was leaving. He had plans to get off the mountain. And while in her hopeful, starry-eyed phase she'd thought they could make it work, who was she really kidding? They'd talked a lot about the past, but the future and present were noticeably absent from their discussions.

Doc Tia came in, papers in her hand. "How are you feeling?" She checked the monitors and studied Ella's face. "That cut on your cheek should heal quickly. Probably won't even leave a scar."

"I'm fine. Ready to get home and get a hot shower."

Doc shook her head as she handed Ella some papers. "Not for a couple of days. Baths only. It's all right here in your discharge paperwork. You can read over it while I disconnect your IV." It was basic information about not getting her stitches wet and signs of an infection along with a prescription for an antibiotic.

"Don't you normally have a nurse do that?"

"I do. But you're special. And the sheriff will want to know how you're doing." She put a bandage over the spot where the IV had been. "You're all set to go. Are you sure you're okay?" Her soft brown eyes studied Ella's like she could see the truth in her soul.

Ella swallowed. "I am. I promise."

Doc waited a bit as if deciding to believe her. "Okay. Is there someone you can call to pick you up?"

Ella set the papers aside and pulled her phone out of her hiking pants. Dead.

"You can use that phone on the wall there. Then you can wait out front."

Ella eased off the gurney and gingerly made her way toward the phone, punching in Mom's number. Man, she was sore. She needed a hot shower, but she couldn't get her stitches wet for two days. So a bath it would be. Better than nothing.

"Ella! I was half tempted to come find you myself. Where are you?" Mom's voice was threaded with worry.

"Urgent care. But I'm fine. Can you come get me?"

"Be there in a few minutes." She hung up, and Ella made her way to the waiting area.

It was empty. Except for Lucas.

She frowned. What was he doing here? Was his fiancée hurt? She couldn't make the connection. Then again, she was tired and had lost some blood.

He stepped over to her and wrapped her in a hug. "Ella. I'm so glad you're safe. I was so worried. Are you okay?"

She shrugged out of his hug and moved to the chairs. It felt weird and awkward. She found it hard to believe hugging him had ever felt natural. "I'm fine. Just needed a few stitches."

He followed her, sitting close, pressing his knees next to hers. "Let me take you home, and you can tell me all about it."

"My mom's coming. She'll be here any minute. Why are you here?" She shivered. Her jacket was soaked in blood and had gone in the trash. Both her shirts had their sleeves cut off so her wound could be dressed, so someone had loaned her a hoodie. The advantage of knowing everyone here.

Lucas slipped his arm around her and pulled her close. "I came to get you. I was the one who told the sheriff yesterday I thought you were missing and in danger. She didn't believe me until today. But, Ella, this whole event has made me rethink everything." He took her hand. "I never stopped loving you."

The door opened, and Ella turned, hoping it was her mom and she could escape this Bizarro world she'd stepped into with Lucas.

But it was Reese. He spotted her, and she knew the moment he took in Lucas's arm around her. His face hardened, and he spun on his heel and left.

Ella got to her feet, shaking off Lucas. "Reese, wait."

But he was already climbing in his Bronco and pulling away.

Tears pooled in her eyes. The evening air chilled her. She was tired; Lucas was irritating her, and she just wanted to go home.

Lucas came up, putting his own coat around her shoulders. The warmth felt good but the source did not. "Lucas, I'm not interested. We aren't meant to be together. Go back to Sophie."

He started to protest, but her mom pulled up. She thrust Lucas's coat at him as he sputtered something she shut out as she climbed into Mom's car and shut the door.

Then promptly burst into tears.

———

Reese drove blindly away from the urgent care. He didn't know where he was going. When Marissa had picked up Raul and him from the sheriff's station, she'd brought them home where he quickly showered and changed clothes so he could come back and get Ella from urgent care as soon as she was ready.

Apparently he wasn't the only one with that idea. Lucas. The man made his stomach turn. But if Reese was honest with himself, Lucas was more suited to Ella than he was. He had a steady job and didn't make life-or-death decisions that got people killed. And he sure had come running fast to make up with her when he'd learned she was hurt.

Ella hadn't seemed to mind too much, from what he could see.

Lorde's words rang in his head. He should have told Ella when he had the chance. But he hadn't wanted to ruin the closeness they had developed, hadn't wanted to see her condemnation in her eyes. But Lorde had put it all out there, raked it all up again. That was what he hated about small towns. Everyone was in your business. There was no privacy.

Once he was upstairs in his garage apartment, he booted up his computer and opened his email. There it sat. The email from

Armando asking again when he thought he'd be free to come join him in San Diego.

Raul getting hurt again had put a crimp in his plans. He would stick around until Raul was healed. As painful as it would be to see Ella with Lucas. But his brother had risked his life for Reese. It was the least he could do.

Then the best thing he could do was join Armando and get off this mountain and out of this small town.

The thought of not seeing Ella turned his blood to ice. But he had to think of what was best for her. And being with a broken man like him wasn't it.

CHAPTER
TWENTY-ONE

Shannon stifled a yawn as she sat at her desk the next day. She hadn't slept much last night. Tony had brought Zach home, but by the time she got home, he was in bed. Either asleep or pretending to be. And she'd left the house before he'd been up. They'd have to talk and soon.

Their conversations during spring break had been short. Zach had been sullen and surly, verging on disrespectful. She got that he was disappointed with his dad and taking it out on her. She was the convenient parent. And the one that wouldn't leave him. No matter what.

He'd tossed out that he thought he'd go live with his dad after graduation. She hadn't said anything. Dan never had Zach for more than a few days at a time. He'd see soon enough that life with Dad wasn't all movies and fun trips. The sad part was she knew Dan would never let Zach live with him. But she wouldn't tell Zach that.

She stood from her desk and left her office. She stopped at Donna's desk. "I'm walking down to the Jitter Bug Too if anyone needs me."

Donna nodded, and Shannon headed out the back of the town center building, hoping to find a moment of peace. The chilly air helped awaken her. Her heavy shoes clomped along the wooden sidewalk in town, providing a nice cadence for her thoughts.

She hoped Tony would show up for their coffee date. Perhaps she could apologize for her shortness with him. Figuring out how to let someone into her life other than Tia and her therapist was going to take some work. But she was up for it. One way or another, Zach wouldn't be living under her roof full-time once he graduated and left for college. And she wanted a life outside of work. She needed it. For too long her focus had been Zach, work, and this town.

She pulled the door open to the Jitter Bug Too, the bells tinkling overhead and the smell of fresh-brewed coffee and buttery baked goods enveloping her and tugging her inside.

Cassie looked up from behind the counter and smiled. "Hey, sis. How are you?" She moved to the machine and pulled an espresso.

"Eh. And I didn't tell you what I wanted."

"I know what you need." Cassie grinned.

"You're not wrong." Shannon glanced around the shop. No Tony. Would he even show?

Cassie pushed over the espresso. "Go sit. I'll bring you a blueberry scone."

Shannon took her coffee and slid into the back booth. One sip had her eyes opening a bit wider. Cassie was right. She needed this.

The bells tinkled again. Shannon looked up. Not Tony. But it was Walt. He nodded in her direction then placed an order with Cassie before coming over to the booth.

"Mind if I join you?"

"Go ahead. Got any updates?"

Cassie brought over their pastries and Walt's coffee then left.

"We hit the grow site this morning. What a mess. We're lucky they didn't burn down the whole mountain. They had burn barrels, chemicals, fertilizer. We've got quite a bit of clean up to do. Some of it will require haz mat because of the chemicals. If those spread into the wildlife, it'll create even more destruction. So there goes my budget and manpower."

"Anything pointing to who's behind it?" Shannon bit into the scone. Her sister was a genius with baked goods.

"Nope. But the body is tentatively identified as Brandt. His wallet was still on him. He had decomposed too much to make it a positive ID. We'll need dental records."

"And Brandt was an employee of Belle Lumber. Think any judge will get us any kind of search warrant based on that connection?"

Walt shook his head. "Nope, but I've kicked it up the chain of command. The tech guys and white collar crime will look into the records they can access."

Shannon sat back. "Lorde's good at hiding his tracks."

Walt nodded. "Yeah, but he'll slip up at some point. We'll get him."

She hoped so. "We have Cory Grant's phone. We were able to get a subpoena for his phone records. Now we're just waiting for the phone company to comply. We may get something there. Cory didn't have anything to say, and he lawyered up. He's off the SAR team, but I'm not sure much will happen beyond that until we come up with something more concrete."

Walt finished his coffee. "We'll keep fighting the good fight. I'll keep you updated if anything else turns up." He got to his feet.

"Thanks, Walt."

Walt left and then the shop was silent other than the burble of the coffee machines and Cassie puttering around. She finished her scone and let Cassie talk her into another cup, regular coffee this time. But after an hour she realized Tony wasn't going to show. Likely he'd gotten busy or something had come up. It happened. She wasn't going to text him. She needed to get back to work anyway.

She got to her feet. "Thanks for the refresh, Cassie. It hit the spot."

Cassie gave her a sympathetic look. "Have a good afternoon!"

"Thanks, sis." On impulse, she came around the counter and hugged her before heading out into the crisp air and the problems that still awaited her.

Tony sat with Ella in her living room drinking coffee. He'd wanted to check on her after everything she'd been through. Her mom, Lori, had let him in, gotten him some coffee, then headed back to her office to work from home. She hadn't wanted to go in today in case Ella needed her. But Ella seemed in good, if subdued, spirits.

"So how are you doing? Really." Tony leaned forward. This was something he was good at. Not like yesterday when he was trying to support Shannon and just made a mess of it.

Ella shrugged. "Sore. Tired. Felt great to be in my own bed last night." She let out a long breath. "I'm sure I'll be processing everything for a while. But mostly I'm grateful for Reese. I couldn't have gotten through all of that without his skills. We were actually having a pretty good time until the last day." Myriad emotions crossed her face, and he suspected she and Reese had gotten close on the trip.

Tony chose his words carefully. "Reese has been a loner for a while. He could use a good friend. You might have to be a bit persistent though. He might try to push you away. But I don't think he means it."

She laughed without humor. "Yeah, I thought we'd kinda gotten past that."

"Don't give up on him."

She bit her lip and nodded.

She had more thoughts than she was sharing. He'd learned

when to prod and when to leave it be. As friendly as Ella was to everyone, she kept her relationships at a surface level, never letting anyone get too close. She'd never shared the reason why, but he suspected—after a few things Lori had said—that it had something to do with her dad.

He also suspected Reese had become something more than a guide on this trip, maybe even more than a friend. If the two of them could find their way forward without hurting each other, they could help each other heal. If they would just be vulnerable enough to let it happen.

He prayed for her then rose and took his coffee cup to the sink. He poked his head in Lori's office door and said goodbye.

As he left, he noted the time. Shannon had mentioned meeting for coffee today. They hadn't talked since yesterday when he'd dropped off the food at the station. But he wanted to swing by the Outfitters and see how Raul and Reese were doing. He suspected Reese would be there and not home resting. Then Tony had a sermon to prepare. It was a busy week with all the visitors. He couldn't quite fit in coffee today.

Shannon would know how it was. Her job was just as unpredictable.

He shot her a quick text saying he wasn't going to make it, though she'd probably figured that out considering it was past the time they usually met. As he drove back into town, he considered that he wasn't exactly being honest with himself either. Her shortness with him stung. Mostly because he'd hoped they were developing a different kind of relationship. Perhaps that was presumption on his part.

She was just doing her job. He accepted that. But maybe it wasn't the right time for him to get into a relationship. Maybe they just couldn't make it work.

If he was completely honest with himself, he wasn't ready to open himself up to her completely. He knew it would mean revealing his secret about his dyslexia upfront and waiting for her reaction. It shouldn't be as big of a deal as he had made it.

Considering his near panic attack Monday when Anne asked him to read to the kids, he wasn't ready.

People talked openly about having dyslexia these days. But no one in his life had known about it except Janelle and his parents. He'd created a whole life around coping with it. And he didn't know how people would feel if they knew their pastor struggled to read.

He just didn't want to find out.

He would take a step back from Shannon and give himself some time to think and pray about the situation. He certainly didn't want to rush into anything.

And what would Shannon think? Would she notice he'd pulled back? Or would she think it was the way their schedules were working out? He didn't want to hurt her. But he couldn't explain it without saying more than he wanted to.

He knew more than most that people and relationships were complicated and messy. But he'd been able to sidestep most of that by being a widower. But if he wanted to move forward in life, he was going to have to get back in it.

He swung into the Outfitter's parking lot. He should practice what he preached. He just couldn't quite bring himself to do it.

CHAPTER
TWENTY-TWO

Reese and Raul were at the shop going through their gear. Reese had swung by the sheriff's department earlier in the day to pick up their equipment. Now it was time to see what they could salvage. Raul was on crutches, so he wasn't much help. He mostly perched on a stool behind the counter and talked to the customers.

Pastor Tony came through the door. He grinned. "I figured I'd find both of you Vega boys here. Didn't think you'd take any time off after being shot at and chased through the woods." He shook both their hands. "How are you guys doing? Any worse for wear?"

"Nah." Raul shrugged. "I'm back on crutches, and I have an appointment with my orthopedic surgeon down the hill next week. But Doc Tia checked me out and said to stay off it, keep the brace on it, and all the typical stuff."

"Good to hear." Pastor Tony's gaze slid to Reese. "What about you?"

"Fine. Had worse in the Army." No one was in the store, so he added, "No nightmares."

"That's good. Up to running Saturday?"

"Sure."

Pastor Tony was quiet a minute. "I just stopped by to see Ella before coming over here. Have you seen or talked to her since yesterday?"

Reese crossed his arms over his chest. "No, I picked up our gear from the sheriff's department this morning. I've got to go through it." His excuses sounded lame to his ears. The pastor would pick up on it for sure.

Pastor Tony nodded and met his gaze. "She seems to be doing okay. But I'm sure she'd like to hear from you."

Reese was noncommittal. Lucas was probably taking care of her. Though Pastor Tony didn't mention his presence.

Pastor Tony chatted for a few more minutes, mostly with Raul. When customers came in, he said goodbye and left. Reese used it as a good excuse to head back to the workroom and go through the gear.

The tents were in good shape. So were the sleeping bags and bear canister, surprisingly enough. As he cleaned the gear and set it out to dry, he came to Ella's pack. The backpack itself belong to the shop, but it contained a lot of her personal gear. After staring at it a minute, he opened it and pulled out the common gear. He got to the first-aid kit. The bloody bandages. He stopped. How was she doing really? Pastor Tony said she was okay, but what did that mean? She'd obviously been well enough to get discharged from urgent care. He'd seen that yesterday. He frowned as he remembered the scene he'd come upon at the urgent care, Ella in Lucas's arms. Was Lucas taking care of her?

He felt like part of him was missing. He had gotten used to her company, her soft questions, her quiet listening. Her clear enjoyment of nature. She hadn't complained once, and she'd been shot. He could ask around about how she was doing. It was a small town. Someone would know.

He pulled her personal items out. Her hat, two shirts, another fleece. They smelled like her. Soft, warm, with a hint of a soothing floral. Lavender? He didn't know. It was all he could do not to bury his face in them.

The squeak of crutches came behind him. Raul.

"How'd everything hold up?"

"Good. Nothing's damaged. I'm kinda surprised. Our pursuers should have damaged the tents and sleeping bags in case we circled back to them." Reese continued to pull out Ella's personal items.

"Would you have?"

"I thought about it. If we had decided to go down the backside of the mountain into the high desert, we would have needed to. But it seemed too risky."

Raul nodded toward Ella's belongings. "You going to take them by her house?"

"I thought you could call her and have her come pick them up."

Raul was quiet a moment. "You should take them to her. You two have unfinished business."

When Reese had come home yesterday from urgent care, Raul had commented on how quick his trip had been. Reese had mentioned that Lucas had picked Ella up and hadn't said anything else. Apparently Raul was filling in some blanks on his own.

"She's back with Lucas. There's nothing else to say."

"You don't know that. If it's true, give her a chance to tell you. She's an honorable woman. She's not going to string you along."

Reese turned and leaned against the workbench. He hadn't said much to Raul about what'd happened on the trail between Ella and him.

Raul hopped up on a stool and set his crutches to the side. "I've seen the two of you together. She lights you up in a way I've never seen before. I can only imagine what happened out there in the woods between the two of you. Don't let that chance slip away. If she goes back to Lucas—and I don't think she will —you shouldn't let her go without a fight. Without making sure you've done everything you can."

Reese stared at the pegboard holding coils of rope behind Raul's head. He knew equipment; he knew order. He didn't know women. "Lorde told her about Afghanistan. That I got my men killed." He scrubbed a hand over his face before meeting Raul's gaze.

"Then tell her the truth."

Reese scoffed. "That is the truth. I made a bad decision and men died. I got this stupid TBI and had to leave the Army."

"That's not the whole truth, Reese." Raul clasped his shoulder. "Tell her the whole truth. She deserves to know." He paused. "And I think you can trust her with it."

Raul was right. And Reese didn't want to admit it.

The front door dinged. They had a customer. Raul reached for his crutches but didn't leave the stool.

"I've never told you, Reese, but I'm proud that you were in the Army, that you were a Ranger. Your skills got you and Ella out of the woods alive. But more than that, you were your own person. You broke the mold and expectations and did what you were called to do. I've always admired that about you." He slid off the stool and onto his crutches. Just before he got to the sales floor he turned. "Get out of here. I can manage without you for a bit."

Reese stared at Raul's retreating back, stunned at his words. Words he never thought he'd ever hear anyone in his family say. Had he even heard him right? He shook his head and pushed off the worktable. He stuffed Ella's items into a bag and emptied the backpack. At the bottom was a soft, leather-bound journal with a pen strung through the thong tying it together.

He studied it a minute, curious as to what her thoughts had been about the trip. He didn't remember seeing her write in it. Other than that first night, they hadn't had any time alone. He ran his finger over the leather before tossing it in the bag with the other items. If he wanted to know her thoughts, he needed to ask her directly.

He headed out the back.

When Mom took a break for lunch, she warmed up a casserole and made a plate for Ella. She'd told Ella she'd decided to work from home today in case Ella needed her.

"I'm not an invalid, and I'm not sick. I can make my own lunch," Ella protested as she joined Mom at the kitchen table.

"I know. But a number of townspeople dropped off food. I'm going to have to freeze some of it. We'll never get through it all."

Ella took a bite. Turkey tetrazzini. Yum. "Why on earth did people bring food?"

"Because you were missing. Those who could were out looking for you. Those who couldn't wanted to feel helpful. And for many people, that means bringing food."

Ella thought about that for a minute. "I thought nobody knew what was going on other than the sheriff and her team. I mean, I figured people would find out, but..."

"Once Raul texted Jonas, everything flew into motion. You know the grapevine. People started showing up at work with food. Tom Asher told me to go home because I was more of a distraction than a help. There was more food on the porch, and people kept coming." She reached a hand over to Ella's and squeezed. "People were worried about you, baby girl. What would the town do without you? People rely on you. And you're special to us."

"Huh." Ella wasn't sure what to make of that. Mom chattered on about who had brought what, but Ella's mind mulled over Mom's words. Ella was used to the small town rallying around people in need. It had just never been her.

She'd need to spend some time with the journal Anne had given her. She hadn't had time to write in it on the trail, but it would be good for her to go back through the events and process them by writing them down. But it was with her gear; she'd have to pick it up. She thought about seeing Reese again; she hadn't heard from him, but before she could go down that thought trail, there was a knock at the door.

"I'll get it." Ella jumped up before Mom could. She was nearly done anyway, and Mom would need to head back to work.

Anne stood at the door, book in hand. "Hey, Ella. I had to see for myself that you were in one piece." She leaned in and gave her a hug, the library smell of paper and ink faintly clinging to her.

"Come on in. Do you have a minute? I spotted some of Cassie's spice cake on the counter and thought I'd have a piece. Want one?"

"Of course."

The women moved into the kitchen. Mom waved to Anne on her way back to work, and Ella set about making some tea and slicing cake.

Anne took a bite. "Mmm. This was why I brought you a book instead of food. I knew you'd have more than you could handle."

Ella shook her head. "Yeah. I didn't expect that. I didn't even know until today that the whole town knew Reese and I were missing." She stumbled a bit over Reese's name. She thought about Pastor Tony's words. She needed to reach out to Reese.

Anne put her fork down. "Ella, you are a key part of this community. Of course everyone is going to be concerned about you. Everyone loves you. We were worried about you."

"But I didn't miss any events. We're still on spring break."

"Ella! We don't love you for what you do for us. We love you for who you are." Anne's gaze on her was steady and full of love.

A kind of slow dawning came over Ella. Mom had said something similar, but she was her mom—a little biased. But Anne's words were true, she realized. She'd known them in her head. But now, she felt them in her heart. She was loved by this little town. It had grown to become the family she'd always wanted, even if it was quirky and obsessed with food. And yes, people would leave and it would hurt. But more people would stay.

And she would be okay.

And on the heels of that… She'd been living a lie by pushing others away, keeping them at a distance, thinking she was protecting her heart. When all she was doing was denying herself the joy of deep friendships with people who loved her.

Tears welled in her eyes, and she reached over to hug Anne. "I didn't get to write in that journal you gave me. Wish I had it with me now. It's still with my backpack and personal gear, which I need to get from Reese. But I think I might have plenty to fill it with now."

Anne gave her a soft smile. "Then your trip accomplished its purpose. It got you to think about your life in a new way." She took a sip of tea. "And what about Reese? Did you get to know him better?"

Ella gave a laugh threaded with a bit of embarrassment. Her cheeks heated. "Yeah, I did." She gave Anne the quick summary of their conversations and their impromptu prom.

Anne smiled, sipping her tea, which encouraged Ella to keep talking. They finished the cake and tea.

Anne tapped the book. "This is my own private copy, so there's no rush to return it. At least it's a non-calorie treat. But I should get back."

Ella walked her to the door.

Anne took her by the shoulders and held her gaze. "Ella, you are a strong woman, worthy of love. And if Reese can't provide that for you, you have a whole town to love you."

Ella nodded, unable to speak, letting Anne's words pour over her and soothe the sore places of her heart. She wanted to believe they were true.

So she would. As long as she could. Even when it didn't feel real.

Anne left, and Ella went back into the kitchen to clean up. There was a knock at the door. She should expect that people would be dropping by all day to see how she was doing. She hurried to answer it, not wanting Mom to be interrupted from her work.

She pulled the door open.

Reese.

Her heart rate picked up, and heat rushed through her body. He looked good—clean shaven and combed hair. But she'd loved his rugged look too.

He met her gaze and held it. "Hey." He lifted a bag. "I brought your stuff back."

"Hey yourself." She grinned and backed inside. "Come on in. I have too much cake here for Mom and me to eat."

He hesitated but followed her in, setting the bag on the couch. "Guess the town has been at work. Marissa said when Raul got hurt they had enough food for a month."

"Mom reminded me that people show their love with food when they feel helpless." She pointed to the three desserts sitting on the counter. "Spice cake, brownies, or sour cream apple pie?"

He hesitated for a moment. "At the risk of you never wanting to go in the woods with me again"—he gave her a wry smile—"could we take a walk?"

She smiled back, curious about what he wanted to say, and a little nervous. She thought about Anne's words and kept them close to her heart. "Let me get my coat and put my boots on."

A minute later, they were outside, down the stairs, and walking along the street. She was still stiff, but it felt good to move around. And since Reese wanted this conversation, she was going to wait until he started it.

"How are you feeling?" he glanced at her.

"Fine. A little sore. The stitches itch. I wish I could take a real shower. Washing my hair in the bathtub was a challenge. But it was nice being in my own bed last night."

He nodded distractedly. "Look, I'm— I'm just going to say this. If you want to go back to Lucas, that's fine. But I want to hear it from you. Not the town grapevine." Pain-filled eyes met hers.

Oh, Reese. She stopped in the middle of the street. "I know what you thought you saw. But if you'd waited two more seconds you would have seen me push Lucas away. He startled me and had me wrapped in a hug before I even knew what was happening. I had no idea he was going to be there, and I have no interest in anyone..." She reached out and touched his cheek. "In anyone but you."

His hand reached up and covered hers. "You're sure?"

"Positive." She smiled as he lowered his forehead to hers. She thought he was going to kiss her, but then he pulled back.

"I have to tell you something."

"Okay." She steeled herself. He was going to tell her he was leaving. That had been his plan all along.

"It's about Afghanistan."

What? That wasn't what she was expecting. Maybe she should concentrate on what he was saying instead of trying to anticipate it.

"Lorde mentioned that I'd gotten my men killed in Afghanistan. I had wanted to tell you what happened while we were on the trail, but it never seemed like the right time. But you deserve to hear it from me."

She thought about the comment Cory had made before she and Reese had left for the waterfall, about how Reese had gotten men killed. She had dismissed it as part of male posturing and Cory exaggerating. But Beckett Lorde had known about it too. A thread of worry worked its way through her heart. But she was committed to hearing him out.

"We were outside the wire—the secure base area—on a mission. We got some intel over the radio that there was a large gathering of people on our route and were advised to go another way. I was the leader; the decision was up to me. Did we take the chance on our regular route that the people were just gathering and weren't hostile, that we wouldn't have a confrontation? Or did we just avoid it all together? But could it be a trap if we pushed into another dangerous area. There was no good way to go. I made a choice, and it was the wrong one."

He stared straight ahead, his voice flat. "We turned down a street. It quickly began to narrow, and as soon as I saw it was deserted, I knew it was a bad sign. But we couldn't turn around. It was too tight. Shooters came out of the doorways and upper windows. We were sitting ducks. Someone had an RPG and blew up the transport vehicle we were in." He swallowed. "I woke up in the hospital. The blast gave me a concussion, a traumatic brain injury. Two of my men died. I still have nightmares about it."

He stopped in the street and turned to her, his gaze questioning.

She threw her arms around him, hugging him tight to her. "Oh, Reese, I'm so sorry you went through that."

There was a second delay and then his arms were around her, holding her tight, burying his face in her neck.

If she had her way, she'd never let him go.

CHAPTER
TWENTY-THREE

Shannon knocked on Zach's doorframe then pushed the door open. He was hunched over his desk, headphones on, playing video games with his friends. He wasn't happy with her. She'd grounded him for lying to her about Isaiah's parents not being home. It didn't seem like they'd gotten into any trouble; they'd just played video games, and he'd wanted to get out of the house. She tried to have some compassion on him for being stuck at home during spring break. But lying was a nonstarter. And she made sure he knew that's what he was grounded for.

He looked up and flipped off his headphones. "What?"

"Just thought you might want to go to Little Bear Lookout tonight." It was a peace offering. She'd come home, gotten out of her uniform and into fleece-lined jeans and flannel shirt and pulled her hair out of its bun to let its waves fall around her shoulders. Comfort was her priority. Though she'd chosen one of her nicer flannel shirts, aware that Tony could be there.

Zach stared at her for a minute. "I thought I was grounded."

"You are. You'll be with me. But you can hang out with whomever of your friends shows up as long as we're there."

"Okay. Thanks." He pushed up from his desk.

"I'll meet you in the car."

She climbed in the Jeep and started it, flipping on the heater. Would Tony be at the Lookout? They needed to talk. He was right. She had a great team, which was obvious with the search for Reese and Ella. And while they hadn't caught the shooters or nailed Lorde, she had confidence they would. And Tony had been part of it.

Zach slid into the car, and they headed toward Little Bear Lookout. She turned onto the two-track and spotted Tia unlocking the chain draped across the road that kept out trespassers. She waved to her and leaned out the window. "I'll lock it." They both drove through, and Zach hopped out to lock the chain behind them.

When they pulled up to the lookout, Zack spotted some friends but turned to her. "Thanks, Mom, for letting me come."

"I hate that you've had a crappy spring break. Let's try to find some way to make it up, okay?"

He came around the car and gave her a quick hug before loping off.

Shannon let out a sigh. Small mom win. She headed over to Tia and joined her on the bench. "Hey, friend. How was your week?"

Tia laughed. "Not as interesting as yours." Her gaze slid around the gathering crowd. She nudged Shannon's shoulder. "Look who's here."

Tony and Ryan stood off to the side talking with Marco and Jonas. Tony's gaze met hers, and he gave a nod but went back to talking. The community event the church had sponsored last night had seemed to go well, thanks to him and Ryan and all the volunteers who showed up to make the tourists feel welcome.

Tia lowered her voice. "What's up with the two of you?"

Shannon shook her head. "I need to talk to him and apologize, but we keep missing each other."

"You'll get through it. You guys have a lot of potential. I'd hate to see it fall apart over something that could be resolved with a conversation."

"I know. But tonight's not the time. But soon. I wanted to have coffee with him yesterday, and he couldn't make it. Our schedules are not our friend. But it'll happen." Shannon's gaze drifted in Tony's direction again. With her position, friendships were few and far between. She'd figure out a way to make it work.

"I see Zach got an early release from his prison sentence." Tia gave her a wry grin.

"I'll get no Mother of the Year awards. I know he's had a raw deal on spring break. I could wring Dan's neck for disappointing him. But Zach can't lie to me. Still, it seemed like letting him come hang out with his friends with most of the town watching was a safe way to go."

"Good call, Mom. He's got to spread his wings."

"I know. It just terrifies me."

Tia looked at her. "We need a girlfriend day. Let's pull out our calendars and get something down or it won't happen. I don't even care what we do."

As she and Tia made plans, Shannon glanced around the gathering crowd of townspeople, people under her care.

And it was good. It wasn't perfect. But it was good.

REESE LOOKED OVER AT ELLA SITTING IN THE PASSENGER seat of his Bronco, hoping they'd get a minute alone. Ever since he'd unburdened himself to her two days ago, he'd felt lighter and closer to her. She'd just held him, and slowly his muscles had unlocked, and he'd softened into her.

Today she'd invited him to watch the sunset over the lake at Little Bear Lookout, a place only known to the locals. A place he'd never been invited to and wasn't quite sure where it was.

"Turn here." She pointed to a small break in the trees.

He wheeled onto a two-track and soon was stopped by a chain across the road with a NO TRESPASSING sign swinging from the middle. He frowned. "This the right place?"

She grinned as she hopped out. "Yep." She pulled out a key and unlocked the hasp that held the chain, carrying it across the road and re-locking it once Reese had driven through.

As she climbed back in, he raised his eyebrows. "You guys are a sneaky bunch."

"We have to be to keep this place to ourselves. But before you drive off, here." She handed him a key.

"What's that?"

"It's your copy of the key to the chain lock. Only locals can have it. But you're one of us now, so that's your copy."

He closed his fingers around the small piece of metal. It was much more than a key. He swallowed, nodded, not able to speak, before driving forward.

Reese recognized the general area. Back when he'd been in high school, kids had partied back here. He'd shown up a couple of times, but he didn't belong with that crowd either. He guided the Bronco back through the narrow trail, tree branches occasionally brushing the sides, his chest feeling a bit funny at being included as one of the townspeople. He was no longer an outsider. And after his decision today, he planned to stay that way. He couldn't wait to tell Ella. If he could get her alone.

The road opened up and appeared to drop off. In front of them was the expanse of Holcomb Lake. The road dipped and spread out into a parking area that already contained a few cars. The sun hung low on the horizon.

He found a spot for them and pulled into it, slipping the key onto his keychain before grabbing their picnic dinner from the back seat and following Ella. Someone had created some split-log benches and strung them out on the steep overlook facing the lake with a perfect view of the sunset. A stone fire pit sat in the middle, a fire already roaring to ward off the chill. The sheriff and Doc Tia already occupied a bench close to the fire. A few others stood around it.

Ella waved to them. She pointed to the end of one bench. "You can put our stuff there." She dropped a blanket on the seat. Then she ran over to hug a woman about her age before dragging her back over. "Reese, this is Amanda Elliot, my co-teacher and dear friend. She just got back from spending spring break with her parents in Palm Springs. Amanda, this is Reese Vega, outdoor master and saver of my life." Ella's face glowed as he and Amanda greeted each other.

Did she really mean what she said? Ella wasn't the type to lie or exaggerate. The funny thing in his chest grew stronger, warmer.

"I hear you two had quite the trip," Amanda said. "Mine was nowhere near as exciting."

Ella touched the scabbed scratch on her cheek. "We can catch up after church tomorrow. I think I might need a vacation to recover from our adventures. Too bad school starts on Monday."

"Yeah, and Easter is only twenty days away. Speaking of which," Amanda glanced over her shoulder. "I see Ryan's here. I need to talk to him about helping out with that." She clasped her hands together quickly before touching Ella's shoulder. "I'll talk to you later. Nice meeting you, Reese."

"You too." Amanda headed over toward the group of Pastor Tony, Ryan, Marco, and Jonas. He thought about joining them for a moment but really didn't want to leave Ella. Plus he'd run with Pastor Tony this morning and caught him up.

"I want to show you something. Up for a short hike?" Ella reached for his hand and led him off to the side where a trail led along the bluff and disappeared.

"With you? Of course."

"You aren't worried about being alone with me?" She exaggerated an eyelash flutter.

"I was hoping for it." This was one hike where he was happy

to have someone else lead. And flirt with him. So different from the hikes he usually led with women he didn't want flirting with him. Maybe he could get Ella to come with him on them more often. It would make it more enjoyable.

A path wound down a short way along the cliff face, ending on a bluff hidden from above that hovered over the lake.

"This is my favorite place. Not too many people know about it."

Reese moved behind her and pulled her back against his chest, his arms wrapped around hers across her middle. He couldn't think of anything more perfect. This was a different perspective of the lake, one he hadn't seen before. Like a lot of things in his life lately.

"I have some news," he said.

She twisted in his arms, brow furrowed.

"Good news. Raul offered me a partnership in the Outfitters and I accepted. I wrote my buddy in San Diego today and told him I'd be staying up here. Running the family business." His throat tightened over those last words. He never thought he'd say them.

Ella's face brightened like the sun peeking over the mountain ridge. "Really? You're staying?"

"I am. If you don't mind. I know I can be kind of a jerk sometimes. I'm working on it."

She twisted all the way around in his arms, placing her hands on his chest. "Yeah? Well, you don't mind that I'm a bookworm and know everyone in town? That we won't be able to go out to dinner without talking to five people between the door and our table?"

He grinned. "I'll adjust." He brushed a strand of hair back from her face. "I'm not going anywhere. I want to figure this thing out between us. I'd do anything for you, Ella. I love you."

Her breath caught with a small gasp. Then she smiled. "I love you too, Reese. I'm glad you're staying."

He slid his hand around her neck and pulled her close,

giving her a kiss full of promise and the future, hoping it would say more than he could. Blood rushed through his veins as he pulled her closer, and she responded in kind.

He slowly became aware of voices floating to them. Reese pulled back. The wind carried conversation and laughter to them.

Ella grinned. Her lips were rosy, as were her cheeks, and not just from the cold. "I've got something to show you." She tugged out her phone and swiped through it.

There was the photo they'd taken together at the beginning of the trip, Holcomb Lake in the background. Even then, before their adventure, they'd looked like they belonged together.

He took the phone from her. "Let's take another." They turned to put the lake behind them. After a few adjustments to keep them from being complete silhouettes from the descending sun, he took a few pictures of them.

Ella kissed his cheek then pocketed her phone. "Let's grab our dinner. The sun's about to go down."

They climbed back up to the top of the cliff as Zach and Isaiah squeezed past them at a jog.

"Careful," Ella cautioned them.

"We will be, Ms. Sommer." Zach shot her a grin.

She shrugged at Reese. "Sorry. Always a teacher to these kids, even those I didn't have in my class."

More people had arrived. Marco, Jonas, Pastor Tony were already there standing in a group talking. There was a couple he hadn't met before. The man was tall with dark hair, the woman a bit shorter blonde.

Ella waved to them as she began unpacking their dinner. "Claire, Alex, come meet Reese."

The couple, along with a middle-school girl, made their way over. "Reese, this is Claire and Alex Wilder and their daughter, Lizzie. They just bought that Victorian one block off Holcomb Springs Road and are turning it into a B-and-B. They moved out here from Michigan."

Reese shook hands with both of them.

"Nice to meet you," Claire said. "My grandma moved with us too, but she wasn't up to coming tonight."

"I can't wait to see what you've done with the place," Ella said.

"Stop by any time. We are *always* there." Claire laughed. "We hope to open before Art Fest in June."

Pastor Tony made his way over, saying hi to Claire and Alex before they moved off, called over by Stan and Wally and their wives. "Glad to see you two are no worse for wear. And, Reese, I have an idea to run by you. The Spread the Love event raised money for the community center. As we were brainstorming things for kids to do there, especially in the winter, we came up with the idea of a climbing wall. Think you might be interested in teaching classes there?"

A warmth enveloped him. He was being treated as a member of this community, as someone with something to contribute. He glanced at Ella, who smiled. "Uh, yeah. I'd be interested."

Pastor Tony lightly smacked his shoulder. "Good. We'll talk more about it later." He moved off to talk to someone else, the opposite direction of the sheriff. Interesting. He'd thought maybe… Well, he was no expert on relationships And there was only one he was really interested in. He pulled Ella closer.

As the sun neared the horizon, everyone found their seats, as if the show was about to begin.

Ella handed him a bowl of steaming stew she'd poured from a thermos. The savory scent filled his senses, smelling like home and comfort.

As they ate, he thought about how leading wilderness trips as a favor to his brother had led to this moment. What he had originally regretted offering to do had turned out to be the best thing that had happened to him. And something he'd never expected—repairing his family relationships—was slowly beginning to happen. Marissa was hosting a family dinner tomorrow. He was bringing Ella to meet his parents. He'd let his guard down, gotten close, and his heart was full. If he and Raul could get close, maybe there was a chance for him and his parents as well.

The sun touched the horizon, melting into it. He slipped his arm around Ella's shoulders. "Ready to make some memories?" He gazed into her eyes, warmed by the love he saw there. Unbelievable, undeserved, and unexpected. But that's what made it a gift.

"Absolutely."

Hey, this is Anne Cartwright, the librarian. If you want to know something about this town, ask me. I know. Believe me, I know.

Do you want to know if Shannon and Tony can figure things out?

Does Beckett Lorde ever get caught? And what happens with Cory Grant?

Want an invitation to Brett and Cassie's wedding?

I've got you covered. I can get you special access to all these details and more. Go to (or just click) https://BookHip.com/DAHXSDC and you'll get the bonus epilogue containing the wedding and more, as well as access only available to my guests of Insider Updates.

Some of your favorite characters (that might possibly be me) will make an appearance on occasion, and JL has specials that only her Insiders have access to. It's totally worth it.

You'll also get the prequel novella to the Hometown Heroes series, *Promise Me*— Grayson and Cait's story. It's adorable. I haven't met them yet in person, but I hope they'll come up to Holcomb Springs soon.

I promise I won't share your email address with anyone but JL, and you can unsubscribe at any time, but why would you want to miss out?

Here's the link again: https://BookHip.com/DAHXSDC.

Do you know how I spend most of my day? As a librarian, I recommend books to people. You can do that too. If you enjoyed this book, please leave a review. It's simply telling other readers what you loved about this book. It can be as simple as "I couldn't put it down. I can't wait for the next one." It helps raise the author's visibility and lets other readers find her. Because I can't talk to everyone. But I'm trying!

Keep reading for a sneak peek of *Under an Indigo Moon*, the next book in this series. You will love it!

—Anne Cartwright, librarian and historian, Holcomb Springs

ACKNOWLEDGMENTS

This book would not be possible without the patience and willingness to read early drafts by Jennifer Lynn Cary. Jenny gets an extra dose of thanks for helping me brainstorm when I got stuck. Many thanks to my early readers!

An extra thanks to my dad, David Crosswhite, for getting me started with this idea and talking with me about all the things that could go wrong in the wilderness.

Much thanks and love to my children, Caitlyn Elizabeth and Joshua Alexander, for supporting my dream for many years and giving me time to write.

And most of all to my Lord Jesus, who makes all things possible and directs my paths.

AUTHOR'S NOTE

I've played around with the idea for this book for a long time. I remember being on a long drive and talking to my dad on the phone and somehow getting on the topic of criminals in the wilderness, particularly the Sidney Poitier movie, *Shoot to Kill*.

Many of my stories have a long germination time. I have more ideas than I have time to flesh them out.

As you may have noticed if you've read my previous two series (Hometown Heroes and In the Shadow) that I've changed our location from the Southern California beach town of Laguna Vista to the Southern California San Bernardino mountains.

While the town of Holcomb Springs doesn't exist, there is a Holcomb Valley that was the site of a gold rush in the 1860s. I took the liberty of imagining what would have happened if that boomtown—known as Belleville—had continued on to become a resort town similar to Big Bear or Lake Arrowhead. I liked the idea of having a small town on the edge of the wilderness with all of the problems and possibilities it can bring. And it was within driving distance of Laguna Vista, so all of our old friends could come up and visit.

Also, if you have read *Inn at Cherry Blossom Lane*, you'll

recognize Alex and Claire. If you haven't read it yet, you'll want to. You can go here https://BookHip.com/RRCKMX to get a free copy.

Starting a new series is always fun. It's great to think about new characters and new adventures while continuing to visit previous characters like old friends. I hope you enjoy what's to come.

ABOUT THE AUTHOR

My favorite thing is discovering how much there is to love about America the Beautiful and the great outdoors. I'm an Amazon bestselling author, a mom to two navigating the young adult years while battling my daughter's juvenile arthritis, exploring the delights of my son's autism, and keeping gluten free.

A California native who's spent significant time in the Midwest, I'm thrilled to be back in the Golden State. Follow me on social media to see all my adventures and how I get inspired for my books!

www.JLCrosswhite.com
Twitter: @jenlcross
Facebook: Author Jennifer Crosswhite

Instagram: jencrosswhite
Pinterest: Tandem Services

facebook.com/authorjennifercrosswhite
twitter.com/jenlcross
instagram.com/jencrosswhite
pinterest.com/tandemservices

SNEAK PEEK OF UNDER AN INDIGO MOON

HOLCOMB SPRINGS, CALIFORNIA, PRESENT DAY

The metal key warmed in Carissa Carver's hand, the teeth cutting into her palm as she cradled it. Odd how the future could be held in such a small item.

The real estate agent and notary public had left the Sleepy Bear Lodge's one meeting room. Leaving her alone with the folder holding the paperwork proof that she'd mortgaged—or as the French said, pledged until death—her future. She shot up a prayer, again, that she was doing the right thing.

It wasn't a huge lodge, but it had a pool and a small day spa. According to Yelp reviews, it was the best in the area. The *area* vaguely included their new town in Wildernessville, California. Real name, Holcomb Springs. But it could have been the other side of the moon as foreign as it felt to them being from Arizona. The boys were in the pool now, and she'd gotten a massage at the "spa" earlier. It was a treat after two days on the road, to celebrate this new stage of their lives.

She, Carissa Carver, *was* an architect, and now she was doing something risky. Her friends and family didn't equate her with risky. They didn't expect her to pull up her roots and move four hundred miles away either. Then again, she didn't expect her husband to, well, never mind. A lot of *nevers* became *had tos*.

Squeezing her hand into a fist—the metal pinching her skin—she lifted it to her nose. The cucumber lotion on her hand merged with the metal, creating a new scent: their future. She had just bought a house. Sight unseen. Well, almost. She'd been on a video tour. It had a new roof, a remodeled kitchen, and new appliances.

She shoved the key into her pocket. A short walk down the hall and she was at the indoor pool. As she opened the door, the tang of chlorine and dampness made her eyes sting.

Her sons, Brandon and Alex, splashed with abandon, shedding days of confinement in a moving truck cab. Waves sloshed over the curled concrete edge, wet footsteps dotted the deck.

"Watch, Mom, watch me!" Six-year-old Alex scrambled over the pool's edge, the water tugging his too big swim trunks back over his small hips while he grabbed at them. With a burst, he was out of the pool, tucked in a ball, and hurling back into the water.

Brandon whooped as his brother surfaced and then waded toward her. At ten, he shouldn't have dark rings under his eyes. The responsibility of having a little brother with Asperger's was aging him too quickly. Alex had no sense of danger; it fell to Brandon to be her extra set of eyes. "Did we get the house?" He swiped water from his face.

She reached into her pocket and showed him the key.

"Cool! Let's go see it!" He hauled himself out of the water. "Come on, Alex. We're going to go see our house."

"Hang on." She touched his clammy shoulder. "We need to get dinner, and it's going to be dark soon. We'll look at it tomorrow."

Brandon's shoulders seemed to fall to his hips.

Alex ran up, arms clutched to his chest, jumping up and down. She gave him a straight arm like the Heisman football trophy to keep him from throwing his wet body on her. She was in jeans and a stretchy cotton tee. No more business casual for her, but she didn't want to go for the wet T-shirt look either. Satisfied he would stay if she removed her hand, she took two steps back to the towel rack and grabbed two fluffy bits of terry cloth and tossed them to her boys.

The look on Brandon's face hurt. So many disappointments, this didn't have to be one. "Dry off and change, and we'll go."

———

The GPS was useless. Her iPhone's service cut in and out, leaving the device guessing as to their true location. She finally figured out—the old-fashioned way by looking at the addresses she could see—she needed to be going in the opposite direction. By the light of the moon, she squinted at the infrequent reflective numbers on the side of the road. They seemed to be getting closer. Old sturdy trees grew over the road, and she slowed, peering through solid branches and leaves.

A bit of moonlight peaked through thick pine branches to shine on a small section of white picket fence. She stopped the moving truck that had been their home on wheels for the last two days and contained all their earthly goods. The house sign was missing a number, but the ones there matched her paperwork.

This was their new home.

"Look boys! A picket fence!" She'd always wanted one, but they weren't much in vogue in southwest-inspired Arizona where rocks took the place of grass. Not much grass here either. Instead, a layer of pine needles coated the ground.

"Cool! A fortress for my Lego mini-figs," Alex commented.

Carissa was pretty sure that meant it was a good thing.

She turned as Brandon leaned over Alex in an attempt to get a clearer look. "That'll keep the ball from rolling into the street when we play catch. Sweet."

Okay, this was good. The boys seemed happy with her choice.

Black lumps squatted around the yard, but she'd expected the landscaping would need some trimming. She scrunched in her seat to maneuver her line of sight around the pine's arms to see the house. It was an old farmhouse, late Victorian, but it looked solid. She let her foot off the brake and inched forward. A glint of something from the backyard. The pond. If she could keep Alex from drowning in it, the boys would love it.

It had taken her entire 401k to fund this next segment of life. A benefit from her very nice architectural firm in her very nice city with her very nice house. If she could rehab this house and sell it for enough money, she was hoping it would adequately provide for the kids and her while she figured out the other parts of the equation. Yeah, she'd have to pay the piper, in this case the IRS. But what choice did she have? Life required money. This was the only gamble she'd ever made in her life, and she hoped it would pay off.

It just had to.

"Mom, look, there's sparks floating around."

She smiled at Alex's view of the stars. They were so much more visible up here in the mountains than they'd been in Arizona. No city lights.

Stars, a picket fence, and moonlight. All it needed was a porch swing. She envisioned her boys running around the back-yard, laughing while she lounged in the porch swing set in motion with her toe, a cold glass of iced tea dripping down her hand.

For once, she'd made a good decision.

Buy *Under an Indigo Moon* at https://www.jlcrosswhite.com/books/under-an-indigo-moon/

BOOKS BY JL CROSSWHITE

Sign up for my latest updates at www.JLCrosswhite.com and be the first to know when my next series is releasing.

Romantic Suspense

The Hometown Heroes Series

Promise Me

Cait can't catch a break. What she witnessed could cost her job and her beloved farmhouse. Will Greyson help her or only make things worse?

Protective Custody

She's a key witness in a crime shaking the roots of the town's power brokers. He's protecting a woman he'll risk everything for. Doing the right thing may cost her everything. Including her life.

Flash Point

She's a directionally-challenged architect who stumbled on a crime that could destroy her life's work. He's a firefighter protecting his hometown… and the woman he loves.

Special Assignment

A brain-injured Navy pilot must work with the woman in charge of the program he blames for his injury. As they both grasp to save their careers, will their growing attraction hinder them as they attempt solve the mystery of who's really at fault before someone else dies?

In the Shadow Series

Off the Map

For her, it's a road trip adventure. For him, it's his best shot to win her back. But for the stalker after her, it's revenge.

Out of Range

It's her chance to prove she's good enough. It's his chance to prove he's more than just a fun guy. Is it their time to find love, or is her secret admirer his deadly competition?

Over Her Head

On a church singles' camping trip that no one wants to be on, a weekend away to renew and refresh becomes anything but. A group of friends trying to find their footing do a good deed and get much more than they bargained for.

Writing as Jennifer Crosswhite

Contemporary Romance

The Inn at Cherry Blossom Lane

Can the summer magic of Lake Michigan bring first loves back together? Or will the secret they discover threaten everything they love?

Historical Romance

The Route Home Series

Be Mine

A woman searching for independence. A man searching for education. Can a simple thank you note turn into something more?

Coming Home

He was why she left. Now she's falling for him. Can a woman who turned her back on her hometown come home to find justice for her brother without falling in love with his best friend?

The Road Home

He is a stagecoach driver just trying to do his job. She is returning to her suitor only to find he has died. When a stack of stolen money shows up in her bag, she thinks the past she has desperately tried to hide has come back to haunt her.

Finally Home

The son of a wealthy banker poses as a lumberjack to carve out his own identity. But in a stagecoach robbery gone wrong, he meets the soon-to-be schoolteacher with a vivid imagination, a gift for making things grow, and an obsession with dime novels. As the town is threatened by a past enemy, can he help without revealing who he is? And will she love him when she learns the truth?